STALKING THE
PRAIRIE DEVIL . . .

Longarm shifted quietly to a more comfortable position, seated in the grass with his back against a
wheel and the rifle across his bent knees as he
chewed an unlit cheroot to pass the time and keep
awake.

A million years went by . . .

Somewhere in the night a coyote howled and once a
train hooted far across the prairie.

Then he heard something.

He didn't know what or where it was coming from,
but he suddenly knew he wasn't alone on the lonely
prairie. He realized he'd stopped breathing, straining his ears in the dead silence all around.

A big gray cat was walking around in Longarm's
gut for some fool reason, as he told himself he
didn't believe in ghosts . . .

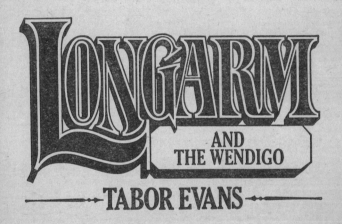

LONGARM

AND THE WENDIGO

—◆— TABOR EVANS —◆—

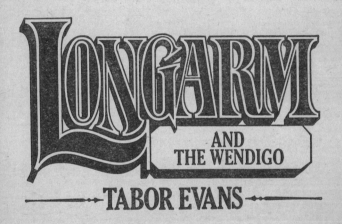

A JOVE/HBJ BOOK

Requests for permission to make copies of any part of the
work should be mailed to: Permissions, Jove Publications, Inc.,
757 Third Avenue, New York, NY 10017

Library of Congress Catalog Card Number: 78-71600

First Jove/HBJ edition published January 1979

Printed in the United States of America

Jove/HBJ books are published by Jove Publications, Inc.
(Harcourt Brace Jovanovich) 757 Third Avenue, New York,
NY 10017

Chapter 1

It was a glorious morning in Denver and Longarm felt like hell. The tall deputy squinted as he left the musty brown darkness of the Union Station to get punched in the eye by a bright morning sun in a cloudless sky of cobalt blue. A sharp breeze blew from the snow-topped Front Range, behind him to the west, as he walked stiffly east toward the Civic Center. The mile-high air was clear and scented with summer snow and green mountain meadows. Longarm wondered if he was going to make it to Larimer Street before he threw up.

At the corner of Seventeenth and Larimer he found the all-night greasy spoon he'd aimed for and went in to settle his guts. He wasn't hungry, but ordered chili and beer as medication.

The beanery was nearly empty at this hour, but Longarm recognized a uniformed member of the Denver Police Department seated at another stool down the counter and nodded. He'd only nodded to be neighborly, but the copper slid his own stein and bowl over next to Longarm's and said, " 'Morning, Uncle Sam. You look like somebody drug you through the keyhole backwards! You spend the night drinking, whoring, or both?"

"Worse. I just came up out of Santa Fe on a night train that had square wheels and no seats worth mention. Rode shotgun on a gold shipment bound for the mint, here in Denver. Spent the night hunkered on a box in the mail car, drinking the worst coffee I've tasted since I was in the army. I suspicion they use the

5

same glue in Post Office coffee as they put on the back of their stamps."

He took a huge gob of chili, washed it down with a gulp of beer, and added, "Jesus, you can't hardly get real chili this far north of Texas. Pass me some of that red pepper to the lee of your elbow, will you?"

The copper handed him the pepper shaker and opined, "Oh, I dunno, the cook here makes a fair bowl of chili, for a white man."

Then he watched with a worried frown, as Longarm proceeded to cover his beans with powdered fire. To the policeman, Longarm was sort of interesting to study on. The Denver P.D. was sincerely glad the deputy marshal was a lawman rather than on the other side; arresting anything that big and mean was an awesome thought to contemplate.

The Deputy U.S. Marshal was civilly dressed in a threadbare business suit of tobacco tweed, but a bit wild and wooly around the edges. His brown flat-topped Stetson had a couple of large-caliber holes in it and the craggy face under the brim was weathered as brown as an Indian's. The big jaw masticating chili under the John L. Sullivan mustache needed a shave, and though he wore a shoestring tie under the collar of his townsman's shirt, he somehow managed to wear it like a cowhand's bandanna. They said he packed a derringer in addition to the double-action .44 in that cross-draw rig he wore under the frock coat. They said he had a Bowie in one of the low-heeled army boots he stood taller than most men in. But the big deputy was one of those rare men who didn't look like he *needed* weapons. When he was in one of his morose moods, like this morning, Longarm looked able to knock a lesser man down with a hard stare from his gunmetal eyes.

The copper asked, "You aim to *eat* that shit with all that pepper in it, or are you aiming to blow yourself up?"

Longarm chewed thoughtfully and decided, "That's better. Chili's no good unless it makes a man's forehead break out in a little sweat. I can still taste that damned Post Office coffee, but I reckon I'll live, after all."

"You must have a cast iron stomach. You, ah, wouldn't want to let your friendly neighborhood police in on it, would you, Longarm?"

"In on what? You want me to fix your chili right for you?"

"Come on. They never detailed a deputy with your seniority to ride with the Post Office dicks. Somebody important robbing the mails these days?"

Longarm took a heroic gulp of beer and swallowed before he belched, with a relieved sigh, and replied, "Jesus, that felt good. As to who's been robbing the midnight trains between here and Santa Fe, I don't know anymore than yourself about it. I just do what the pissants up at the Federal Building tell me."

"I hear since the Lincoln County War's run down there's about eighty out-of-work gunslicks searching for gainful employment. You reckon any might be headed for my beat?"

Longarm studied for a moment before he shook his head and said, "Doubt it. Denver's getting too civilized for old-fashioned owlhoots like we used to see over at the stockyards. Your new gun regulations sort of cramp their style. To tell you the truth, I sort of dozed off once we were north of Pueblo. Colorado's getting downright overcivilized of late, what with street lamps, gun laws, and such."

"By gum, I run a cowboy in for a shooting just two nights ago, over on Thirteenth and Walnut!"

"There you go. That's over on the other side of Cherry Creek where the poor folks live. 'Fess up. You ain't had a real Saturday night in the main part of town this year, have you?"

"The hell we hasn't! I'll bet Denver's still as tough a town as any! I disremember you saying you heard any shooting in Santa Fe! I'll bet the hands riding into Denver of a Saturday night are just as mean as any you met down New Mexico way!"

"No bet. Santa Fe's got sissy as hell since the new

governor said folks can't shoot each other any more in Lincoln County. Hell, I was in Dodge last month and you know what they got? They got uniformed police and honest-to-God street lamps in Dodge now! Things keep up this way and we'll likely both be out of a job!"

Leaving the policeman nursing his injured civic pride, Longarm paid the silent, surly Greek behind the counter for his breakfast and resumed his walk to work, feeling almost human. He knew he rated the day off for having spent the night on duty, but these new regulations about paperwork meant he had to report in before he could go home to his furnished digs for some shut-eye.

The Federal Building sat at the foot of Capitol Hill. Longarm went in and climbed to the second floor, where he found a door marked *UNITED STATES MARSHAL, FIRST DISTRICT COURT OF COLORADO.*

He entered, nodded to the pallid clerk pecking at his newfangled typewriting machine, and made his way to an inner door, where he let himself in without knocking.

His superior, U.S. Marshal Vail, glared up with a start from behind his big mahogany desk and snapped, "Damn it, Longarm! I've told you I expect folks to *knock* before they come busting in on me!"

Longarm grinned and was about to sass the plump, pink man behind the desk. Then he saw Vail's visitor, seated in an overstuffed leather armchair near the banjo clock on the wall and tipped the brim of his hat instead, saying, "Your servant, ma'am!"

The woman in the visitor's chair was dressed severely in black, with a sort of silly little hat perched atop her coal-black hair. She was about twenty-five and pretty. She wasn't quite a white woman. Maybe a Mexican lady, dressed American.

Marshal Vail said, "I'm glad to see you on time for a change, Longarm. Allow me to present you to Princess Gloria Two-Women of the Blackfoot Nation."

Longarm managed another smiling nod before the

girl cut in with a severe but no less pretty frown to say, "I am no such thing, Marshal Vail. Forgive me for correcting you, but, John Smith and Pocahontas notwithstanding, there is no such thing as an Indian princess."

Vail shrugged and asked, "Aren't you the daughter of Real Bear, the Chief of the Blackfoot, ma'am?"

"My father was war chief of the Turtle Clan. My mother was Gloria Witherspoon, a captive white woman. There are no hereditary titles among my father's people, and even if there were, no woman could inherit the rank of war chief."

Vail looked annoyed but managed a wan smile as he nodded and asked, "Just what is your title, then, ma'am?"

"I'm a half-breed. On rare occasions, I'm called *Miss*."

Longarm ignored the bitterness in her almond eyes as he leaned against the back of another chair and suggested, "I don't reckon your family tree is what you've come to Uncle Sam about, is it, Miss Two-Women?"

Vail cut in before she could answer, saying, "I've got the lady's complaint down, Longarm. It's your next job."

Longarm didn't think it was the time to point out that he rated the day off. He knew it wouldn't do any good and the odd little bitter-eyed woman interested him. So he nodded and waited for Vail to fill him in.

The marshal said, "This lady's daddy sent her to see us, Longarm. A bad Indian's gone back to the blanket. I got his wanted papers here somewhere . . . anyway, I want you to run up to the Blackfoot reservation in Montana Territory and—"

"Ain't you assigning me to a job for the B.I.A., Chief?"

The girl said, "The man my father is worried about isn't a problem for the Bureau of Indian Affairs, sir. They don't know he's alive. My father reported him to the Indian agent at Fort Banyon. They told him they'd file a report on the matter, but of course we know they won't. Like myself, Johnny Hunts Alone is nonexistent."

Longarm asked, "You mean he's . . ."

"A half-breed. You don't have to be so delicate. Half-breed's one of the nicer things I'm used to being called."

Vail found the "wanted" flyer he'd been rummaging for and said, "He may not exist to the B.I.A., but Justice wants him bad. Matter of fact, we don't have him down as an Indian, half or whatever. We've got him as one John Hunter, age thirty-six, no description save white, male, medium height and build. When he ain't hiding out on reservations he robs trains, banks, and such. We got four counts of first degree on him in addition to the state and federal wants for armed robbery."

Longarm pursed his lips and mused, "I remember seeing the wanted flyers, now. Funny, I had him pictured in my head as just another old, uh . . ."

"White man," Gloria Two-Women cut in, stone-faced. Both men waited as she continued, "Like myself, Johnny Hunts Alone is a Blackfoot breed. In his case, his *mother* was the Indian. They say his father was a Mountain Man who, uh, married a squaw for a trapping season. She gave him his half-name of Johnny, hoping, one would presume, his father might come back some day."

Longarm asked, "Was he raised Indian, then?"

"To the extent that I was, I suppose. I've never met him. They say he ran away to look for his white father years ago."

Vail explained, "The way I understand it, this Johnny Hunts Alone, John Hunter, or whatever, can pass himself off as white or Indian. He sort of raised himself in trail towns, hobo jungles, and such till he took to robbing folks instead of punching cows. The reason he's been getting away with it for years is that we could never find his hideout. According to this little lady's daddy, the jasper's up at the Blackfoot

10

reservation right now. Miss Gloria, here, will introduce you to her daddy and the chief'll point the owlhoot out to you. Seems like a simple enough mission to me."

Longarm sighed and said, "Yeah, it always does. You mind if I ask a few questions? Just the result of my suspicious nature."

Without waiting for permission, he stared soberly at the girl and asked, "How come your Blackfoot relations are so suddenly helpful to Uncle Sam, Miss Two-Women? Meaning no disrespect, the Blackfoot have a reputation for truculence. Wasn't your tribe sort of cheering from the sidelines when Custer took that wrong turn on the Little Big Horn a few summers back?"

"Like the Cheyenne and Arapahoe, the Blackfoot were allied with the Dakota Confederacy, if that's what you mean. Since you're so interested in the history of my father's people, you probably know the survivors have been penned like sheep in one small corner of Montana."

"I read about it. Did this Johnny Hunts Alone take part in the Great Sioux Uprising of '76?"

"Of course not. Do you think my father would inform on a fellow warrior?"

"There you go. So why *is* your daddy so anxious for us to arrest one of his people?"

"Honestly, don't you know anything about Indians? The renegade is *not* a Blackfoot to my father and others like him. Johnny Hunts Alone ran away before he was ever initiated into any of the warrior lodges. When our people were fighting for their lives against the Seventh Cavalry he was off someplace robbing banks."

"So your dad and the other chiefs don't owe him much, huh?"

"Not only that, but the man's a known thief and a troublemaker. Thanks partly to my mother, Real Bear speaks English and can read and write, so perhaps he's more aware than the others of what a wanted fugitive on our reservation could mean to us."

"What's that, ma'am?"

"Trouble, of course. Our tribe is . . . well, frankly, licked. Most of us are resigned to making the best of a bad situation. But there are hotheads among my father's people who'd like another try at the old ways. Some of the Dream Singers have been having visions, and meetings have been held in the warrior lodges of which I don't feel free to tell you the details. My father is one of the more progressive chiefs. He's trying to cooperate with the B.I.A. He's trying to lead his people into the future; he's man enough to face it. An outlaw hiding among the young men, boasting of how many whites he's killed—"

"That makes sense, ma'am. As you were talking just now, it came to me I'd heard your daddy's name before. Real Bear was one of them who voted with Red Cloud against the big uprising. Though, the way I hear tell, he did his share of fighting once his folks declared war. You mind if I ask you some *personal* questions, ma'am?"

Vail cut in to point at the clock above Gloria's head as he snapped, "She might not mind, but I do, dang it! You folks have a train to catch, Longarm! You can jaw about the details along the way. Right now I want you to get cracking. I'll expect you back here about this time next week, with Johnny Hunts Alone, John Hunter, or whomsoever, dead or alive!"

It wasn't until he'd escorted Gloria Two-Women aboard the northbound Burlington that Longarm gave serious consideration to her race. Under most circumstances, he wouldn't have given it much thought, for she was a pretty little thing and his mind was on the job ahead.

As the conductor nodded down at the railroad pass they were traveling on, Longarm asked, "What time are we due in Billings? I make it about twelve hours before we have to change trains, don't you?"

"We'll be getting into Billings around ten this evening, Marshal. Uh . . . you mind if I have a word with you in private?"

Longarm glanced at the girl seated across from him, gazing stone-faced out the window at the passing confusion of the Denver yards, and got to his feet to follow the conductor with a puzzled frown. The older man led him a few seats down, out of the girl's earshot, before he asked in a low whisper, "Is that a lady of color you're traveling with, Marshal?"

"You're wrong on both counts. I'm only a deputy marshal and she's half white. What's your problem, friend?"

"Look, it ain't *my* problem. Some of the other passengers has, uh, sort of been talking about the two of you."

"Do tell? Well, I'm a peaceable man. Long as they don't talk about us where we can *hear* it, it don't mean all that much, does it?"

"Look, I was wondering if the gal might not be more comfortable up front in the baggage car."

Longarm smiled wolfishly, and took the front of the trainman's coat in one big fist as he purred, "She ain't a *gal*, friend. Anything in skirts traveling with *me* as her escort is a *lady*, till *I* say she's something else. You got that?"

"Loud and clear, Marshal. This ain't *my* notion!"

"All right. Whose notion might it be, then?"

"Look, I don't want no trouble, mister!"

"Old son, you've already got your trouble. You just point out who the big mouth belongs to and then maybe *you'd* best go up and ride in that baggage car!"

"I'm just doing my job. Forget I mentioned it."

"I'd like to, but I got a twelve-hour ride ahead of me and I don't aim to spend it fretting about my future. I'm going to ask you one more time, polite. Then I'm likely to start by busting your arm."

"Hey, take it easy. I don't care who rides this durned old train. It's them two cowhands up near the front of the car. I heard 'em say some things 'bout niggers and such and thought I'd best head things off."

Longarm didn't turn his head to look at the two young men he'd already marked down as possible

13

annoyances. He'd spotted them boarding the train. They looked to be drovers and one was packing a Patterson .44 and a bellyful of something stronger than beer.

Longarm let go the conductor's lapel and said, "You go up to the next car. I'll take care of it."

"I got tickets to punch."

"All right. Go on *back* to the next car."

The conductor started to protest further. Then he saw the look in Longarm's cold blue-gray eyes, gulped, and did as he was told.

As Longarm sauntered back the way he'd come, Gloria looked up at him with a bemused expression. He nodded and said, "We'll be picking up speed in a mile or so. You want a drink of water?"

"No thanks. What was that all about?"

"We were talking about the timetable. Excuse me, ma'am. I'll be back directly."

He walked toward the front of the car, shifting on the balls of his feet as the car swayed under his boots. One of the two men in trail clothing looked up and whispered something to the heavier man at his side. The tougher-looking of the two narrowed his eyes thoughtfully but didn't say anything until Longarm stopped right above them, letting the tail of his coat swing open to expose the polished walnut grips of his own Colt, and said, "You boys had best be getting off before we leave the yards. Might hurt a man to jump off a train doing more'n fifteen miles an hour or so."

The one who had whispered asked, "What are you talking about? We're on our way to Billings, mister."

"No you ain't. Not on this train. You see, I don't want you to be upset about riding with colored folks, and since I aim to stay aboard all the way to Billings, we'd best make some adjustments to your delicate natures."

The heavyset one with the gun looked thoughtfully at the weapon hanging above Longarm's left hip and licked his lips before he said, "Look, nobody said *you* was colored, mister."

14

"Is that a fact? Well, it's likely the poor light in here; I'm pure Ethiopian. You want to make something out of it?"

"Hey, come on, you're as white as we'uns. *You* wasn't the one we was jawing 'bout to that fool conductor!"

His companion added, "You just wait till we gits that troublemaker alone, mister. He had no call to repeat a gent's observings."

"Boys, this train's gathering speed while we're discussing your departure. You two aim to jump like sensible gents or do I have to throw you off unfriendly-like?"

"Come on, you can't put us off no train! We got us tickets to Billings!"

"Use 'em on the next train north, then. I'll tell you what I'm fixing to do. I'm fixing to count to ten. Then I'm going to draw."

"Mister, you must be loco, drunk, or both!"

"One!"

"Look here, we don't want to hurt nobody, but——"

"Two!"

"Now you're getting us *riled*, mister!"

"Three!"

"Well, damn it, Fats, *you* got the durned old gun!"

"Four!"

The heavyset one went for his Patterson.

He didn't make it. Longarm's five-inch muzzle, its front sight filed off for such events, was out and covering him before Fats had a serious hold on his own grips. The drover snatched his hand from his sidearm as if it had stung his palm as he gasped, "I give! I give! Don't do it, mister!"

"You did say something about disembarking, didn't you, gents?"

"Look, you've made us crawfish. Can't we leave it at that?"

"Nope. You made me draw, so now you're getting off, one way or the other. Let's go, boys."

After a moment's hesitation, Fats shrugged and said,

"Let's go, Curley. No sense arguing with a crazy man when he's got the drop on us."

His younger sidekick protested, "I can't believe this! I thought you was tough, Fats!"

But he, too, slid out of the seat and followed as Longarm frogmarched the two of them out to the vestibule between the cars. Fats looked down at the blurring road ballast and protested, "Hey, it's goin' too fast!"

"All the more reason to jump while there's still time. It'll be going faster, directly."

"You got a name, mister?"

"Yep. My handle's Custis Long. You aim to look me up sometime, Fats?"

"Just don't be in Billings when we gits there, mister. We got us *friends* in Billings!"

Then he jumped, rolling ass-over-teakettle as he hit the dirt at twenty-odd miles an hour. Longarm saw that he wasn't hurt, and as the younger one tried to protest some more, he ended the discussion by shoving him, screaming, from the platform.

Longarm holstered his gun with a dry smile and went back to where he'd left Gloria. The petite breed's face was blank but her eyes glistened as she said, "You didn't have to do that to impress me. You've already called me 'ma'am.'"

Longarm sat down on the seat across from her, placed his battered Stetson on the green plush beside him, and said, "Didn't do it for you. Did it for myself."

"You mean they offended your sense of gallantry?"

"Nope. Just made common sense. They got on drunk and ugly and we have a good twelve hours' ride ahead. Had I given 'em time to work themselves up all afternoon, I'd likely have had a killing matter on my hands by sundown. This way, nobody got hurt."

"One of them might dispute you on that point. I was watching out the window. The fall tore his shirt half off and left him sort of bloody."

"Any man who don't know how to fall has no call wearing cowboy boots."

16

"What am I supposed to do now, call you my Prince Charming and swoon at your feet?"

"Nope. I'd rather talk about the lay of the land where we're headed. You said your daddy, Real Bear, is the only one who can point out this Johnny Hunts Alone to me. How come? I mean, don't the other Indians know a stranger when they see one?"

"Of course, but you see, it's a new reservation, just set up since our tribes were rounded up by the army in '78. Stray bands are still being herded in. Aside from Blackfoot, we have Blood and Piegan and even a few Arapahoe gathered from all over the north plains. My father doesn't know many of the people living with his people now, but he did recognize Johnny Hunts Alone when the man passed him near the trading post last week."

"The owlhoot recognize your dad?"

"Real Bear didn't think so. My father knew him over fifteen years ago and they've both changed a lot since, of course. It wasn't until my father got to my house that he remembered just who that familiar face belonged to!"

"In other words, we're traveling a far piece on the quick glance and maybes of one old Indian who might just be wrong!"

"When you meet Real Bear, you'll know better. He doesn't forget much. Aren't you going to ask about our house?"

"Your house? Is there something interesting about it, ma'am?"

"Most white people, when they hear me mention my house, seem a bit surprised. I'm supposed to wear buckskins, too."

"Well, I ain't most people. I've been on a few reservations in my time. What have you got up there, one of them government-built villages of frame lumber that could use a coat of paint and a bigger stove?"

"I see you *have* seen a few reservations. Ours is a shambles. The young white couple the B.I.A. sent out from the East doubtless mean well, but . . . you'd have to be an Indian to understand."

Longarm fished a cheroot from his vest and when she nodded her silent permission, thumbnailed a match and lit up, pondering her words. He knew the miserable fix most tribes were in these days, caught between conflicting policies of the army, the Indian agency, and loudmouthed Washington politicos who'd never been west of the Big Muddy. He took a drag of smoke, let it trickle out through his nostrils, and asked, "What's this other trouble you mentioned about the young men wanting another go at the Seventh Cav?"

"The boys too young to have fought in '76 aren't the real problem. Left to themselves they'd just talk a lot, like white boys planning to run off and be pirates. But some of the older men are finding civilization more than they can adjust to. You know about the Ghost Dancers?"

"Heard rumors. Paiute medicine man called Wovoka has been preachin' a new religion over on the other side of the Rockies, hasn't he?"

"Yes. Wovoka's notions seem crazy to our Dream Singers, but the movement's gaining ground and even some of our people are starting to make offerings to the Wendigo. You'd have to be a Blackfoot to know how crazy *that* is!"

"No I wouldn't. The Wendigo is your Dad's folks' name for the devil, ain't it?"

"My, you *have* been on some reservations! What else do you know about our religion?"

"Not much. Never even got the Good Book that *I* was brought up on all that straight in my head. Blackfoot, Arapahoe, Cheyenne, and other Algonquin-speaking tribes pray to a Great Spirit called Manitou and call the devil 'Wendigo,' right? I remember somethin' about owls being bad luck and turtles being good luck, but like I said, I've never studied all that much on anyone's notions about the spirit world."

"Owl is the totem of death. Turtle is the creator of

18

new life from the Waters of Yesteryear. I suppose you regard it all as silly superstition."

"Can't say one way or another. I wasn't there. It might have took seven days or Turtle might have done it. Doubtless sometime we'll know more about it. Right now I've got enough on my plate just keeping track of the here-and-now of it all."

"Does that make you an atheist or an agnostic?"

Longarm bristled slightly. The last person to call him an atheist had been a renegade Mormon night rider who had left him to die in the Great Salt Desert. He had had plenty of time to ponder on the godless behavior of those who accused others of godlessness. "Makes me a Deputy U.S. Marshal with a job to do. You were saying something about devil worship up where we're headed, Miss Gloria."

She shrugged and replied, "I don't think you could put it that way. People making offerings to the Wendigo aren't Satanists; they're simply frightened Indians. You see, it's all too obvious that Manitou, the Great Spirit, has turned his back on them. The Wendigo, or Evil One, seems to rule the earth these days, and so—"

"Is he supposed to be like *our* devil, with horns and such, or is he a big, mean Indian cuss?"

"Like Manitou, the Wendigo's invisible. You might say he's a great evil force who makes bad things happen."

"I see. And some of your folks are praying to him while others are taking up Wovoka's notions about the ghosts of dead Indians coming back from the Happy Hunting Ground for another go-round with our side. I don't hold much with missionaries, since those I've seen ain't been all that good at it, but right now it seems you could use some up on the Blackfoot reservation."

"We have a posse of divers missionaries on or near the reservation. My father would like to run all Dream Singers off, Indian as well as white. I hope your arrest of Johnny Hunts Alone will calm things down enough for him to cope with."

Longarm nodded and consulted his Ingersoll pocket

watch, noting that they had a long way to ride yet. The girl watched him silently for a time before she murmured, "You're not as dumb as you pretend to be."

Longarm smiled. "Pretending such things sometimes gives a man an advantage. Speaking of which, you've got a pretty good head on your own shoulders. I can see you've been educated."

"I graduated from Wellesley. Does that surprise you?"

"Why should it? You had to go to school someplace to talk so uppity. I know those big Eastern colleges give scholarships to bright reservation kids. It'd surprise me more if you'd said you'd learned to read from watching smoke signals."

"You are unusual, for a white man. By now, most of your kind I've met would have demanded my whole history."

"Likely. Most folks are more curious than polite."

"You really don't care one way or the other, do you?"

"I likely know as much about you as I need to."

"You don't know anything about me! Nobody knows anything about me!"

Longarm took a drag on his cheroot and said, "Let's see, now. You're wearing widow's weeds, but you're likely not a widow. You're wearing a wedding band, but you ain't married. You were born in an Indian camp, but you've been raised white and only lately come back to your daddy's side of the family. You've got a big old chip on your pretty shoulder, too, but I ain't about to knock it off, so why don't you quit fencing about with me?"

Gloria Two-Women stared openmouthed at him for a time before she blurted, "Somebody gave you a full report on me and you've been the one doing the fencing. Who was it, that damned agent's wife?"

"Nobody's told me one word about you since we met, save yourself. You knew I was a lawman. Don't you reckon folks in my line are supposed to work things out for themselves, ma'am?"

Before she could answer, the candy butcher came through with his tray of sweets, fruits, sandwiches, and bottled beer. Longarm stopped the boy and asked the girl what she'd like, adding, "We won't stop for a proper meal this side of Cheyenne, ma'am."

Gloria ordered a ham on rye sandwich, a beer, and an orange for later and the deputy ordered the same, except for the fruit. When the candy butcher had left them to wait on another passenger, she insisted, "All right, how did you do that?"

"Do what? Size you up? I'm paid to size folks up, Miss Gloria. You said your mama was a white lady, and since you're about twenty-odd, I could see she must have been taken captive during that Blackfoot rising near South Pass in the 'fifties. When the army put 'em down that time, most white captives were released, so I figured you likely went back East with your ma when you were, oh, about seven or eight. You may talk some Blackfoot and you've got Indian features, but you wear that dress like a white woman. You walk white, too. Those high-buttoned shoes don't fret your toes like they would a lady's who grew up in moccasins. You sure weren't riding with the Blackfoot when they came out against Terry in '76, so I'd say you looked your daddy up after he and the others settled down civilized on the reservation just a while back. Here, I'll open that beer for you with my jackknife. It's got a bottle opener and all sorts of notions."

He opened their drinks carefully, aiming the warm beer bottles at the aisle as he uncapped them. Then he handed her one and sat back to say, "I was born in West-by-God-Virginia and came West after the War. I fought at Shiloh. . . ." Longarm's voice trailed off.

"You were doing fine. What made you stop?" Gloria asked.

"Reckon both our tales get a mite hurtful, later on. We're both full-grown, now, and some of the getting here might best be forgot."

"You know about my mother deserting me once she was among her own people, then? How could you know that? How could anyone know so much from mere appearances? Is that orphanage written on my breast in scarlet letters, after all?"

"No. I never met your mama, but I know the world, and how it treats a white gal who's ridden out of an Indian camp with a half-breed child. You ought to try to forgive her, Miss Gloria. She was likely not much older than you are right now, and her own kin likely pressured her some."

"My mother had a white husband waiting for her. I wonder if she ever told him about me. Oh, well, they treated us all right at the foundling home and I did win a college scholarship on my own." She sipped her beer and added in a bitter voice, "Not that it did much good, once I tried to make my way in the white man's world. I was nearly nine when the soldiers recaptured us, so I remembered my father's language and could identify with that side of my family. You were right about my reading about the new reservation and running back to the blanket, but how did you figure out my widow's weeds?"

"Generally, when folks are wearing mourning, they mention someone who's dead. On the other hand, one of the first things I noticed was that chip on your shoulder and your hankering to be treated with respect. I'll allow some folks who should know better can talk ugly to any lady with your sort of features, but widow's weeds and a wedding band gives a gal a certain edge in being treated like a lady."

"It didn't stop those two cowboys you put off the train."

"They were drovers, not cowhands, ma'am. And neither had much sense. Most old boys think twice before they start up with a lady wearing a wedding band, widow's weeds or no. They were likely drunker than most you've met. So 'fess up, that's the reason for the mournful getup, ain't it?"

She laughed, spilling some of her beer, and answered, "You should run away with a circus! You'd make more as a mind reader than a lawman!" Then she sobered and added, "You're wrong about the ring, though. I am married, sort of."

He didn't rise to the bait. She'd tell him in her own good time what she meant by "sort of" married. From the smoke signals he'd been reading in her eyes, she couldn't be married all that much.

Chapter 2

They had to lay over in Billings for a grotesquely routed train that promised to take them close enough to the Blackfoot reservation. Gloria said they'd be able to hire a buckboard for the last few miles, and Longarm's saddle, Winchester, and other possibles were riding with him to where he could commandeer a government mount from the army. The local train connecting up with the line north wasn't leaving Billings before morning and they got in a little after nine-thirty. They spent an hour over steak and potatoes before Longarm had to deal with the delicate matter of hotel accommodations.

It wasn't checking in with a woman he was worried about. He had enough cash to pay for separate rooms. But even in the dim light of a gaslit town, Gloria's Indian features drew stares, and some of them weren't friendly. Billings was only a few miles from the old battleground of Little Big Horn and the local whites had long memories as well as buried kinfolk in the vicinity. As they entered the lobby of the Silver Dollar Hotel he murmured, "Should anyone ask, remember you're a Spanish lady from Sonora."

"I'll do no such thing!" she murmured, adding, "I'm a Blackfoot and proud of it!'

"Maybe, but I've got to do the fighting, so I reckon you'd just best hush and let me do the talking, hear?"

He strode over to the hotel desk and flashed his federal badge at the night clerk. "We need two rooms. I'll take one with a bath."

24

The clerk nodded impassively and shoved the registration book toward the deputy. "I can fix you up with adjoining rooms, bath between. This lady, uh, your missus?"

"Of course not. What would I want with two rooms if we were married up? Do I look like a sissy?"

The clerk laughed as Longarm registered for them both, signing Gloria in as "Miss Witherspoon."

Unfortunately, the girl glanced over his shoulder to protest, "That's not my name, damn it!"

A couple of sleepy-looking gents lounging among the potted ferns of the lobby sat up to stare with greater interest as Longarm sighed and said, "Now, Miss Gloria, let's not make a fuss about it. You said your mama's name was Witherspoon, and—"

"I am Gloria Two-Women. My mother abandoned me and I'll not bear her name, even for a night."

The clerk raised an eyebrow. Longarm quickly touched the side of his forehead and confided, "She's a federal witness I'm taking up to Fort Benson. She's a mite, uh, confused."

"She says her name is 'two women,' Deputy."

"There you go. I told you how it was. She's only one woman at a time as anyone here can plainly see."

One of the lobby-loafers got slowly to his feet as he said, "I can plainly see she's *Indian*, too! What are you, mister, a squaw man?"

"Paying for two rooms, friend, I don't reckon it's your concern. I am also a U.S. Deputy Marshal and you are stepping on the tail of my coat, so why don't you go back yonder and warm your seat some more?"

"I rode with Terry in '76 and I don't give two hoots and a holler who you work for, mister. You got no call to bring Indians in here!"

Longarm saw two others rising, now, and the desk clerk was muttering unfriendly things about the town marshal. He took Gloria's elbow in his free left hand, nodded, and said, "We'll be on our way, then, gents."

He half-dragged the girl outside, as behind them the lobby rang with jeering laughter. He started up the boardwalk with her, chewing his unlit cheroot, too steamed to say much.

She marveled, "You just let them run us out like we were trash!"

"Nope, it was your hankering to see a fight that got us run out. If you aim to sleep this night, you'd best stuff a sock in that pretty mouth of yours next place we try!"

"Why didn't you stand up to them back there? I thought you were a man!"

"Was, last time I looked. I likely could have whupped the whole lobby, if it had made a lick of sense. But I was looking for a couple of rooms, not another Little Big Horn."

"Oh, you know you could have backed them down!"

"Maybe, but then what? You like to sleep in hotels angry folks are throwing rocks at all night, Miss Gloria? Suppose I *had* bullied us a brace of rooms? Then suppose those browned-off vets had gone looking for some help? I'm supposed to be a *peace* officer, not the biggest boo in Billings. We'll try a block up the street and maybe this time you'll have more sense."

"I can't believe it. You were so brave when those men were annoying us on the train."

"Yeah, I can see I made a mistake back there. You like to see white men humiliated, don't you?"

"I just have to stand up for my rights, damn it."

"What rights? They were going to give us two rooms and a bath, weren't they? Where does it say in the Constitution you have a right to be a pain in the neck?"

"I'm not ashamed of being what I am."

"Like hell you ain't. Look, I know the sort of sass you've had to take off white folks in your time. You want to put feathers in your hair and do something about it, it ain't my never-mind, but let's eat the apple a bite at a time, huh? Your daddy sent you to fetch a U.S. Deputy Marshal to bail him and his folks out of a fix. Suppose you let me get there peaceably before you start another uprising!"

"I don't have to put up with insults, just because of my race."

"Yes, you do. No matter what your race is, somebody don't figure to like it. I was chased from hell to breakfast by Apache last summer, just for being white. When we get where we're going, you'll likely see me catching a few dark looks from your daddy's folks, too. The thing is, there's enough trouble in this world for all of us, even when we don't go looking for it. I see a hotel sign up ahead. This time, damn it, I'll thank you to be that Mexican lady I told you about!"

"*They* take a lot off your kind, too."

"That's true. If we were checking into a hotel in Texas I'd say you were a Blackfoot. Hereabouts, they ain't mad at Mexicans."

He escorted her into a smaller, shabbier hotel and this time there was no incident at the desk. There was no adjoining bathroom to their two small rooms upstairs, either, but Longarm didn't comment. There were chamber pots under the beds and he supposed it might be a good lesson for the young woman.

He let her into her own room and handed her the key, with a warning about opening to anyone but himself, then gave her a terse goodnight nod. He went to his own room, and before lighting the lamp, stared down into the street for a time. He'd been watching in the glass windows to see if they'd been followed from the other hotel, but it seemed as if his crawfish act had satisfied the local Indian fighters.

He locked the door and sat on the edge of the brass bedstead, tearing up a newspaper he'd found on the dressing table. He crumpled the shreds of newspaper and threw them on the threadbare rug between the bed and the locked door before he hung his gun rig on a bed post, put his watch and derringer under a pillow, and got undressed.

Nude in the darkness, he scratched his chest morosely as he thought of the bath he'd missed. He needed a shave, too, and there were soot and fly-ash

27

in his hair from the long train ride north. Well, he'd just have to bear with it for now. Damn that fool squaw!

As he was sliding under the covers there came a soft rap on his door. Longarm got up, drew the .44 from its holster, and went over to the door, standing to one side as he asked, "Yeah?"

"It's me, Gloria. Are you still awake?"

"Yep, but I'm naked. What can I do for you, ma'am?"

"I want to apologize for the way I acted down the street."

"Forget it. We're both worn out from all that riding, smoke, dust, and such. You get some shut-eye and I'll see you in the morning."

"Can I come in for a moment? I'm too keyed-up to sleep."

He went over to the bed and slipped on his pants before going back to open the door. The girl was wearing a white shift and was barefoot. Her tawny skin seemed darker against the white cotton in the dim light and her hair smelled like wilted tea roses. He shut the door and locked it behind her as she stepped on a paper ball and exclaimed, "Good heavens! What's all this paper doing on the floor?"

"Old Border Mex trick. Keeps folks from pussy-footing in on you while you're snoring."

"Do things like that happen often, in your line of work?"

"Not often. *Once* would be too often, though. I don't have a chair in here for you. You can sit on the bed and I'll sort of stand here while you tell me what's on your mind."

She went to the bed, slipped the shift off over her head and sat down, stark naked, before she said, "I want to sleep with you."

Longarm blinked but managed not to gasp his surprise as he waited a breath to steady his voice. "Just like that?"

"What's the matter? Don't you want to sleep with me?"

"Well, hell, sure! But I sort of figured—"

"I know what you've been figuring, all day. Most men would have made their move by now. This time tomorrow, we'll be on the reservation where it'll be a federal offense for you to trifle with me. I knew this was the one night you'd have to try and, damn it, you just move too *slow*, Longarm!"

Grinning, he unbuttoned his pants, let them fall around his ankles, and stepped out of them. She lay back as he loomed over her, wrapping arms and legs around him as he sank into her tawny body with both feet braced firmly on the rug. She thrust her body to meet his own hungry thrusts and her open mouth was a warm pit of savage desire as she sucked his tongue almost to the point of pain.

He let himself go without attempts at finesse or mutual orgasm, the first time. Then, having made her acquaintance, he moved them both to the center of the bed and got down to serious lovemaking, murmuring, "Still think I move too slow?"

"Let me get on top. I like to take charge."

"I noticed." He grinned, rolling off to let her have her way. And have her way she did. Every time Longarm tried to respond with movements of his own she'd kiss him and whisper, "Just float with me, darling. Mama knows what she's doing. I'll take good care of baby. You'll see!"

Longarm knew better than to argue with a lady, so he lay there, spread-eagled and as puzzled as he was delighted by the lovemaking of this strange, dark little woman.

It was too good to last forever; she'd literally wrung him out like a lemon and as she took his limp flesh between her moist lips he sighed, "You've got to let it rest up a mite, honey. I don't reckon I could get it up again with a block and tackle right now!"

She laughed and threw herself down beside him, resting a head on his shoulder as she fondled him and purred, "We'll see about that. Did you—?"

Longarm silenced her with a finger on her lips. "Don't say nothing. I've just been looking up through a knothole in the bottom of heaven and I want to hear the angels sing some more."

"Am I as good as a white girl?"

"That's a fool thing to say. You're at least as good as *any* kind of gal, white, red, or even blue. I disremember doing it with a blue gal, but I doubt she'd teach me anything you left out."

"You're sure I satisfied you completely, darling?"

"You've got your hand on how satisfied I am. If I was more satisfied I'd be dead."

"Then why did he leave me, the brute?"

Longarm nodded in sudden understanding as he sighed and said, "Likely crazy, if you ever done him like that. Who are we talking about, the brave you're 'sort of' married up with?"

"My husband's a white man, the son of a bitch!"

"Oh. I was wondering what we were trying to prove just now. When did this lunatic run off on you, Gloria?"

"About a year ago. He was a soldier at the fort. He said—he said he loved me."

"Yeah, most men do, when they marry up with someone. What happened to him? He get transferred out?"

"Of course. There's not much you don't know about Indian matters, is there? My father warned me it would happen, but I thought Roger meant it. You know what my father tried to tell me?"

"Sure I do. The new army regulations say no soldier can trifle with a reservation gal unless his intentions are honorable. Your Roger had to marry you or leave you be, and seeing you're so pretty . . ."

"Roger said he considered me a white girl! He said he'd take me with him when he left the fort. He said he'd told his folks about us and that they'd be proud to have me back East. He said . . . he said . . . God damn it, you know what he said. You men all say the same things when you mean to do a woman wrong!"

"Well, he likely meant it at the time, honey. I know what it's been like for you, but—"

"You know nothing, white man! You don't know what it's like to grow up wishing you were white, or

30

even black, for God's sake, if only you could belong *somewhere!*"

"You seem to be accepted by your tribe, Gloria."

"A lot you know! Why do you think they call me Two-Women? If my father hadn't been a chief—"

"Now just back up and study what you're saying, honey. Your father *is* a chief."

"Perhaps, but if he'd been just another brave—"

"If? If? Hell, if the dog hadn't stopped to pee he'd have caught the rabbit. Everything in life's an 'if,' and we have to make do with the ifs the Good Lord gives us. Try 'if' another way and your mama never would have been taken by Blackfoot. Or you could have been born dead, or a boy, or some other Indian kid named Mary. You know what you're doing, honey? You're picking a fight with 'if' instead of living with all you got!"

"That's easy for you to say. But if you'd been born a breed . . ."

"Well, I wasn't born a breed. Or the Prince of Wales, either: I was born on a hard-scrabble farm to folks too poor to spit. I'd have settled for being a Hindu maharaja with elephants and dancing gals to play with, and my complexion could be damned. So don't go cussing me for being white. It wasn't my idea and it ain't been all that easy."

"What would you have done if you'd been born an Indian, or colored?"

"Can't say. It never happened. I'd likely be another jasper, but I'd likely have managed to make do with what I was. Those ifs don't give us much choice."

"You'd have made a terrible Indian. You think too West Virginian."

"Likely you're right. Seems to me your own head's screwed on funny, though. If you don't like the name Two-Women, how come you almost got me shot by insisting on it over at that other hotel this evening?"

"It's my name, the only name I have."

"What's wrong with your mother's name, Witherspoon?"

"Those people rejected me. My father's people accepted me, however grudgingly, as at least a half-person." She shuddered as she added, "Not that I don't have to put up with sly remarks on the reservation. Some of the older squaws got quite a laugh when my soldier boy deserted me as the cast-off squaw he must have considered me."

"Gloria, I suspicion you fret too much over things. Your Daddy must think highly of you or he'd never have sent you on a mission for his tribe."

She fondled him almost painfully, as she asked, "How am I as a lover? Am I really the best you've ever had?"

Longarm was only half-lying as he nodded and ran a hand over her moist flesh, assuring her, "I don't like to brag, but I've been with some nice gals in my time and, yes, you are purely the best I've ever got next to."

"Do you think you'll always remember me as the best lay you ever had?"

"I'll have to. Anything better would kill me, but what's this about remembering? We're just getting started."

"No. After this night, you'll never be able to touch me again."

"I won't? Well, sure, we'll have to be careful once we're up near the reservation and all, but—"

"Never," she insisted, adding, "You can do it all you want tonight, if you're man enough, but one night of love is all I give. To anyone. I suppose you think I owe you an explanation?"

He said, "No. I suspicioned it was too good for you to be really enjoying it. I heard about an actress back East who plays the same trick. She's had men duelling over her, blowing out their own fool brains and beating on her door at all hours with flowers, books, and candy."

The beautiful breed's voice was downright nasty as she asked, cruelly, "Are you suggesting you'll be different, Mr. Longarm?"

"Oh, I'll want you. I'll likely remember this night

as long as I live and some night, alone on the trail, I'll do some hard wishing, most likely. But I don't reckon I'll play your game."

"Pooh, you don't even understand my reasons."

"Sure I do. You're a pretty little thing all eaten up inside with hate for us menfolks. One fool man betrayed your love and now you reckon you can get back at us all by turning the tables. You're playing love 'em and leave 'em 'cause you got loved and left. Your revenge is to drag us poor old boys into bed and pleasure us crazy, leaving us with nothing but the memory of the best lay any man could ever dream of, and no way to ever get it again. I'll allow it's mean as hell, but it ain't original."

She sat up suddenly to snap, "I suppose, now, you're going to try and say you lied before? I suppose you're going to pretend it won't bother you never to have me again?"

Longarm thought before he answered. He knew, now, that much of what he'd just enjoyed had been an act of curious cruelty.

He decided the hell with it. Real women were complicated enough and it wasn't as if the supply was likely to run out.

She insisted, "Well, am I? Am I not the greatest lay you've ever had, or ever will have?"

He feigned a mournful sigh and said, "Yeah, I know when I'm whipped. If you don't let me call on you this weekend I'll likely wind up jerking off under your window. Can't we make an exception, just this once?"

Her voice was triumphant as she chortled, "No. I swear by Manitou you'll never sleep with me again. Two-Women has spoken!"

He rolled over as if to fall asleep. He figured it was the least a man could do, considering.

After a time, bored with her game, Gloria got softly out of bed and tiptoed back to her own room, the victor of her own grotesque game of revenge. Longarm got up and locked the door, muttering, "Thank God. I was afraid I'd never get any sleep tonight!"

Chapter 3

Longarm could see there was trouble long before he and Gloria reached the cluster of frame buildings in the rented buckboard he was driving. A huge crowd of Indians stood around the reservation agency across from the log trading post the center had grown up around.

It was midafternoon as they arrived and the sun floated above the purple Rockies far to the west. The Blackfoot reservation occupied an expanse of rolling short-grass prairie fifty miles across, but the tracks of the Iron Horse crossed the reservation and they'd been able to get off and rent the buckboard at another town just over the horizon to the east.

Gloria sat primly at his side, less friendly than ever, having not quite managed to claim him as her latest victim the night before. Longarm had been too gallant to make the obvious remark about black widow spiders when he found her dressed and coldly formal at dawn.

An Indian ran over as Longarm reined in near the edge of the crowd, and shouted something to Gloria in the high, nasal dialect of her tribe. The girl blanched and gasped, "Oh, God, no!"

Then, before Longarm could ask her what was up, she was out of her seat and running through the crowd, who gave way with expressions of compassion for the pretty little breed.

Longarm shouted to anyone who'd listen, "What's going on? Anyone here speak English?"

A short moon-faced man in faded denims and a

very tall black hat came over to say, "I am Yellow Leggings. When I was young I killed a soldier and took his horse with me to Canada. Heya! That was a good fight we had at Greasy Grass! Were you there?"

"No, I'm still wearing my hair. What's all the fuss about?"

"I was a Dog Soldier. Now I am only a reservation policeman and they do not pay me on time. Wendigo has struck again. This time He-Who-Walks-the-Night-Winds took Real Bear. The people are very frightened."

Longarm nodded, sweeping his gunmetal gaze over the silent, unblinking faces crowded around him. He turned back to Yellow Leggings. "Where'd it happen?"

"In his house. The almost-girl you rode in with lives there, too. I think it was a good thing she was not home last night. The Wendigo would have torn her apart, too."

"Which house was his?"

"That one, north of the agency. The agent and some of the Indian police are in there now. I didn't want to go inside. I am not afraid of man or beast, but I don't like to be near spirit happenings. I told them I would stay out here and keep order."

"Can you get somebody to tie this mule to a post, Yellow Leggings? I'd better see what's going on."

"Go, then. I will see to your wagon and the things in back. I never steal in peacetime."

Longarm jumped down with a nod of thanks to the older Indian and elbowed his way through the crowd. Somewhere ahead of him, a woman screamed shrilly in mindless grief.

He went to the indicated cabin of unpainted lumber, and finding the door open, went inside.

Gloria was being comforted on a couch by a thin, blonde white woman and an older, fatter squaw. Gloria was still screaming, her face buried in her hands. Longarm saw that there was another room and went to the entrance as a harassed-looking young white man came out, blinking in surprise to see another white.

Longarm said, "I'm U.S. Deputy Marshal Custis Long. You must be the Blackfoot agent?"

"I am, and you have come to the right place, lawman. I hope you have a strong stomach."

Longarm followed the man into the bedroom, where two Indian police in those same tall hats stood over what looked at first like a badly butchered side of beef on the bed.

Longarm suppressed a wave of nausea as he recognized the form on the blood-soaked mattress as that of a man. From the blood on the walls and ceiling it looked as if he might have been skinned alive.

The agent said, "His name was Real Bear. You'll have to take my word for it, he was an Indian."

"He was the man I came up here to see. How long ago did it happen?"

"Nobody knows. They found him like this about an hour ago. We were supposed to hold a meeting this afternoon and I sent one of my police over to fetch him. Now you know as much as I do."

"Not quite. You say he didn't turn up for a meeting. What was the meeting about?"

"Just the usual stuff. Complaints about the government rations being late, as usual. Some trouble about stolen livestock. Nothing that can't wait, now."

"One of your Indians said something about *another* Wendigo killing. Has anything like this happened before?"

"Not here at the center. Some of the old folks have been jawing about spirits out on the prairie, but I don't seem to be missing anybody. To tell you the truth, I didn't take it too seriously. I'm shorthanded here, and I've been having trouble with the damned army again, and—"

"I know people in the B.I.A. Anybody think to look for sign?"

One of the Indian policemen looked up to say, "No sign. No footprint. Nobody see Wendigo come. Nobody see Wendigo go. We find only . . . this."

Longarm touched a finger to a blood spatter on the

wall and said, "Dry. Must have been done last night in the dark."

The agent snorted and said, "Tell me something I haven't figured out an hour ago! Of course he was killed at night! Who in hell's going to walk out of here covered with blood and carrying a man's skin, in broad daylight?"

Then, before Longarm could answer, the agent suddenly ran to the window, leaned out, and threw up.

Neither Longarm nor the Indian police said anything as he recovered, turned wanly from the window, and said, "Sorry. Thought I got it all the first time. I, uh, never saw a thing like this before."

Longarm's voice was gentle as he said, "It ain't a thing you see every day. Maybe we'd best go outside to talk about it."

"I have a duty to investigate," the young man said.

"Sure you do. So have I. But this'll keep. If these other peace officers can't find sign to read in here, the two of us ain't likely to. I see our next best bet as some solid jawboning on the whys and wherefores."

"Well, we'd best take the chief's daughter over to our place and put something strong in her. Right now I could use a drink myself!"

"Let's go, then. Which one of these peace officers is the ranking lawman, hereabouts?"

Both Indians and the agent looked surprised. Then the agent nodded at the taller of the two and said, "I guess Rain Crow, here, has the most seniority."

Longarm nodded at the Blackfoot and said, "Glad to know you, Rain Crow. You can call me Longarm. I reckon you'd best come along while we put some twos and twos together."

Rain Crow asked, "You want me to come with you, in the agency?"

"You're a lawman, ain't you?" Longarm shot a quizzical glance at the agent, who quickly nodded and said, "Of course. I'm assigning you to help the marshal, Rain Crow. He'll need a guide around the reservation and help with his horses and—"

"I'll get a *boy* from you to wrangle for us," Longarm cut in, adding, "I'm going to need *men* like Rain Crow as my deputies."

To his credit, the young agent caught on and nodded as the Indian followed them out of the blood-spattered bedroom.

Out in the other room, they found the couch empty. The agent nodded again and said, "Good. I see Nan and old Deer Foot managed to get poor Gloria out of this god-awful place. We'll likely find 'em in our kitchen."

"Nan would be your wife, Mr. . . . ?"

"Durler. Calvin Durler. My wife Nan and I have been out here about a year. I'm afraid we're still pretty green."

"You talk like a farming man, Calvin. I was born in West Virginia, myself."

"I'm afraid we're from farther east. Our home was in Maryland."

"Tidewater Maryland or the Cumberland?"

"Cumberland, by God. I'm not *that* much of a dude!"

"There you go. I suspicioned you had hair on your chest, Calvin."

The youth laughed and said, "I'm still ashamed of throwing up like a baby, but I thank you for the neighborly way you took it."

"Hell, you never threw up on *me*, Calvin. Maybe if more folks got sick to their stomachs when folks they knew got killed, we'd live in a more peaceable world."

The three men went outside and elbowed their way through the upset, questioning Indians to the larger agency residence. Calvin Durler led his guests to the side door and they went in to find Nan Durler brewing coffee in her sparsely furnished, whitewashed kitchen. Her husband asked, "Where's Gloria?" and the blonde woman replied, "In the bedroom. I made her lie down. Deer Foot's with her."

"Deer Foot's our housemaid," offered Durler to Longarm, who'd figured as much.

38

The agent took a brandy snifter from a sideboard and poured two glasses, holding one out to Longarm. The deputy held it out to the Indian, saying, "Where's mine, Calvin?"

The agent and his wife exchanged glances. Then Durler said, "I didn't make up the regulation, Longarm, but it's against the law to give an Indian a drink."

"Yeah, I heard," said Longarm, placing the glass, untasted, on the sideboard.

The Indian said, "I know what is in your heart, but it is all right. I will not be offended if you white men drink without me."

"You may not be, but I would," said Longarm. "When my deputies can't drink, I can't drink. Maybe we'd best all have some coffee."

Durler nodded eagerly and said, "That's just what I need, a hot cup of coffee. I'll pour it, Nan."

But Nan Durler, who'd been watching and sizing up the play, shook her head and said, "The three of you gents sit down. It's my place to pour for guests."

With the niceties out of the way for the moment, Longarm faced the other white man and his new Indian sidekick across the plank table and said, "All right, I'm a man with an open mind, but I can't buy a spook dropping down out of the sky to skin folks alive. So what we have is a human killer as well as his victim."

He saw the hesitation in the Indian's eyes and asked, "You got another notion, Rain Crow?"

"I don't know. The Dream Singers say Wendigo walks the night because our people have turned from the old ways. I know you think this is foolish, but—"

"Hold on. Foolish is a strong word, Rain Crow. I ain't one to sass my elders. Some of the old folks, red or white, just might know things I don't. I'll go along with evil spirits, if I cut an evil spirit's trail. I have to say, though, most of the men I've seen killed have been killed by other men, up to now. Chief Real Bear sent word to us about a rogue Blackfoot breed named

Johnny Hunts Alone. Does that name mean anything to either of you gents?"

Durler looked blank and shook his head. Rain Crow frowned and said, "I have heard the name. The old ones say his white father rode with us long ago, in the Shining Times of the beaver trade."

"Real Bear reported that he'd come back to the reservation. You're a reservation peace officer, so you likely know a lot of folks hereabouts."

"I know many people, many. But this man you speak of is a half-breed."

Longarm nodded. "Yep, somewhere in his mid-thirties. What's his being a breed have to do with it? You have breeds living among you, don't you?"

"Of course, but not many, and they are known to everyone. Real Bear's daughter in the other room is half white. There is the Collins family and the Blood woman called Cat Eyes. Then there is Burning Nose and—"

"In other words, breeds are rare enough for every-one on the reservation to take note, or likely gossip some about 'em?"

The Indian smiled. "The old women like to tell dirty stories and everyone knows how breeds come into the world. Yes, if there was a half-white Blackfoot called Johnny, I would have heard about him."

"You think Real Bear was lying, then?"

"No. He was a good person. If he said this man was among us, it must be so. Yet it is not so. I don't have an answer for this."

"Try it another way. Could a breed be passing him-self off as a full-blooded Blackfoot?"

"This is more possible than that Real Bear lied, but he would have to look like a full-blood and he would have to act like a full-blood. You know how it is with breeds."

"No, Rain Crow, I don't know any such thing. You don't like breeds, do you?"

The Indian looked uncomfortable. Longarm said, "They have the same troubles on our side of the fence,

Rain Crow. Most white folks suspicion breeds of all sorts of things."

"You think they're bad people, too?"

"No, I think they've got a hard row to hoe. Whites don't trust 'em because they're part Indian. Indians likely wonder if they can fully trust a man who is half white. I reckon a breed gets looked at sort of closer than the rest of us. Though, when you think on it, the best chief the Comanche ever had was a breed named Quanna Parker and the worst renegade who ever scalped a white man was a lily-white bastard named Simon Girty. So I'd say breeds are likely no better or worse than most folks, but I'll go along with you on Johnny Hunts Alone having a hard time passing himself off as a full-blood. Not just because he's a breed, but because he was raised mostly white. He'd have to be clever as old Coyote to pass muster here on the reservation."

"Heya! You have heard the tales of Coyote?"

"Sure. You ain't the first Indian lawman I've worked with. Let's study more on where this jasper might be hiding. You know the layout, Rain Crow. Where would you be if you were a white-raised Blackfoot?"

"The reservation is very big. It has five towns and much open range. How do you know he didn't leave when Real Bear recognized him?"

"Come on, Rain Crow, you ain't going to play cigar store Indian on me, are you?" Longarm prodded gently.

The young Blackfoot looked away and said, "You don't think Wendigo killed Real Bear. You think he was killed by a real person."

"There you go. And Real Bear was a good man with a good heart, so if he was killed by a real person—"

"Heya! The only one who'd want him dead would be someone who was afraid he'd been recognized! Someone who didn't want Real Bear to tell on him!"

"Now you're talking like a lawman, old son. So do you reckon we should look for spooks, or—"

"I will start asking the old ones about the Shining Days when the man called Johnny Hunts Alone lived among us," said Rain Crow, getting to his feet and leaving without ceremony.

As soon as the policeman was gone, Longarm grinned at the agent and his wife and said, "I'd purely like some of that brandy, now."

Durler laughed and poured each of the three of them a shot, saying, "You sure have a way with Indians. I swear to God, I haven't been able to get much cooperation from any of my charges."

"I noticed. Maybe you could start by *talking* to them."

Durler protested, "Nan and I have been doing our best to make friends with our charges and—"

"That's the second time you've called them your *charges*," Longarm cut in. "Before the army whipped 'em down and fenced 'em in, they thought of themselves as *men*."

"I see how you played on Rain Crow's pride, Longarm, but I've got responsibilities here, and damn it, they act like children around most white men."

"Sure they do. That's probably because every time they *haven't* acted like children, lately, somebody's shot at them! You take away my gun and smack me alongside the head every time I try to think for myself and I'll act childish, too. But I wasn't sent up here to tell you how to do your job for the B.I.A. I ain't buttering up your, uh, charges, to *steal* your job, neither. You see, I ain't about to track down a renegade hidden out amidst all these folks unless I get some of 'em on my side."

"You think you can talk the Blackfoot into turning the renegade in?"

"Well, *one* Indian did it. Now that I'm here, it'll only take one more."

"In other words," Durler said, "you think some of the Indians are hiding him from us?"

"He has to be hiding somewhere. What *else* are the Blackfoot hiding from you?"

"Hiding from me? I don't know. What would they be keeping from me?"

Longarm shrugged and said, "A reservation's like a jail in some ways. There're always things the cooped-up folks don't want the warden, or the Indian agent, to know. If Real Bear was working for our side, Johnny Hunts Alone would be on the other."

Durler nodded and said, "You mean the trouble-makers might be hiding him from you. If only we knew who the troublemakers were."

Longarm's eyebrows rose a notch, then he frowned and asked, "Don't you know which Indians are bucking you, Cal?"

"Not really. All of them seem a little sullen and none of 'em come right out and say they aim to scalp me. I think some of 'em might be drinking when I ain't looking."

"I smelled firewater when a couple passed me to windward, but you always have drinking on a reservation. It's as natural as small boys smoking corn silk behind the hen house. How about Dream Singing? Gloria Two Women made mention of some Ghost Dancing her daddy was worried about."

Durler laughed and shook his head, saying, "Oh, I'm not worried about that crazy new religion of Wovoka and his raggedy Paiutes. We got a notice about it from headquarters. The army says it's not serious."

Longarm looked disgusted and said, "Army didn't think much of Red Cloud's brag over in the Black Hills, either. 'Fess up, Cal. Do you *know* if there are any Ghost Dancers on this reservation?"

Durler shot a sheepish glance at his wife, who seemed very interested in her fingernails at the moment. Then, seeing she wasn't going to help or hinder, he sighed and said, "Damnation, Longarm, I've got over fifteen thousand sections of damn near empty prairie to cover!"

"I know. How much of it have you ever really looked at?"

"Not one hell of a lot, as you likely suspicion. But it ain't as if I haven't been trying to do my job! I've got six villages, a model farm, and more damn paper work than ten Philadelphia lawyers could handle! I'm putting in a sixteen-hour day and I'm still swamped, as Nan can tell you!"

His wife looked up to nod grimly as she muttered, "He's up past midnight, every night, with those infernal books of his!"

Longarm looked away, uncomfortable with the message he thought he might be reading in Nan's upset eyes. To steer the conversation away from a topic he thought might be getting under both their skins, he said, "I know you've a lot of corn to shuck, Cal. How are you getting on with the other white folks?"

"What white folks? We're up to our necks in Blackfoot. They hate us for being white and the whites in town and over at the army post hate us for feeding the rascals. The only white who ever comes out here is the sutler who owns the trading post across the way. He comes when the spirit moves him, which ain't often. I'm supposed to issue cash to my Indians, but Washington's slow in sending it and the sutler doesn't give credit."

"I know the type. He likely has an uncle in Washington, too. It's all cash and carry? No swapping for furs and hides or—? Never mind, that was a fool question, wasn't it?"

Durler smiled thinly, glad to be able to pontificate on something he knew better than his visitor. He said, "Yeah, the Shining Times are gone and so are most of the buffalo. The Indians still hunt a mite. Not enough game left for trading the old ways. We give each Indian family a small cash allowance and the trading post sells 'em the most expensive salt and matches this side of the Mississippi. Like you said, somebody likely has an uncle."

"That council meeting Real Bear never made it to was something about missing livestock, wasn't it?" the marshal asked.

"Some of the Indians complained of white cow thieves. Don't know if it's true or not. Along with the demonstration farm, which grows mostly weeds, we have a reservation herd, which sort of melts away as you look at it each sunup. It's a toss-up who's worse as a farmer—a Blackfoot or a cowboy. I know for a fact some of 'em have run steers for private barbecues. There are a lot of hard feelings between us and the local whites, so it wouldn't surprise me all that much if a few government cows wind up wearing a white man's brand."

"Surprise me more if they left you alone. What reservation brand have you registered with the territorial government?"

Durler said, "Oh, most of 'em are delivered with *U.S.* stamped on their hides. I haven't been able to teach my Indian herders all that much about branding, and as to a registered brand, well . . . "

"Good night!" Longarm exclaimed. "And you've still got one cow left! You sure live in the midst of Christian neighbors, Calvin!"

"Look, I'm an Indian agent, not a cowhand. I *thought* I was a farmer, before I tried to grow stuff in this prairie sod. They told me the Indians would help us, but—"

Longarm shoved himself away from the table and got to his feet, saying, "I've got to get over to the fort and borrow a horse from the remount sergeant. I'll be back before sundown and we can jaw some more. You got an ice house or something we can store the body in?"

"Store it? Ain't I supposed to *bury* Real Bear?"

"Sure, after I get a sawbones to look him over and tell me what he died from."

"Come on, we know how he died! He was skinned alive."

"Maybe. I'd like an M.D. to give me an educated guess as to bullets, poisons and such, though. He'll keep a day or so in this dry, thin air, so you put him in a shady spot with maybe some chopped ice in the box with him. I'll show you how when I get back. I want to make it over to the fort and back by daylight."

He tipped his hat to Nan and ducked out the side door as the agent followed him toward the buckboard. The crowd of Indians was still in place, standing sullenly silent and not appearing to notice either white man as they crossed the village street. Longarm found a young boy seated on the trading post steps with the reins of his rented mule in hand. He gave the kid a nickel and a smile for his trouble. The kid put the coin in his britches and went away without saying thanks or looking back. Longarm couldn't tell whether they were all pissed at him, the agent, or white folks in general.

It occurred to Longarm that unless he found the killer of Real Bear pretty quickly, things were likely to get ugly hereabouts.

Fort Banyon was little more than an outpost, manned by an over-aged second lieutenant and a skeleton platoon of dragoons. A cluster of log buildings surrounded a parade ground of bare earth and was surrounded in turn by a rail fence, broken in places. Everything from the tattered flag drooping from the flagstaff of lodgepole pine to the threadbare uniforms of the men lounging on the orderly room steps told Longarm there hadn't been a general inspection for some time and that morale was low, even for a frontier garrison.

He wasn't challenged as he drove through the open gateway and across the parade to the orderly room. The C.O., a dumpy man with a florid face and an unbuttoned officer's blouse, came out on the porch to stare at him morosely as Longarm hitched the mule to a rail. As the deputy walked over to the steps the officer asked, "Did you bring mail from town?"

"No sir. I'm a Deputy U.S. Marshal, not the mailman. I need a mount. I generally ride a gelding at least fifteen hands high. Got my own saddle and bridle."

46

"What are you talking about, mister? This is an army post! We don't sell horses!"

"Aw, hell, Lieutenant, this argument I keep getting from you fellows is as tedious as shitting on an ant pile. I know you're supposed to give me an argument and we both know that in the end, I'll get the horse. So what say we agree it's a hell of a note how the Justice Department imposes on the army and I'll be on my way."

Before the officer could reply, his first sergeant came out to join him. The C.O. said, "Lawman. Says he wants a horse."

The sergeant shook his head at Longarm and said, "We're short on mounts, mister. We're here to keep an eye on them Blackfoot, not to be a remount station."

"Yeah, I noticed how scared you are of Indians. Your pickets damn near shot me as I came in. You look like an old soldier, Sarge. Do we have to go through all this bullshit? You know damn well I'm riding out of here on one of Uncle Sam's ponies, and if you keep me here much longer I aim to make you feed me supper, too!"

"You've got requisition papers, I guess?" the sergeant said.

"Sarge, I've got carte blanche. I'm covering first degree murder. Federal. So give me something to sign and I'll be on my way."

The two army men exchanged glances. Then the lieutenant shook his head and said, "Nope. I'm short-handed on men and mounts. Maybe you can borrow a pony over at the reservation agency. They're federal, too."

"Yeah, and my legs drag when I ride Indian ponies. I ride with a McClellan saddle and too much gear for one of those skinny critters I've seen over yonder. Maybe if Custer hadn't shot all those Indian ponies they'd *have* one fifteen hands high, but he did, and they don't."

"You don't like our army, mister?" the lieutenant bristled.

"Why, boys, I like it more than I can tell you. Hell, if I was *mad* at you, I'd likely try and give you a hard time."

"You feel up to giving a platoon of dragoons a hard time, mister?"

"You mean *whup* all thirty-odd of you? Not hardly, Lieutenant. I'm a friendly cuss. So why don't you lend me a mount and I'll tell you what; I'll just forget about a few old reportables, next time I wire the government."

"Reportables? You must be drunk, lawman! You got no power to report doodly shit about *army* matters!"

"Well, I ain't connected up with the Inspector General's office, though, now that you mention it, I do have some drinking pals in Denver who work for the I.G. All us lawmen sort of exchange information."

He looked around thoughtfully before adding, innocently, "But you're likely right. I don't figure the I.G. would be interested in little things like no guards posted or a few busted fences or that flag nailed up there night and day without proper hoisting lines. Tell me something, Lieutenant. How *do* you hold proper flag ceremonies twice a day, the way you've got it sort of up there for keeps?"

The officer scowled and started to bluster. Then he shrugged and told the sergeant, "Give the blackmailing son of a bitch a horse."

"Does the lieutenant want him, ah, well-mounted?"

"By all means, Sergeant. He's a fellow federal officer," the C.O. said sweetly.

Longarm followed the first sergeant down the barracks line to the corrals as some of the enlisted men who'd heard the exchange followed. Longarm sighed wearily. He'd been through this same hazing so many times, he knew the routine better than most soldiers did.

They got to the remuda corral, where a civilian in buckskins perched atop a corral rail, jawing with a uniformed stable hand. The first sergeant introduced the civilian as a scout named Jason, they winked at the horse wrangler and said, "Cut old Rocket out for this nice deputy, will you?"

The stable hand grinned and took a throw rope from the gatepost as Longarm said, "I'll trot back and fetch my saddle."

"Don't you aim to watch us pick your pony, mister?"

"No, I know you'll do right by me. By the time you get that bronc roped and steadied I'll have time to fetch my saddle, walk to town, get a drink, and walk back."

He knew he was only half jesting, so he strolled back up the line to the buckboard, removing his Winchester and possibles from the saddle in the wagon bed with slow deliberation. He knew that while they might even try to kill him, they wouldn't steal his gear, so he left it in the buckboard.

As he turned with the McClellan braced on one hip, he saw that the civilian scout, Jason, had followed him part of the way up the company street. Jason was almost as tall as Longarm and a bit older. There were a few gray hairs among the greasy thatch on his head and in his spade-shaped beard, and his suntanned face was creased with friendly laugh-wrinkles. Jason fell in at Longarm's side as they walked back to the corral, saying, "They treated me the same way when I was first posted here, mister. I ain't generally a tattletale, but I reckon they've gone overboard with old Rocket!"

"Bad bronc, huh?"

"No. Rocket's a killer. I can see you know which end of the horse the bit goes in, but if I was you I'd pass on Rocket. It's not like it was a shameful thing to do. There ain't a man in this outfit who is ashamed when it comes to old Rocket."

"I thank you for the warning, Jason. If I live, you can call me Longarm."

"Where do I send your possibles after the fool horse throws you and stomps on your head?"

Longarm didn't answer. He saw that the soldiers had roped and blindfolded a big gray gelding and led him into an empty corral next to the remuda. As the others held Rocket, Longarm threw his saddle over the broad back and cinched it, asking, "Ain't most of these grays assigned to army bands?"

The stable boss grinned and said, "Yeah, old Rocket was a mite, uh, spirited for parades. So they sent him out here to fight Indians. You ain't scared of spirited horses, are you, lawman?"

"Let's get it over with," said Longarm, getting the bridle on over the blindfold after punching Rocket in the nose to make him open his mouth for the bit.

He put a foot in the stirrup and hoisted himself up into the saddle, ready for anything. But nothing happened. The big gray stood as placid as a plough horse while Longarm settled in the saddle and got a firm grip on the reins. He muttered, "One of that kind, huh?" Then, in a louder tone, he said, "All right, yank the blinds and give me room."

The soldiers scattered as the stable boss pulled the bandanna blindfold out from under the bridle and joined his messmates on the surrounding rails. The big gray blinked at the sunlight, took two steps backwards toward the center of the corral, and tried to jump over the late-afternoon sun, as someone shouted, "Hot damn!"

Longarm yanked hard on the reins to force the gray's head down and to one side as they came down. The Spanish bit he'd rigged his bridle with had been purchased with such emergencies in mind, and while he customarily rode with a gentle hand on the reins, he could hurt a horse with the bit if he had to, and right now he had to.

Rocket didn't like it much. He was used to army bits as well as having his own way. With his head held down almost against Longarm's left stirrup, he had to buck in a tight circle; any good rider can stay aboard a bucking horse as long as it bucks in a repeated pattern. Some of the soldiers might not have known this, so they were impressed as the big lawman rode easily, swaying in tune with the mindless anger of the killer bronc.

Then Rocket saw he wasn't getting anywhere bucking in a circle, so he danced sideways and threw his full weight against the corral rails. He had intended his rider's right leg to take most of the shock, but Longarm saw it coming, kicked free of the right stirrup, and got his leg up in time. The big gray followed up his knee-breaking attempt with a sideways crabbing the purpose of which was to throw Longarm before he could get his leg back down in place. Longarm expected that, too, so it didn't work.

The big gray fought to raise his head, trying to get the cruel bit between his teeth. Then, when he saw that the enemy tormenting him had the bit well-set, he decided, as long as his muzzle was down by the man's left foot, that he might as well bite it off.

Longarm snatched his toe back as the big yellow teeth snapped at it, then he kicked the gray's muzzle, hard. Rocket tried a couple more times before he gave up on that one, his nostrils running blood.

They circled the corral a few more times, spinning like a top, but the gray was tiring, and like any bully, Rocket didn't like to get hurt; Longarm was the meanest critter he'd ever been ridden by.

"You got him, mister!" someone shouted. "Just stay on a few more minutes and that old bastard will be your asshole buddy!"

Longarm shouted, "I don't want to marry up with him, I want to *work* with him!"

He steadied the gray as he stopped bucking, rode him once around the corral at a weary trot, and reined in by the rails, climbing quickly off and perching by the boss wrangler, maintaining his hold on the reins. Rocket saw an opportunity and pulled suddenly back to unseat him, but Longarm leaned back and gave the Spanish bit a vicious yank, drawing more blood. After that, Rocket stood very still indeed as Longarm said, "That was sure interesting. Now, I'd like to pick out a gelding fifteen hands high and if you give me another bronc I'll *kill* the son of a bitch. Then I'll come for *you*, personal."

"You made your point when you stayed aboard old Rocket, mister. We was just having a little friendly fun. I'll issue you Betsy. She's a good steady mare."

"No you won't. I said I'd pick a gelding. I reckon I earned it, don't you?"

The wrangler noted the chilly look in Longarm's eyes and nodded soberly. "Yep, I'd say it's time to quit while I'm ahead."

Chapter 4

Longarm got back to the Indian agency near sundown, riding a tall chestnut and leading the mule and buckboard.

Calvin Durler came out to help as he unhitched and unsaddled in the agency corral. Durler said, "Nan's got a room fixed up for you and we have Real Bear in the root cellar, wrapped in a wagon tarp. Nan didn't like it much, but what the hell, we haven't harvested enough to mention, so the cellar's mostly empty and I put her preserves on the other side."

Longarm nodded. "I'll run the body into town come sunup. The army post has no surgeon but they tell me there's a county coroner in Switchback. You do have a telegraph line here, don't you?"

"No. We're supposed to, but they never installed it. I use the one at the federal land office in town on government business. The land agent's sort of mad about it, too. Who'd you aim to wire?"

"My office. They figured I'd just come here, arrest the jasper Chief Real Bear pointed out, and be on my way back by now. I don't reckon they'll think Johnny Hunts Alone got the drop on me if I don't get in touch tonight. You're sure I won't be crowding you folks?"

"Hell, we're delighted to have white folks to talk to. Nan and me don't go to town much. The locals seem to blame us for past misdeeds of the Blackfoot, and maybe some Comanche, too! We've got us some champion Indian-haters in this territory!"

"Well, Montana was all Indian land up till a few

short years ago, so the locals are mostly the same people who drove the Indians back into this one corner to start with. How's Gloria Two-Women taking her daddy's murder, now? Did you get her calmed down enough for me to talk to yet?"

Durler shook his head exasperatedly. "Oh, she's jumped the reservation again. Says her name is Wither-something-or-other, now."

Longarm arched an eyebrow. "Do tell? When did all this happen?"

"While you were over getting this horse. Gloria said a lot of crazy things, then she sort of took herself in hand and went over to her house to pack her duds. Deer Foot helped, but it's a funny thing—Gloria won't speak Blackfoot anymore. She says with her daddy dead she's not an Indian anymore. How do you figure that?"

Longarm shrugged. "Likely makes as much sense for her to try to make it as a white woman, after all. If I'd been here, I'd have suggested she try living in Oklahoma, where breeds have an easier time than most places. Maybe she knew that, though. She didn't say where she was going, huh?"

"Nope. Just rode to Switchback to catch a train. They could probably tell you at the station where she took it to, if you really want to question her about what happened."

"Hardly seems worth it," Longarm sighed. "She was with me when her daddy was killed, so we know she didn't do it. I, uh, got to know her pretty well on the train ride up from Denver, so I don't reckon she left anything out I could use. Real Bear never pointed out the renegade to her, so even if she was here, she couldn't identify the jasper for us. Is Rain Crow back with anything, yet?"

"He was by here an hour ago. He hasn't found out much we didn't know already. He did say the old ones don't think a man did it. They say the Wendigo punished Real Bear for turning his back on the old ways and accepting a breed as his daughter." Durler

54

shook his head wearily and added, "It's as well Gloria lit out. She was a proud little thing and some of the talk about her is right ugly."

Longarm studied a crow flying past and tried to appear disinterested as he asked, "Oh? What sort of gossip are the old squaws spreading about the gal?"

Durler shrugged and said, "The usual back-fence bullshit about any gal who lives alone, if she's pretty. She lived right next door, so Nan and I can tell you she was proper. They say she was married to a white man once. It was before we got here, so I can't say what went wrong. As far as I know, she was a perfect lady."

"I'll remember her as perfect, too," said Longarm, shifting his weight to meet the younger man's eyes again as he changed the subject. "I noticed you've got corn in the feed troughs. You been shipping it all this way with all this free grass around?"

"I grew the corn on my so-called model farm. The soil hereabouts is piss-poor or I'd have grown a real crop."

Longarm laughed and said, "You must be one hell of a farmer, Cal. If you'd asked me if you could grow corn on this reservation I'd have said it was impossible!"

Durler stared morosely down at the tawny stubble all around and said, "It damn near was. Like I said, it's poor soil and the Indians shirked such honest toil as I assigned 'em."

Longarm knew it wasn't his job, but he couldn't keep his mouth shut about such an obvious greenhorn notion. He said, "There's nothing wrong with the soil, Cal. It's the crop that was all wrong. You're a mile above sea level and damn near in Canada. About the only farm crop you can grow up here is barley. Corn's a lowland crop. Needs at least twenty inches of rain a year to survive."

"Yeah, I noticed our fields were a mite dry. I had Indians haul water to the corn. They didn't cotton to it much, but I knew Indians ate corn, so . . ."

"Cal," Longarm cut in, "it ain't my call to tell you

55

how to run your spread, but there's Indians and there's Indians. Your Blackfoot lived on wild game, roots, and such, before the army showed them the error of their ways. It's no wonder they've been shirking. No offense intended, but you ain't showing them how to farm the high plains. You're showing them how to make the same mistakes every other nester who's been dusted out has made, over and over."

Durler's jaw had a stubborn set to it as he snapped, "I'll admit I don't know this country, damn it, but what am I to do? My job is to make small-holders instead of hunters out of the Blackfoot. They gave me the job because I was a fair farmer, back East!"

"I don't doubt it, Cal. There are abandoned homesteads all over the prairie left by men who came out West with the skills they learned in other parts. You just can't farm out here the way you do back East."

"Will you show me how, then?"

"I don't aim to be here all that long. For openers I'd say to drill in some rye and barley next time. Then I'd get some of the old-timers to advise me about the climate, soil, and such."

"None of the nesters will talk to me, damn it!" the agent said sourly.

"I didn't mean *white* old-timers. These Indians were here long before it got so civilized. I know they're not keen on farming and you'll have as much to show them as they have to show you, but you'll do better *talking* to them than *lecturing* them. You get my drift?"

"Hell, only a handful speak English."

"I know. It would make your job a lot easier if you and Nan learned Blackfoot."

"Good God! We'd never be able to in a million years! I don't know one word of Blackfoot!"

"Sure you do. They speak Algonquin, which is about the easiest Indian language there is for a white man to pick up. Damn near every Indian word we already know is Algonquin."

"I tell you, I don't know word-one!"

56

"How about squaw, papoose, moccasin, tomahawk, or skunk, or possum?"

"Those are Algonquin words?"

"So are tom-tom, pow-wow, wampum, and succotash. I'll bet you know what every one of those words means, don't you?"

"Sure. I reckon they must have been the first Indian words the white folks learned when they got off the boat."

"There you go. You're halfway to learning the lingo already. You don't have to learn to speak it perfectly, but they'll respect you for trying. My Spanish is awful, but most Mexicans brighten up when I give 'em a chance to laugh at me, rather than the other way around. A little gal in a border town once even helped me learn a bunch of new words." Longarm smiled. "The lessons were purely enjoyable."

The agent chuckled. "I'll see if we can get Deer Foot to teach us some Blackfoot. Meanwhile, supper should be almost ready."

They went inside and found Nan Durler as good as her husband's word. The fare was simple, but well-cooked, and like most country folk, the three of them ate silently. It was something they didn't think about; witty dinner conversation is a city notion.

Nan had made a peach cobbler for dessert and insisted on Longarm's having two helpings before she'd let him step out onto the porch for an after-dinner smoke. He'd expected his host, at least, to join him. But he found himself alone on the steps, puffing a cheroot as he watched the stars come out over the distant Rockies.

It was peaceful outside, now. The Indians had drifted off home after jawing about the murder of their chief all afternoon. Somewhere in the night a medicine drum was beating softly, probably to keep the Wendigo away. Longarm judged the drum to be a good two miles distant, so he decided Rain Crow could tell him, later, what the fuss was all about.

He was halfway through his smoke when Nan Durler

57

came out to join him. She said, "Calvin's at his books again. Sometimes he spends half the night on those fool papers for the B.I.A."

Longarm nodded without answering as the blonde sat beside him on the steps. After a while she shuddered and said, "They're at that old drum again. Sometimes they beat it half the night. I don't know if I hate it more when the Indians are whooping it up or when they're quiet. Back home we had crickets and fireflies this time of year."

"Night noises are different on the prairie. I sort of like the way the coyotes sing, some nights."

"It wakes me up. It's no wonder the Blackfoot think the Wendigo walks at midnight out here. Some of the things I hear from my window are spooky as anything."

"Well," Longarm observed, "you're pretty high up for rattlers, hereabouts. I can't think of much else that can worry folks at night."

"The other night, I heard the strangest screaming. Calvin said it was a critter, but it sounded like a baby crying."

"Thin, high-pitched hollerings? Sort of *wheeeeee wheeeee wheeeee*?"

"Yes! It was awful. Do you know what it might have been?"

"No 'might' about it, ma'am. It was a jackrabbit."

He didn't add that jackrabbits screamed like that as they were being eaten alive by a silent coyote. He didn't think that part would comfort her.

She shuddered again and said, "I guess it could have been 'most any old thing. Sounded like it was getting skinned alive . . . oh, dear . . . "

"I'll be hauling the body into town, come morning, ma'am. I could wrap him in a tarp and leave him out in the buckboard overnight if it frets you to have him in your root cellar."

Nan grimaced and said, "Leave him be, but let's not dwell on it. I'm going to have to take at least two of the powders the doctor gave me if I'm to sleep a wink tonight."

58

Longarm asked cautiously, "Oh? You take sleeping powders often, ma'am?"

Her voice was bitter as she said, "Just about every night. My husband seems more interested in his books than in sleeping and I get so . . . so *lonely* when the wind starts to keen out on the prairie!"

"Most folks get used to the prairie after a time, ma'am."

"Most folks have neighbors, too. The Indians look through us, and you know we're outcasts to the other whites around here, don't you?"

Longarm shrugged and said, "Well, who wants to butter up to the grudge-holding kind, ma'am? There are likely others over in town who aren't so narrow-minded."

"I doubt it. You should see the looks they give us when we ride in from the reservation! You'd think the Indian Wars were still going on!"

Longarm noticed that she'd somehow moved closer to him and decided she was probably too upset to have realized it. He shifted away a little and said, "The Blackfoot were hostile Indians and it hasn't been all that long, ma'am. Some folks are sore about the Civil War and *those* memories are almost old enough to vote. You've got to remember some of your neighbors, red and white, were swapping lead not five years ago this night."

She moved closer, as if uneasy at the gathering dusk and asked, "Have you fought Indians, Longarm?"

He saw that there wasn't much room left for his rump, so he stayed put as he answered, "Yep. You name the tribe and I've likely traded a few shots with 'em."

"But you don't seem to hate Indians at all."

He tried to ignore the warmth of her thigh against his as he looked away and suggested, "I've been lucky about Indians. They never tried to do more than lift my hair. I mean, they never killed a woman or kid of mine. I was over at Spirit Lake just after the Sioux first rose under Little Crow and it was mighty ugly, but none of the dead white folks were my kin. I've left some squaws keening over their own dead in my time, so I can afford to forgive and forget. But it was right ugly out here until recently. The soldiers and other whites have done some terrible things, too, and not every Indian is the noble savage some have written about. Ugly feeds on ugly, and like I said, it wasn't all that long ago. We have to give both sides a mite more time to get used to having one another as neighbors."

Nan's hand was suddenly on Longarm's knee as she said, "You think Calvin is a fool, don't you?"

"I never said such a thing, ma'am!"

"You didn't have to. I've seen the mockery in your eyes. To you he's just a green kid, isn't he?"

Longarm got to his feet, not knowing how else to get her hand off his knee, as he said, "Getting sort of chilly, ain't it?"

She remained seated, looking up at him oddly as she asked, "Are you afraid to answer me?"

Longarm shook his head and said, "I thought I had, ma'am. You asked did I think your man was a fool and I said he wasn't one. He's younger than me and has a few things to learn. But he'll do."

"For you, maybe. Where are you going? It's early yet, and I'll never get any sleep this night."

"I'd be proud to sit out here and jaw some more," he said as tactfully as he could, "but I've got to get some shut-eye, and like I said, there's a chill in the air."

"I noticed," she said, looking suddenly away.

He saw that she didn't intend to go inside, so he said goodnight and left her sitting there, nursing whatever was eating at her. He noticed that she didn't answer, either. She surely seemed a moody little gal.

He went to his room and locked himself in from force of habit before sitting on the bed to pull off his boots. He frowned at the door for a time, then he said, "You're getting a dirty mind, old son. You just leave that damned door locked, hear? Her man is just down the hall, and damn it, a gent has to draw the line *some* damned where!"

The town of Switchback, as its name indicated, was a railroad community where the trains added a second engine to negotiate a sudden scarp in the high plains before going over the mountains to the west.

Longarm left the dead Indian with the county coroner and walked across the rutted street to the land office, where he found a federal official named Chadwick in charge. Chadwick was about forty and looked like a superannuated buffalo hunter, except for his broadcloth suit. Longarm told the land agent his reasons for calling and Chadwick led him back to a lean-to shack behind his office, where he kept the telegraph setup.

A writing desk stood under a long shelf of wet cell batteries. A sending and receiving set shared the green desk blotter with paper pads and some leather-bound code books. Chadwick asked if Longarm knew how to send, and seeing that the lawman needed no further help, left him to his own devices.

Longarm got on the key, patched himself through to Denver Federal, and sent a terse message:

CHIEF REAL BEAR MURDERED STOP STILL LOOKING FOR FUGITIVE STOP INVESTIGATING BOTH CASES STOP SIGNED LONG DEPUTY U S MARSHAL DENVER

Then he left without waiting for a reply. If he gave Marshal Vail a chance to contact him, he'd probably be saddled with all sorts of foolish questions and instructions.

He accepted a cigar from the land agent, and as they shared a smoke, filled his fellow federal man in on what had happened. Chadwick shook his head and said, "I heard the medicine men are jawing about evil spirits again. You don't think it means more Indian trouble, do you?"

"Don't know what it means. While I'm here, I'd best ask you some questions about the situation. You have many cattle spreads hereabouts?"

"Of course. That's what I'm doing here in Switchback. Since the rails came through and Captain Goodnight brought the longhorns north, Montana's turned to cattle country. Ain't that a bitch? Five, six years ago this was all buffalo and redskins!"

"I noticed the electric lamp over the railroad yards. Anyone wanting to claim more land would come to you, wouldn't they?"

"Sure. Most of the good stuff's been filed on, though. I guess you want to know how many offers I've gotten on the reservation, right?"

"I admire a man who thinks on his feet."

"Knew what you suspicioned the minute you told me about the dead Indian. But you're barking up the wrong tree. I've had requests to extend the open range west into the reservation, but everyone knows by now that my hands are tied. Land and B.I.A. are both under the Department of the Interior, but I can't file claims on Indian-held land and neither can anyone else."

"So there'd be no money in it for white folks hereabouts to trifle with the Blackfoot. How about revenge?"

"You mean some white man killing Indians just for the hell of it, like Liver-Eating Johnson? Maybe, if he was sort of crazy. This Indian you brought in was killed right on the reservation, right?"

"Next door to the agency."

"There you go. You show me a white man who can creep to the center of a reservation, kill a chief, and creep back out without leaving sign, and I'll show you a white man who can out-Indian an Indian! I was out here when the Blackfoot were still in business killing folks, and while I don't like 'em all that much, I'll give 'em the edge on skulking. You know what I suspicion? I suspicion that old Indian was killed by one of his own! I don't know a white man in the territory who could have pulled it off the way you say it happened."

"I'd say you've got a point," Longarm agreed. "Most Indian-killers pick 'em off along the edges of the reservation. I've got a warrant on a breed named Hunter or Hunts Alone. Any of the spreads hereabouts hire a breed hand, lately?"

"A breed, working on a Montana spread? Hell, they'd hire a nigger first. Not as if they have. I've never seen a nigger cowhand, have you?"

"Yep. First man ever killed in Dodge City was a colored hand called Tex. Someone shot him the first day of the first drive up from Texas and they've been shooting ever since. I'll take your word for it that most Montana hands are white, though. How about the railroad or some other outfit?"

"You mean here in Switchback? I know just about every man in town, at least on sight. I don't miss much, either, and I don't like Indians. If there was a half-breed working in Switchback, even swamping out saloons, I'd have seen him, maybe five minutes before I ran him out of town. I could tell you *stories*, Longarm!"

"I've heard 'em. Found some fellows after Apache worked 'em over, too. We don't have a good description of Johnny Hunts Alone, though. He could take after his pa's side of the family. No telling how white he might look."

"Didn't you say Chief Real Bear said he was on the reservation?"

"Yeah," Longarm said. "I see what you mean. He couldn't look *too* white, unless some of the others have fibbed about not noticing."

"He's got to look nigh pure white or pure Indian, then, whether he's hiding out with them or us. You can't have him both ways."

"You're right. I thank you for the smoke. I'd best get over and see what the doc can tell me."

Longarm left the land office and went back to the coroner's. Inside, he found Real Bear even more messed up than when he'd been found. The coroner seemed cheerful, considering, as he looked up from the god-awful mess in his zinc-lined autopsy tray and said, "They fractured his skull before they started taking him apart. He was struck from behind with a blunt instrument and most likely never knew what hit him."

"That's some comfort. You can't tell what the weapon was, huh?"

"If I could I'd have said so. You mind if I keep his skull? Save for being stove in a little, it's a beaut."

"I told his kin I'd bring him back for a proper funeral, Doc. Are you a headhunter? I took you for a Presbyterian."

"I'm writing a paper for the Smithsonian on hereditary bone structure. The Mountain Men spent more time screwing squaws than trapping beaver and some of the skull formations out here are getting interesting as hell."

"Going to bury him head and all anyway. But while we're on the subject, Doc, I've got papers on a Blackfoot breed who may be passing as anything. Is there anything I should be watching for?"

"You mean like the mark of Cain? It would depend on both parents. I've met pure-blooded Indians pale enough to worry about sunburn and some Scotch-Irish as white as you or me who have those same high cheekbones and hooked noses. I'd say if your man's part Algonquinoid he might be a bit hatchet-faced for a white, but his complexion could go either way. If you could get your suspect to take down his pants, a lot of Indians have a dark sort of birthmark on their tailbone."

Longarm grinned as he thought of a pretty little squaw he'd had with the lights on and dog-style, but he shook his head and said, "That doesn't seem a decent request, even from a lawman to a suspect. Could you sort of put him back together for me, Doc? I'd like to carry him home in a neater bundle."

"Come back in about an hour. You figure they'll leave the body in one of those tree-houses, or was he a Christian?"

"The Indian agency doesn't let 'em bury folks in the sky anymore. I know what you're thinking, Doc, but forget it. This one's gone for good."

He said he'd be back directly and stepped outside, glad to inhale some fresh air after the medicinal smell of the coroner's lab.

He headed back to where he'd left the buckboard, wondering what his next move ought to be, and suddenly grinned as he spied a wooden Indian standing in front of a cigar store next to a saloon. He muttered, "We were just talking about you!" and changed course to pick up some more smokes.

The unplanned move saved Longarm's life, but only by an inch.

Something buzzed across the back of his neck, followed by the report of a high-powered rifle, and he wasted no time wondering if it had been an angry hornet. He loped for cover at a long-legged run without looking back as another bullet ticked the tail of his coat, and then he dove head-first through the front window of the saloon, sliding across a table on his belly in a confusion of broken glass, scattered chips, and cards, as the men whose poker game he'd broken up flew backwards from the table in all directions, swearing in surprise.

Longarm landed on his shoulder, rolled, and came to his feet with his gun in his hand and facing the shattered window as he shouted, "Hold it! I'm purely sorry about how I came in, but I come in peace!"

A gambling man kneeling in a corner with a drawn derringer got up, saying, "We heard the shots outside, stranger. How'd you get so popular?"

Longarm moved to the other window and looked out, gun in hand. It came as no great surprise to him that the street and boardwalks were devoid of life or movement. Everyone within sound of the shots had taken cover.

The bartender joined Longarm at the window. He had a barrel stave in one hand but his voice was reasonable as he said, "Before you bust *this* window, friend, who's paying for the one you just come through so sudden?"

Longarm kept his eyes on the buildings across the way as he took out his wallet with his free hand and flashed his badge, saying, "Uncle Sam is paying for the glass and a round of drinks for everyone. Get back out of the light, though. That jasper was firing an express rifle!"

The gambling man with the derringer laughed and

said, "Hell, nobody shoots folks I'm drinking with! You want me to see if I can circle in on the son of a bitch for you, Marshal?"

"It's a kind thought, friend, but I imagine he's pulled up stakes, and I don't want gunplay with all those shops across the way likely filled with folks. I guess it's safe for us to have that drink, now."

"Any idea who tried to bushwhack you, Marshal?"

"I'm only a deputy, and I've got lots of folks gunning for me. Getting shot at comes with the job."

He turned from the window to see the dozen-odd men in the saloon lining up along the bar as the bartender poured a long row of drinks. Longarm bellied up to an empty place and called for a shot of Maryland rye as he holstered his .44 and took out a voucher pad. When the barkeep brought his drink, he tossed it back in one throw, grimaced slightly, and explained, "I'm saying I busted fifty dollars worth of window in the line of duty. I can't write off the booze, of course, but figuring a nickel a shot—"

"Hey, that window came all the way from St. Louis, mister."

"That's why I'm saying it was worth fifty instead of the twenty-odd you paid for it. Don't shit me and I won't shit you. I'm an expert on busted windows and I owe a certain obligation to the taxpayers."

"How 'bout seventy five and I'll throw in another round of drinks?"

"Nope. I didn't hurt anybody and I ain't charging for the interesting diversion added to a dull afternoon, so I figure the boys rate one drink on me for such inconvenience as picking up cards and chips off the floor. If you want to argue about the damages, you are free to sue Uncle Sam for more. And now, having done my Christian duty, I'll be saying *adios*."

Without waiting for a reply, Longarm moved over to the swinging doors, risked a peep out front, and stepped out on the plank walk. Nobody shot at him, so he shrugged and went next door to the cigar store he'd been headed for in the first place.

As he stepped inside the richly scented darkness of

the little shop, a female voice snapped, "Freeze right there, you son of a bitch!"

Longarm froze, staring soberly down the barrel of an S&W .45 in the right hand of a big blonde woman wearing the cotton shirt and batwing chaps of a working cowhand. Her face was sort of pretty under the beat-up Stetson she wore cavalry style, dead-center and tipped forward.

Longarm said, "Your servant, ma'am. I'd tip my hat, if you didn't have the drop on me."

"What in thunder's going on out there?" the woman asked.

"I'm a U.S. Deputy Marshal and somebody just took a couple of shots at me. Now you know as much as myself."

The store owner's bald head appeared above the edge of the low counter he'd been hiding behind and he said, "I sure wish you'd put that gun away, Miss Sally."

The big blonde hesitated, then shrugged and lowered the muzzle of her revolver. Longarm noticed she hadn't put it back in the holster riding above her ample hips, so he kept his hands away from his own sides as he put them on the counter and said, "I came in here for some nickel cheroots. Do I save money buying 'em by the boxful?"

"You want some nice scented cheroots I just got in? They smell sort of lavender when you light up."

"Not hardly. I only want to smoke, not smell pretty."

The girl called Sally laughed and said, "He's been trying to sell them sissy cigars for months. You got a name, Marshal? They call me Roping Sally."

"*Deputy* marshal, ma'am. My name is Custis Long. They call me Longarm."

"I can see why. Custis is a sissy name."

"I know. My mama was a gal, Miss Sally."

"Hell, I don't hold with that 'Miss Sally' shit. My friends treat me like I was one of the boys."

The storekeeper explained, "Roping Sally owns the Lazy W. Her cows are scared of her, too."

Roping Sally laughed, finally got around to holstering her gun, and said, "My poor sweet cows are waiting to join up with the Blackfoot, too. So give me my plug and I'll be on my own way, damn it."

Longarm raised an eyebrow and asked, "Are you the owner Calvin Durler's been buying beef from, out at the Indian agency?"

"I'm one of 'em. Got a herd of twenty waiting over in the railroad corral right now. Letting 'em sort of rest and drink their fill before my boys and me herd 'em over to the reservation."

Longarm smiled sardonically and said, "The government pays by weight instead of by the head, huh?"

Her face was innocent, but her voice was mischief-merry as she nodded and replied, "Yep. That's why I'm watering and feeding 'em fit to bust before I run 'em over in the cooler afternoon. As long as that dude's paying by the pound, I may as well sell him plenty of water and cowshit with the beef. Damned Indians lose 'em before it's time to slaughter, anyway."

He nodded. "So I heard. It's no federal matter, I suppose, but watered stock is one thing and cow thieving is another. Don't reckon you have any ideas on who's been running off some of the reservation herd, huh?"

"It ain't me. Sometimes I suspicion the Indians just lose cows down a prairie dog hole. Agent out there's supposed to be making cowhands out of 'em but he don't know his ass from his elbow. He keeps buying beef and they keep getting lost, strayed, or stolen. Makes it a good market for the rest of us, though it does take forever to get paid."

"Well, you don't sell your best stock to Uncle Sam, do you?"

"Hell, do I look stupid? Prime beef goes east to Chicago for the top price and cash on the barrelhead. I don't sell them poor redskins really *dangerous* sick cows, though. Just such runts and cripples as might not make it alive to Chicago's yards. I *shoot* critters with anthrax, consumption, and such. Some folks say I have

68

too soft a heart to be in the cattle business, but it wouldn't be right to feed folks tainted beef."

"I can see you're a decent Christian woman—no offense intended. I have a dead Indian over at the coroner I'll be carrying back to the reservation in a little while. I'd be pleasured to ride out with you."

Roping Sally shook her head and said, "You'd best go on ahead, unless you like to ride right slow. I drive beef at a gentle pace. We'll likely mosey in about sundown."

"No use running weight off twenty head, huh? I knew a trail boss one time who used to haul a tank wagon along and water his stock a mile outside of Dodge."

Roping Sally laughed and took a healthy bite from the cut plug the storekeeper had handed her. She said, "I know all the tricks of the trade, but I fight fair. I figured you for a gent who knew his way around a cow. You rope dally or tie-down?"

"Tie-down. I value my fingers too much to mess with that fancy Mexican dally-roping."

"Tie-down's too rough on the critters. I'm a dally-roper, myself."

"You must be good. I notice you've got ten fingers."

" 'Course I'm good. That's why they call me Roping Sally. If you're out there when we ride in this evening, I'll show off a mite with my border reata. The Indian kids get a kick out of watching me, too."

Her boast gave Longarm an idea, but he didn't mention it. He said, "I'm staying at the agency, so we'll meet around sundown, Roping Sally."

Then he finished buying his smokes and went to see if the dead Indian was back together yet.

Chapter 5

The funeral of Real Bear took about fifteen minutes, Christian time, and maybe twelve hours, Indian time. Longarm didn't hang around to see the Indian ceremony. Calvin Durler read a short service over the open grave in the little burial plot a mile from the agency and Nan Durler threw a clod of earth and a handful of wildflowers on the pine planks of the chief's coffin.

Then, as the three whites moved back, a Dream Singer called Stars Were Falling moved to the head of the grave with a rattle and started chanting as some kneeling squaws with shawled heads began to wail like coyotes.

Longarm and his host and hostess went back to the buckboard. Calvin drove back to the agency house with Nan at his side and Longarm sitting in the wagon bed, his boots dangling over the tail gate.

He'd told Cal the cattle were coming, so, after dropping Nan off at the house, the two men saddled up and rode in the other direction to the fenced-in quarter-section in which the reservation herd was supposed to be kept.

Calvin Durler sat his bay mare morosely as he tallied the small herd in the big pasture, muttering, "Damn. I'm supposed to have thirty-seven head. I only make it thirty-six. I'm missing one. I'm missing the damned kid who's supposed to be watching, too."

Longarm swept his eyes over the nibbled stubble of buffalo grass and said, "I see a break in the fence, over to the left of your windmill and watering tank. What are you missing?"

"I just told you. A cow," Durler said impatiently.

"They're all cows, damn it. Are you short a calf, a heifer, a steer, or what?"

"Hell, Longarm, I just count 'em. I don't know 'em personal."

"Yeah, you're overgrazing too. Takes more than five acres a head of this short grass to graze longhorn. You're treating them like a dairy herd instead of range cows."

"Look, it's the only way I know. How would you do it if you were me?"

"You've got a water tank to keep them from straying more than a few miles. I'd get rid of that foolish barbed wire and let 'em at the grass all about."

"Then how would we catch 'em when it comes time to slaughter?"

"Round 'em up, of course. Don't you have *any* Indians who know how to drive critters in off the range?"

"I can't get 'em to watch the fool cows while they're fenced, and to tell the truth, I don't know much more than they do about working these spooky cattle."

"I see some that ain't branded, too. You do need help and that's a fact."

Before Calvin could defend himself, Longarm squinted off to the east and said, "I see twenty—no, twenty-one head coming out to join you."

Durler looked across the quarter-section and nodded, saying, "That's Roping Sally and two of her hands with the new stock I ordered. Wait till you meet her. She is purely something."

"We met in town this afternoon. Sure sits a horse nice and— Boy, look at that, will you? The herd smelled strangers and was about to spill before she cut and milled the leader. That gal knows her cows!"

"She's crazy, too. Nan says it's not natural for a gal to dress like a man and ride astride like that. Nan's scared of her. Thinks she might be one of those funny gals who are queer for their own kind."

Longarm didn't answer, not knowing about Roping Sally one way or the other. The cowgirl spotted the break in the fence and, thinking in the saddle, swung the leaders for it with a slap of her coiled leather reata. Her two helpers swung in behind the stragglers without being ordered, and together, the three of them worked the little herd through the gap to join the others.

Roping Sally called out something to one of her hands and the man dismounted to repair the fence as Roping Sally loped her big buckskin their way, her long hair streaming from under her Stetson as she shook out a community loop from her coil. She was halfway to them as she twirled the braided leather rope above her head, letting the loop grow larger and larger as she came. Then she flicked her wrist and the loop dropped vertically in front of her like a huge hoop. The well-trained buckskin leaped through it without breaking stride as she twisted in the saddle and recovered her loop with a wild whoop of sheer animal joy.

Durler laughed and said, "Every time she does that I keep saying it ain't possible. How in hell does she do that without hanging up in her own rope?"

Longarm said, "It's not easy. Pretty as hell, though."

Roping Sally reined in near them, reeling in her reata like a fishing line with a series of blurred wrist movements and slapping the coil back in place neatly as she called out, "I found a stray I suspicioned was yours, Cal. Likely a half-weaned calf looking for his mama and halfway to town when he run into us. You gonna take my word on the weights this time or do we have to cut 'em out and run 'em over to your fool scales by the slaughterhouse again?"

Before the agent could answer, Longarm said, "We were just talking about that, Sally. New government policy. Uncle Sam's buying them by the head, now."

"Do tell? What's the offering price per head these days?"

"They're offering ten dollars a head for scrub stock. But seeing you've got some prime beef mixed in with those other cripples, how does fifteen sound?"

"Shit! I can sell 'em to the meat packers at railside for more than that!"

"I know. Maybe you'd do better that way."

She grinned and said, "Might have known you'd wise old Cal up. When do I get my money? Ain't been paid for the *last* beef yet."

Durler said, "I sent the voucher weeks ago, Sally. You know how Washington is."

"That's for damn sure. I'd starve to death if nobody was buying my *good* beef. Say, Longarm, what are you doing in that army saddle? I thought you was a cow man."

"Used to be. Working for Uncle Sam on a government horse and rig these days."

"Hell, I wanted to see if you could throw a rope without hanging yourself. You want to borrow Buck?"

Longarm was about to decline, but he noticed a handful of young Blackfoot had drifted over to watch the sundown diversions.

He remembered the idea he'd had in the cigar store and nodded. By now one of the teenaged hands riding with Roping Sally had joined them and the girl swung out of her dally saddle as he steadied the buckskin for her. She walked over to Longarm with a swish of her chaps and said, "You can tie down if you've a mind to. My reata's a new one."

Longarm dismounted and walked around to the near side of the buckskin. He shot a glance at the girl's mount before he put a foot in the stirrup, muttering, "That's the way it's going to be, huh?"

He swung up in the saddle as the grinning boy passed him the reins and moved away. The buckskin took a deep, shuddering breath and exploded between Longarm's legs.

He'd expected it since noticing the white of the buckskin's rolling left eye, so he was braced for a dispute from the one-woman horse. Buck crow-hopped five or six times, saw he had a rider aboard, and started getting serious.

Roping Sally yelled, "Ride him, cowboy! Wahooooo!" as Buck and Longarm got acquainted. The buckskin shook himself like a wet dog at the top of every ascent through the evening sky and came down with the spine-snapping jolt of a serious bronc who wasn't afraid of sinking up to his knees in bedrock. The Indian kids were shouting now. Longarm didn't know if they were rooting for him or the horse as he noticed Buck was losing interest in killing him. He yanked his hat off with his free hand and started slapping it across the buckskin's face, grunting, "Let's get it all out of you, you old son of a bitch!"

But Buck had had enough. He was sensible as well as ornery and it's tedious to work up a sweat over a man who won't be thrown. Longarm saw that he had the buckskin under control and ran him hard once around the inside of the fence line to get the feel of him as he uncoiled a loop of reata. As he came by at a dead run, he whirled his medium-sized loop just twice to open it, and threw.

The dismounted Roping Sally crabbed sideways as she saw his intention but the leather loop came down around her head and shoulders anyway as she grabbed it, yelling, "You drag me and I'll kill you!"

Longarm let go the coil to keep from doing any such thing as he reined Buck to a skidding stop, whirled him around, and dropped to the earth with a bow of mock gallantry.

Roping Sally looked relieved and said, "I thought you were mad. I forgot to tell you old Buck ain't named after his color."

"It was sort of interesting. You want to do me another favor?"

Roping Sally disentangled herself from her own rope and coiled the other thirty-five feet in, clucking about the way he'd let the oiled leather lay in the dusty stubble before she asked, "What's your pleasure? I don't screw, if that's what you mean."

74

"You see them Indian kids watching? Cal, here, has been trying to get them interested in working cows. I thought maybe you, your hands, and me might show them how much fun it can be."

"I get your drift. What'll we show 'em? More rope work or some fancy cutting?"

"Let's just play it by ear. I don't have a saddle horn or rope, so I'll cut. You three throw some cows down for the hell of it."

He turned to Durler and said, "We're putting on a wild-west show for your kids, here. Why don't you talk us up? You might mention that working cows is almost as much fun as hunting buffalo was, when they had buffalo to mess with."

Durler laughed and said, "I got you, Longarm. You there, Short Bird! Come over here, I want to talk to you."

So, as the Indians watched, Longarm started cutting cows out of the uneasy, milling herd as Roping Sally and her two helpers went through the motions of roping and branding. Longarm enjoyed it as much as the grinning Indian kids, for Sally was a lovely thing to watch in the soft evening light as he worked with her. His army mount wasn't a good cutting horse, but he managed well enough, and every time he sent a steer running her way Sally roped it on the first cast. She roped underhanded, overhanded, and sideways, as if her reata was an extension of her fingers. She caught and stopped them by the horns, by either hind foot, and once she dropped a rolling loop in front of a young steer and grabbed him around the belly as he leaped through the hoop. Her dismounted helpers threw each critter she caught and hogtied it as if for branding. Longarm noticed they never got sloppy, like some hands, and threw a critter on the wrong side. He surmised that every animal she owned was branded on the left rump, the way well-tended cows were supposed to be. It was nice to see serious work. In his time he'd seen cows branded on the right side, either flank, or shoulder.

Some old boys didn't seem to give a damn where they marked a cow, as long as they got done by supper.

It was getting darker and Longarm knew enough showmanship to call a halt before the audience got restless, so he rode up beside Sally and yelled, "That's enough! We've run fifty pounds out of this beef and if they're not interested by now, they never will be."

"Hot damn! You cut good, Longarm! What in thunder are you wasting time with that badge for? Any damn fool can work for Uncle Sam! Takes a *man* to work *cows*!"

"Oh, I don't know about that. I just saw a gal who could show Captain Goodnight a thing or two."

"My daddy wanted a boy. I just grew up as much of one as I knew how."

They rejoined Calvin at the gate and the agent was smiling as he said, "If they didn't enjoy it, I surely did. I still think some of those tricks aren't possible. My wife and I would be pleased to have you and your hands join us for supper, Miss Sally."

"That's neighborly of you, Cal. But we gotta get home. You can send me the receipt for these new cows when you've a mind to."

And then, without another word, she swung her mount around in a tight turn and was off across the pasture at a dead run. Her hands were a bit surprised, but they followed and the three of them jumped their ponies over the far wire without looking back.

Calvin laughed and said, "One thing's for sure, Longarm. Nan's wrong about her not liking men. I think you could have some of that, if you've a mind to."

"Hell, Cal, she chews tobacco!"

"I noticed. Sure built nice, though. I suspicion you touched her heart by catching her with her own rope."

Before Longarm could answer, an older Indian came up at a dead run on a painted pony, shouting, "Wendigo! Wendigo!"

It was the moon-faced Yellow Leggings. Durler called back, "What are you talking about? What Wendigo? Where?"

"North. Out on the prairie. Near the railroad tracks. Wendigo got Spotted Beaver! They just found him!"

"Spotted Beaver, the old man with that band of Bloods? What happened to him?"

"I told you! Wendigo got him! It was a bad thing they found. Wendigo killed Spotted Beaver and flew away with his head!"

"His head was taken, for sure," said Longarm, staring down soberly from the saddle at the god-awful mess that a dozen Indians stood around in the moonlight. It was too dark by the time they'd ridden over with Yellow Leggings to make out every detail, but it was just as well. The corpse spread-eagled on the grassy slope near the railroad right-of-way had been carved up pretty badly.

Rain Crow rode over, holding a coal oil lantern in his free hand as he reined in beside Longarm to say, "No sign. I circled out at least a mile all around. You can see where Spotted Beaver's pony walked. You can see where it ran away. You can see where they rolled in the grass as they fought. That is all you can see. The Wendigo is said to walk the sky at night."

"I don't mean to question you as a tracker, Rain Crow, but a man on foot might not leave much sign in this buffalo grass."

"That is true. We don't know how long the grass has had to spring back from a careful footstep. But we are five miles out on open prairie. You can see where Spotted Beaver left hoofmarks."

"A man can walk five miles in less than two hours, even walking carefully."

"True, but where would a human go? There is nothing north of the tracks for fifteen miles. We are twenty-five miles from the reservation line. Nobody came in to Spotted Beaver's campground. The Bloods knew something was wrong when his pony returned without him. They fanned out as they searched in the sunset light. If a man had been walking, they would have seen him."

"Suppose the killer was waiting out here, killed this

man, then rode Spotted Beaver's mount and— No, that won't work, will it?"

"I have been thinking. The Bloods tell me the old man decided to ride out to look for medicine herbs late this afternoon. He told nobody but his own people, and they were all together when he was killed."

"Yeah. Hard to set up an ambush when you don't know where your victim's likely to ride. Maybe some old boy who just hates *any* Indian did it," Longarm speculated.

"You mean a white man? I have thought of this too. The railroad tracks are not far. But the trains do not stop, crossing the reservation."

"So, while a mean cuss might snipe at a stray Indian from a moving train, he wouldn't cut off his head and mess him up with a carving knife, would he? I'm going to check their timetable, anyway. There might have been a work train out here this afternoon. Though I can't see how a whole work crew would stand by as one of 'em killed and carved an old man up like this."

"You don't think it was the work of the Wendigo, then?" Rain Crow asked.

"I'll be in a fix if it was. I never arrested a ghost before."

Calvin Durler rode over from where he'd been talking to some other Indians and said, "My folks are spooked pretty bad. They keep saying there is an evil spirit on the reservation."

Longarm said, "I won't argue about evil, and I'm not ready to buy a spirit."

"Jesus, they're still keening over Real Bear, and now this! We've got to put a stop to these killings, Longarm! What are you aiming to do?"

"Not sure. I reckon we'll just have to eat this apple one bite at a time. I'll have a word with any Indian who has a mind to talk about it. Then I'll run this body in for an autopsy, too, and see what the railroad has to say about track-walkers and such."

"I guess we've done all we can for tonight, then?"

"No. You go on home and lock your doors and windows. I figure I'm just getting started."

Chapter 6

The old Blackfoot's face was painted with blue streaks and flickered weirdly in the firelight, and though he wore a shirt and dungarees, his long gray hair was braided with eagle feathers hanging down on each side of his narrow skull. He squatted near the fire in a pool of light as the others listened from the surrounding shadows of the open campfire. From time to time he shook the bear-claw rattle in his bony hand to make a point as he half-spoke, half-chanted, "Hear me! This place is not where men should live! Do you see buffalo about you? Do you see the skull-topped poles of the Sun Dancers? No! There is nothing here for us but white man's beef and who-knows-what in the iron drums of food he expects us to eat!"

Sitting their mounts beyond the firelight, Longarm and Rain Crow listened silently as the old man wailed, "In the Shining Times we ate fat cow! In the Shining Times we were *men*! In the Shining Times great Manitou smiled at us and our enemies wet their leggings at the mention of our name! But when the Blue Sleeves came we let them treat us like women. We let them tell us where we could live instead of fighting them like men! I say Wendigo has come among us because Manitou has turned his back on us in shame. I say we should fight again as men. I have spoken!"

Rain Crow started to translate, but Longarm hushed him, muttering, "I got the drift. Who's that other old one coming forward now?"

"He is called Snake Killer. Do you want me to tell them to stop?"

"No. Let them have their say. Nothing here's all that surprising."

Snake Killer was, if possible, even older than the man whose place he was taking at the fire. He wore one tattered feather with a scalp-tip in his gray braids. His legs were bare, but he wore an old army tunic against the chill of the night. Longarm suspected that the tunic might have been issued to a Seventh Cav trooper, once. He could see where the arrow holes had been neatly darned over.

Snake Killer said, "Hear me. I do not count my coups, as all here know about my fight with the chief of the Snakes in the Shining Times. I agree this is a bad place for us. I, too, fear that Manitou no longer smiles on us, but I think it would be a bad thing to fight the Blue Sleeves again. They beat us when there were only a few white men on the high plains, and now there are many. Many. I say we should go north, into the lands of the white she-chief, Victoria. In Canada there are not so many white men. In Canada there are still buffalo along the Peace River. There are other people like us on the Peace River, but I think we could beat them and take their hunting grounds away. It would be a good fight—better than fighting the Blue Sleeves for land they've already ruined forever."

Longarm swung his mount away and rode toward the agency as Rain Crow fell in beside him. The Indian policeman sighed and said, "They are just talking, I think. If you catch Wendigo in time they may not jump the reservation after all. Old Snake Killer likes canned beans and his bones are too brittle for the war-path."

"Yeah, but that same conversation's probably going on around a dozen fires tonight. Have any of Wovoka's missionaries been talking to your folks, Rain Crow?"

"You mean that Paiute prophet who makes medicine shirts and tells of ghosts helping us against the army? I chased one away a few months ago. I know how to

80

read and write. I think a man who puts on a medicine shirt Wovoka says is bulletproof would be foolish. I have seen one. The medicine shirt was badly tanned deerskin with painted signs all over it. They said its medicine would protect the wearer from a soldier's bullets. But when I tested it with my knife it didn't turn the tip of my blade. That's when I chased the man away."

"But not before you decided his medicine was no good, huh?"

"Of course. I am what I am. I was too young to fight in the Shining Times, but my father took hair from two of your soldiers before they killed him. If I thought I could drive all of you back across the big water, I would do it. But I know I can't, so I am trying to learn. They say the Shining Times can never come again and I believe this. So I must be . . . I must be something new."

"Well, you're honest enough, and we'll likely always need good lawmen, red or white."

"It is almost a job for a real person. Tell me, is it true you white men count coup when you kill an enemy? I have heard it said yes and I have heard it said you just get drunk after a victory."

"You heard it partly right both ways, Rain Crow," Longarm said. "Sometimes we hoist a few drinks to celebrate a job well done and the soldiers get medals if they've done something worth bragging about."

"I know what medals are. You wear them on your chest instead of your head. Have you ever heard of an Indian getting one of these medals?"

"Sure. The army's decorated some scouts for gallantry in action."

"I couldn't scout for the army. They never fight anyone I don't like. If they asked me to help them kill Ute or Crow I would scout for them and win many medals. But they always want to kill our allies."

"Well, the killing's almost over, I hope. Save for some Apache holding out down near the other border, the army doesn't have much call for scouts any more.

They've got a white scout over at the fort. You know him?"

"Jason? Yes. He is a good person, for a white man. I asked him why the soldiers were still there and he said he didn't know. He said he just goes where they send him. He said he didn't think the soldiers were mad at us any more."

"Yeah. I'd say their officer is a pissant, though. He's bored and spoiling for a fight. I do hope if your folks decide to act foolish they'll jump north instead of any other way. Wouldn't take much to start that old lieutenant shooting."

They rode back to the agency, where Rain Crow said he'd stable Longarm's mount before going back to his own shanty. Longarm asked if he wanted a cup of coffee first and the Indian said, "No. The woman is nice to us, but she is afraid. Deer Foot says she thinks the agent's wife is going to run away from him one day. When this happens, I do not want to know anything about it."

Longarm said goodnight to the Indian and went inside, thinking of Rain Crow's notion. If the Indians saw it too, he hadn't been as dirty-minded as he'd first supposed. Nan was fixing to run off with the first man who made her an offer and she was a pretty little thing. On the other hand, Calvin Durler was a decent cuss. Being a Christian surely could get tedious.

Inside, he found the Durlers seated at the kitchen table with a tiny white girl dressed like a sparrow. Calvin said, "Longarm, allow me to present you to Miss Prudence Lee. She arrived just after you rode off."

Longarm removed his hat as the agent added, "Miss Lee's from the Bible Society. I keep telling her she'd do better in town, but she says she's come to bring the Gospel to our red brothers."

Prudence Lee dimpled prettily, considering how little there was of her, and said, "We were just talking about the ritual murders, Deputy Long. It's my intention to show the Blackfoot the error of their ways."

Longarm forked a leg over a chair and sat as Nan

Durler shoved a mug of coffee in front of him without looking at him. He grinned and said, "The army's sort of showed them some errors already, Miss Lee. What do you mean by ritual murders?"

"Isn't it obvious that the medicine men have been sacrificing people to their heathen gods?"

"No, ma'am, it's not. I've been told the Pawnee used to make human sacrifices, long ago, but none of the other plains tribes went in for it, even before we, uh, pacified them."

"Come now, I know I'm a woman, but I know the terrible things they've done to captives in the past."

"Captives, maybe. That was torture, not religion. The two killings we just had were simple murder. The men killed were both on friendly terms with such Blackfoot as I've asked." He looked at Durler to add, "Rain Crow and I saw some old boys pow-wowing about a trip to Canada. You'd better see about issuing some rations and back payments."

"My God, I'd better let the army know if they're preparing to jump the reservation, too!" Durler said.

"I wouldn't do that. Not unless you want some dead Indians no Wendigo had to bother killing. Those boys over at the fort are bored and ugly."

Prudence Lee, having warmed to her subject, broke in insistently to ask, "What about the Sun Dance?"

"Sun Dance, ma'am?"

"That business of dancing around a big pole with rawhide thongs punched through living flesh. You can't tell me that's not a blood sacrifice!"

"Oh, bloody enough, I suppose. But we don't let 'em do that any more. Besides, you're missing a point. Indians think it's brave for a man to shed his *own* blood to Manitou. Other people's blood doesn't count as a proper gift."

"Brrr! To think of God's creatures living in such ignorance of the Word! Manitou is what they call their heathen god, eh?" Prudence asked.

"Well, Manitou means 'god' in Blackfoot, ma'am. I don't know how heathen he might be. Seems to me the

Lord would be the Lord no matter what you call Him."

"Agent Durler tells me many of his charges speak English, so I'll have little trouble setting them straight. You did say I could use the empty house next door as my mission, didn't you, Mister Durler?"

Calvin shrugged and said, "If you won't go back to town. You won't be able to sleep there till we repaint the bedroom, though. Uh, you know what happened there, don't you?"

"Pooh, I'm not afraid of ghosts. My Lord is with me, even into the valley of death, forever."

Longarm wondered why she didn't say "Amen," but he knew better than to ask. He took out his watch and said, "Be more room here, if I took Spotted Beaver into Switchback tonight. I'll get there before midnight if I leave soon."

Durler asked, "Will the coroner be up at that hour?"

"Don't know. If he ain't, I'll have to wake him, won't I?"

"He isn't going to like it much," Durler cautioned.

"I don't like not knowing what killed Spotted Beaver, either. The railroad station's open all night and I'll have a few questions for them, too. I'll toss my saddle roll in the wagon and bed down somewhere along the way, once I'm finished in town."

Nan Durler grimaced and said, "You don't mean to sleep out on the open prairie, do you?"

"Why not, ma'am? It don't look like rain."

"It makes my flesh crawl just to think about it! It's so creepy-crawly out there at night!"

"I spend half my nights sleeping out on the prairie," he said. This wasn't strictly true, but he thought it might disabuse her of any notions she might have about his carrying her off to his castle in the sky. Even if he was wrong, he did intend to spend at least one night in the open. This place was too full of women for a man to sleep peaceably in, alone.

Longarm's luck was with him when he drove into Switchback about eleven that night. A lamp was lit

84

over the coroner's office and the saloons were still going full-blast.

He pounded on the coroner's door until the older man came to cuss out at him. Then he said, "Got another one for you, Doc. You don't get *his* skull, either. Somebody beat you to it."

He carried the stiff, wrapped form of Spotted Beaver into the lab and flopped it on the table as the coroner lit an overhead lamp. The coroner said, "Good thing I'm half asleep and my supper's about digested. What in hell tore this old boy up?"

"I was hoping you could tell me, Doc. What say you give him the once-over while I run over to the railroad station. I've got some trains to ask about, too."

He left the coroner to his job and walked the three blocks to the station, where he found the stationmaster dressed but asleep in a cubbyhole office under an electric light bulb. The man awoke with a start as Longarm came in, glanced at the wall clock, and said, "Ain't no trains due for a good six hours, mister."

"I ain't looking for a ticket. I'm a Deputy U.S. Marshal after some information. You have a train stopped out on the Blackfoot reservation this evening?"

"Stopped? Hell, no. There was a westbound freight around four and an eastbound crossing closer to six. No reason to stop, though, and both were on time, so they likely didn't."

Longarm took out a cheroot, stuck it between his front teeth, and spoke around it as he fished in his pocket for a match. "Someone killed an Indian near your tracks. I wondered if you might have some crewmen who lost kin at Little Big Horn or such."

The stationmaster shook himself wider awake and thought for a moment. "I know the boys on both crews. I don't think either of them would be mean enough to shoot at folks as they passed by."

"This jasper got off to work close up with a knife. How fast do your trains run through there?"

"Hmmm, the eastbound's coming downgrade a mite, so it'd be crossing the prairie there about forty-odd.

Westbound might slow to twenty or thirty on uphill grades. I'm going by the timetables, you understand. So we're talking about average speeds. Be a mite faster going down a rise than up, but, yeah, I'll stick with those speeds. You want the names of the engineers?"

"Not yet. Looks like I'm sniffing up the wrong tree. While I'm here, though, do your trains run the same time every day?"

"Not hardly. Depends on what's being freighted where. We get a wire when a train's due in or out, but the timetable varies a few hours from day to day. Why do you ask?"

Longarm took a match from his pocket, igniting it with his thumbnail in the same motion, and touched the flame to his cheroot. "Man figuring to hop a slow freight would have to know when one was coming."

The stationmaster looked astounded. "Hop a freight on open prairie? We don't run freights that slow, Deputy. Be a pisser to reach for a grab-iron doing more'n ten miles an hour, wouldn't it?"

"Yeah. Like I said, I'm likely in the wrong place."

Longarm left the man to sleep away the rest of his night in peace and went back to the coroner's.

The coroner couldn't tell him anything he didn't know already. Spotted Beaver had been killed and cut up, down, and crosswise. Except for the head, nothing important was missing. The coroner found nothing to tell him what had killed the headless trunk, though he muttered laconically, "None of that knifework did him a lick of good. If he was shot or bashed, the evidence left with his head."

"Could you say what was used to rip him up like that, Doc?"

"Something sharp. Wasn't a butcher's meat saw or animal teeth, but name anything else from a penknife to a busted bottle and I'll swear to it."

Longarm asked, "Can I leave him here with you for the night, Doc?"

"Sure. I'll put him away for you on ice. I know you're

driving a long, lonesome ways, but they don't bother me all that much."

"I'm not worried about traveling with a dead man. Done it before in my time. Come morning, though, I aim to ship the remains to Washington for a real going-over at the federal forensic labs. I'll come back before high noon."

"I'll tin his internals in formalin for you, then. What do you figure I missed?"

"Likely not a thing, Doc. But it pays to double-check."

"I don't have the gear to look for obscure drugs or poisons, but you don't think he was drugged, do you?"

"Don't know what to think. Just covering every bet I can come up with till I hit a winning hand."

"Makes sense. How come you're making such a roundabout night of it, though? You could take a room over at the Railroad Hotel and get an early start, since you're due back anyway, before noon."

Longarm kept his true reasons to himself as he said. "I've got an appointment at the agency, come sun-up. They're expecting me back tonight."

He said goodnight and left, going next to the saloon he'd busted up. The night man on duty didn't know him but a couple of the men who'd seen him come through the window wanted to buy him a drink. So Longarm let them, then stood a round in turn as he casually swept the crowd with his eyes from under the brim of his hat. Nobody seemed too interested in him. He told the two boys drinking with him part of what had been going on and repeated that he was heading back to the agency alone.

Then, having spread the word as much as he could without being too obvious, he left. He climbed to the buckboard seat and drove out of Switchback at a trot.

It was after two in the morning now, and the moon was low in the west, painting a long, zigzag chalk line of light where the black mass of the distant Rockies met the clear, starry bowl of the sky. It would be darker soon, and though he knew the mule could see well enough by starlight to carry them safely back to the agency, which wasn't now all that far, he had other plans.

They knew at the agency that he was supposed to be bedded down out here in the nothing-much. He'd told everyone in town who'd listen much the same thing.

He slowed the mule to a walk about three miles out of town and just over the horizon from the top windows of the agency. There was no wind and the night was as quiet as a tomb. Longarm looked up at the Milky Way arching palely against the night sky and muttered, "He-Who-Walks-the-Midnight-Sky, huh? If you're up there you'd best get cracking, Wendigo, old son. You're running a mite late of midnight."

He wheeled off the wagon ruts and reined in fifty yards away on the open prairie. The moon had dropped out of sight behind the Front Range now, and the outlined snow fields were dimming away. Longarm tethered the mule in its traces to a cast-iron street-anchor and put an oat bag over its muzzle, saying, "You'll have to manage through the bit, old mule. Ain't sure how long we're staying hereabouts."

He threw his bedroll to the ground a few yards from the buckboard and spread it out in the darkness. He pulled up some bunches of dry buffalo grass and stuffed some under the weather tarp to make the bedroll appear occupied. Then he took kindling and some dry cow chips from the wagon bed and built a small night fire eight feet from the bedroll, moving back and keeping himself to the north of the little flickering fire as he moved back to the tethered mule and buckboard. He took his Winchester from the wagon boot, levered a round into the chamber, and hunkered down under the wagon.

A million years went by.

Longarm shifted quietly to a more comfortable position, seated in the grass with his back against a rear wheel and the rifle across his bent knees as he chewed an unlit cheroot to pass the time and keep awake.

Another million years went by.

Somewhere in the night a coyote howled and once a train hooted far across the prairie. He muttered, "Must be a special. Stationmaster said the next train was due in six hours and that was two or three hours ago."

Then he heard something.

He didn't know what it was, or where it was coming from, but he suddenly knew he wasn't alone on the lonely prairie. He realized he'd stopped breathing and inhaled slowly through his nose, straining his ears in the dead silence all around.

A big gray cat was walking around in Longarm's gut for some fool reason; he told himself he didn't believe in ghosts. Nobody sensible believed in ghosts, but then, nobody sensible was sitting out here in the middle of nothing-much after making himself a target for whoever might be interested.

He heard the sound again, and this time he grinned as he identified it, muttering, "Man or devil, the son of a bitch is riding a pony!"

The sound he'd heard was someone dismounting, trying not to squeak saddle leather in the process, but not quite managing. Longarm had the sound located, more or less. Someone had reined in on the far side of the wagon ruts and climbed down for a more Apache-style approach than most found neighborly when coming in on a night fire.

Longarm rolled forward, shoving the Winchester into position for a prone shot as he stared into the inky blackness and listened for a footstep. Once he heard what might have been the distant *ting* of a spur on dry grass, but it was hard to tell. Whoever it was, was moving in like a cat. Longarm studied the stars along the skyline, and after a while, one winked off and on. He knew where the other was, now, but it was too far to do anything about. Another star went out and stayed that way. The jasper was standing there, likely studying the fire and what he could see of the bedroll. If he had a lick of sense he'd move a mite closer in. He was way too far out for a decent shot.

Then a distant female voice called out, "Longarm! Look out!" and a rifle flashed orange in the darkness near the vanished star. Longarm fired at the flash and rolled away from his own gun's betraying flame as, much farther off, a third gun fired, twice.

He heard the sound of metal on dry grass, followed by a groan and a thud. Longarm was under the tailgate now, so he rolled over once more and sprang to his feet, his Winchester at the ready.

The feminine voice called out again, closer, and Longarm heard the sound of running boot heels and jingling spurs as Roping Sally shouted, "Are you all right, Longarm?"

"Stay back, God damn it! I can't see a damn thing and I only shoot at one thing at a time!"

"I got him outlined against your fire and he's down! I'm coming in!"

Longarm circled wide. Then, as he got well clear of his night fire, he too could make out the inkblot on the grass. Another shadow stepped over it and kicked it, muttering, "There you go, you mother-loving, bush-whacking son of a bitch!"

As Longarm moved in cautiously, Roping Sally turned to the sound of his footsteps and said in a girlish tone, "He's dead as a turd in a milk bucket, old son! Who got him, you or me?"

"Maybe both of us put one in him, Sally. What in thunder are you up to out here?"

"I saw you come out of the saloon and ride off. Then I spied this jasper running for his pony like he aimed to go somewhere serious, so I sort of tagged along after him. I had him betwixt your fire and me when he dismounted, sneaky-like. So I did the same and, oh, Lordy, I thought you were in that fool bedroll!"

"So did he, most likely. Let's see who he used to be."

As Longarm knelt and turned the dead man over in the fitful glow, Sally said, "Hot damn! I might have known you were setting a trap for the bastard! Who was he, and how'd you know he aimed to follow you?"

Longarm muttered, "Shit—sorry, ma'am. His handle

was Fats. I threw him off a train in the Denver yards and he said he'd remember me. I guess he did. As to knowing he was likely to follow me, I was aiming higher. You see his rifle hereabouts?"

"Over there to the southeast. Looks like an express rifle to me."

"Me too. He was the one who took a shot at me in town the other day, damn it! Poor silly varmint tracked me all the way up here just because I made him look foolish one time. He had a younger sidekick, too."

"He followed you alone, Longarm. You reckon his pal is in Switchback?"

"Hope not. I've got enough on my plate up here. You hear mention of a new hand in the country called Curley?"

"Nope. There's a Curley riding for the Double Z, east of town, but he's been here for at least two years."

"Damn! I can't chance not watching for one more old boy with a poor sense of humor and I can't waste time hunting him down. I've got bigger fish by far to fry!"

"Tell me what the bastard looks like and me and my friends'll be proud to round him up for you," Sally offered.

"Can't do that, Roping Sally. No telling how many innocent drifters might get hurt if I turned you loose with a private posse!"

"Well, can I tell you if I see or hear tell of folks named Curley?"

"Sure, Sally. But just don't get excited before you talk to me about it, hear?" Longarm cautioned.

"I'll be sly as hell. What are we to do with this rascal here?"

"I'll put him in the wagon bed and see if they'll bury him for me someplace. Might be papers out on him, somewhere. He took things too seriously for a boy with a clean record."

"Hot damn! You mean I might get a reward for shooting him?"

"If there's anything like that I'll see that you get the

money, but you'd best let me take credit for gunning him, Sally. I don't want any of his friends dropping by to pay you a call some night."

"Aw, hell, I was aiming to brag on it some," Sally said disappointedly. "Lots of folks in this county treat me like a sissy!"

"You're all man, Roping Sally, but let's not build you a rep as a gunslick if we can help it. It can make for nervous nights. Believe me, I know!"

"I'll do as you say. Where you heading now?"

"Hadn't thought about it all that much. I doubt if anyone else is likely to creep into this web tonight. I gave my bed at the agency to a guest of the Durlers. Hmm, I'd best carry you and this jasper back to town and try for some shut-eye at the hotel."

"You can stay at my spread, if you've a mind to. It's just to the northwest of town."

"Uh, I figure to get up with the chickens, Sally."

"Hell, don't we all? You come on home with me and I'll fry you some eggs before we turn in."

Longarm didn't answer. Roping Sally punched him on the shoulder and asked, "What's the matter, are you scared of me?"

"Not hardly. But what'll folks say about it in Switchback?"

"Who gives a hoot and a holler? I don't keep any hands on my spread. The boys I was riding with before live with their folks in town and I hire 'em as I need 'em. Ain't nobody there but me and a mess of critters. I got dogs and cats, Shanghai chickens, a Poland China hog, and my remuda and herd keeping me company, but not one of 'em ever gossips about me worth mention."

Longarm laughed and said, "We'll talk about it along the way."

Chapter 7

Roping Sally's house was a large one-room soddy with a lodgepole roof and a cast-iron kitchen range sharing space with a fourposter bed and enough supplies to stock a general store. They'd stored Fats in the smoke-house and put the mule in with Buck. Longarm sat at an improvised table made of planks laid across two barrels. He smoked as he watched Sally putter at the range with her back to him. He noticed that the seat of her pants was tight and worn shiny between the wings of her flapping chaps, and though she was a mite broad across the beam where she sat a horse, her waistline was as trim as if she'd been cinched up in a whalebone corset. The hickory shirt she wore was tight enough for him to see she wasn't wearing a corset, or much else, under it. She was one handsome woman— considering she chewed cut plug—but Longarm couldn't figure her out. He was either getting into something too good to be true; or just as likely, about to make a terrible mistake.

The girl turned with a grin and plopped two coffee mugs and a pair of tin plates down in front of him, saying, "There you go. Wrap yourself around those eggs before you tell me I can't cook."

"Uh, don't we use some forks or something, Sally?"

"Oh, Lordy, I'm so flusterated I clean forgot the silverware! You've likely suspicioned I don't entertain all that much."

He waited until she'd put some oversized cutlery on

the planks before he said cautiously, "You told me, coming in, you didn't have any fellows sparking you."

"Hell, there ain't a man in Montana worth spit on a rock. Present company not included, of course."

"Sally, you can't tell me somebody hasn't tried," Longarm said skeptically.

"Sure they have. Sissy little things who have to sit down to pee, most likely. I knew they were just after my daddy's cows."

"Oh, you got a daddy hereabouts?"

"Dead. Got thrown and busted his neck, summer before last. He raised me to be a cowhand and he likely raised me right, for I've done right well here, without him. What's the matter with the eggs? You ain't eating 'em."

Longarm put a forkful of rubbery, over-fried eggs in his mouth and chewed hard. He swallowed bravely before he shook his head and said, "You got 'em just right, Sally. I'm a mite tuckered after such a long, hard day, is all."

"Why don't we go to bed then? Which side would be your pleasure?"

"Sally, I'd best spread my bedroll out in the wagon bed, out back."

"What in thunder for? I took a bath last Saturday. Besides, that fellow in the smokehouse tore shit out of your blankets with that old express rifle."

"Sally, how old are you?"

"I'm old enough, I reckon. My daddy and me ran just about the first longhorns north from the Powder River Range to this here territory and I shot my first Sioux before I lost my cherry!"

Longarm brightened and said, "Oh? I was, uh, wondering how soon we were likely to get to that subject."

"My daddy said I wasn't a virgin anymore when I told him about it. He was sore as hell, but there wasn't all that much he could do about it, since the cuss who cost me my cherry was long gone. You want to hear about it?"

"Not really. Just wanted to know where this trail was leading me. You take the right side and I'll take the left and we'll likely wind up in the middle. You want me to blow out the lights?"

"What for? There's stuff all over the floor and we'd likely bust a leg finding our way."

"Suits me. Most gals like to undress in the dark."

Roping Sally looked puzzled and said, "You reckon we ought to take our clothes off just to sleep two or three hours? It's going on four, and my old Shanghai rooster starts crowing any minute now."

"Well," Longarm said, "you're right about it being late, but I sleep better raw, so I'd best blow out the lights."

"I'll do it. You just climb over those boxes and I'll join you."

He did as she told him and had his boots off about the time Roping Sally doused the last lamp. He undressed, frowning and puzzled, then got under the covers as Sally climbed in on the other side, saying, "I took my britches and boots off, but I don't like the way these old blankets scratch when I don't wear my shirt."

Longarm reached for her and snuggled her head against his shoulder as he asked mildly, "You ever think of using sheets?"

"They just get dirty and torn up when I'm too tired to shuck my boots after a hard day's ride. What are you hauling on me like that for?"

"Don't you want me to cuddle you some, first?"

She moved closer and nestled her body into the curve of his as she said, "It sure feels nice. I like the way you run that hand up and down me, too. Feels like you're petting me right friendly."

Longarm slid his hand to her face in the dark, turned her chin up, and kissed her lips. Roping Sally's lips were a mite wind-chapped and her breath smelled like a tobacco shop, but she responded after a moment of hesitation. Longarm wondered why women always seemed to want to back off at the last minute after damned near running a man all around the corral to rope and saddle him. He kept his lips against hers as he moved the hand downward. Sally stiffened as he cupped her mons in his palm and rubbed her lightly through her shirttail. She rolled her mouth aside and whispered, "Are you getting dirty with me?"

Longarm was finding it difficult to keep his amazement concealed. He said levelly, "Honey, there ain't anything dirty about this. It's why the Lord made men and women different, is all."

"I don't know if you ought to do that, though. You're getting me all mushy and funny-like."

But she had her own free hand on the back of Longarm's, now, and when he asked if she wanted him to stop, she pressed it closer and murmured, "Don't know *what* I want. It feels nice as anything, but I ain't sure I ought to let you keep going."

"Sally, it's going on four, I got a long day ahead of me, and this palaver must cease. We've got no time for any more games!"

Suiting his actions to his words, Longarm cocked a leg over her, parted her ample thighs with his knee, and climbed aboard, moving her damp shirttail above her navel as he guided himself into her. Her matted pubic hair was wet with her own desire and though she was tighter than he'd expected, he sank full-depth into her on the first thrust.

Sally gasped, "My God! What are you *doing* to me?"

He tactfully avoided a direct answer. "Could you maybe move your knees up some? You're tighter than a drum, and—"

"Oh, Lord, I'm *ruined*! I swear I think you're *screwing* me!"

Longarm frowned in the darkness, but this was no time to discuss the details. She began to respond with hard, rocking thrusts of her own, even as she sobbed, "You never told me you wanted to get dirty! This is terrible! How will we ever be able to look one another in the eye again, come daylight?"

"I'll stop if you've a mind to," Longarm lied considerately. But Roping Sally dug her nails into his bouncing buttocks, spread her legs wider, and moaned.

Longarm figured she was one orgasm ahead of him by the time he stopped to get his breath back, still in the saddle. Roping Sally was breathing hard, too, but she sighed, "Oh, my, that was more fun than Saturday night after roundup! Can we do it again? I know you've ruined me forever, but now that I know what all the fuss is about I'm sort of getting the hang of it."

Longarm thought of himself as a patient man, but this was too much.

"Sally, what in thunder are you talking about? You're not going to tell me that old sad tale about being a virgin, are you?"

"I don't know what tale you're talking about, but if you mean to ask have I done it before, I ain't. You won't tell anybody, will you?"

"Honey, you told me you lost your cherry years ago and that your pa was pissed at the jasper who did it!"

"Oh, that was when our wrangler put me aboard a spooky bronc when I was maybe thirteen. I rode the bronc, but when I got off, my crotch was all bloody and Daddy was sore as hell. He said the ride had busted my cherry, and—"

Longarm's eyes rolled upward and he slapped his forehead with the heel of his hand. "Oh, Jesus! I see the light and I'm purely sorry, ma'am!"

"You ought to be sorry, you dirty old thing. You just screwed me and I'm a ruined woman, but to tell you the truth, I ain't all that riled. You want to do it some more?"

He stayed inside her, but didn't move, as he cleared his throat and said, "Sally, we've got to talk about this. I know a gent's supposed to do right by a lady and all, but I ain't the marrying kind . . . damn it! I had you down as a tough old cowgal!"

"I'm tough enough, I reckon. You don't think getting screwed is likely to turn me sissy, do you?"

"Not hardly, but . . . shit, I just don't know what to say."

"Are you sore at me? I know folks are supposed to be ashamed to see each other after they've been ruined, but you know what? I still like you, even after being dirty with you."

He kissed her tenderly, and said, "I like you, too, honey. I just ain't been down this trail too many times and I don't know what I'm supposed to say or do."

"Well, you've said we're still pals, and as to *doing*, I wish you'd either take that fool thing out of me or move it *right* some more!"

Longarm laughed and started responding to her mischievous thrusts. In a short while, it didn't seem all that big a fuss. Roping Sally might have been a late-bloomer, but for a virgin, she caught on quickly.

Longarm was awakened at sunup by the sound of flowers and the smell of birds. The morning breeze was banging sunflower heads against the window over the bed and the chickens in the upwind henhouse stank something awful.

He stretched and the blonde head cupped on his naked shoulder murmured, "Don't get up, yet. The chores can go hang this morning. I want to hear some more of those facts of life you were jawing about before we went to sleep."

He scraped a thumbnail through the stubble on his jaw, ran a tongue over his fuzzy teeth, and sighed, "I've got to get back to my job, honey. Besides, I've told you all I know about the birds and bees and how you gals might keep from getting in a family way."

She raised her head shyly, stared at him in the wan gray light, and grinned, saying, "I can look you in the eye, anyway. Likely I ain't ruined after all."

"I told you it came natural, didn't I?"

"Yeah, but Daddy said folks jeered at ruined women-folks. We'd best not tell anybody we've been screwing, huh?"

"I don't think we should do it in the streets of Switchback, but between us, we can likely whup anyone who jeers all that much. Why don't you catch a

98

few more winks? I'll get something to eat in town before I start asking around about the fellow we shot last night."

"I am purely tuckered. When will you be coming back this way again? You *are* fixing to, ain't you?"

"Well, sure, if you want me to. I'm going to be right busy most of the day, but if I get the chance, tonight—"

"Hot damn! I'll take a bath, then. You were right about it being nicer with all my clothes off. Maybe I can find some sheets around here somewhere."

Longarm swung his bare legs out from under the covers and started to dress as Roping Sally watched. When he stood up to pull his tight riding pants up she sighed and said, "Jesus, you're pretty. Did you get them shoulders roping cows or hugging other gals?"

"Little of both, I suspicion. You're built nice, too, Sally."

"I'm in fair shape from hard work and clean living, up to last night, I reckon, but these fool big tits of mine get in the way when I'm wrestling steers to the ground. You sure you weren't funning when you said you liked 'em?"

"I kissed 'em both, didn't I? Go back to sleep, now. I'll try to make it back around sundown."

He finished dressing and went outside. He got the stiff, heavy corpse from the smokehouse and threw it in the wagon bed, tossing a tarp over the late Fats before hitching the mule in its traces. Then he climbed up and drove out across the cattle guard to the road to Switchback in the crisp morning sunlight. Nobody saw him, thank God. He didn't know what he was going to do about Roping Sally and himself, but at the moment he had other things to worry about.

Chapter 8

Switchback kept early hours, so by the time he'd eaten breakfast near the railroad station, had a shave at the barber shop he found open across the street, and asked some more questions about the railroad, the coroner's office was open.

The coroner came out to lift a corner of the tarp as he asked, "What are you doing, starting a collection? I can tell you what killed this one without an autopsy. He was hit front and back with bullets. Either round would have been enough."

"I'm just reporting the killing to you for your county records, Doc. I'll see that he gets buried. You got the specimens for me to ship to Washington?"

"Canned his liver and kidneys along with the heart and lungs. You can have them any time you like. Are you sending them East on the noon express?"

"Yep. I'll see about getting the rest of the remains out to the reservation for burial this afternoon. Got another errand to do, first."

"You want to put this cadaver in my vault for now, or do you feel the need for company?"

"I'd take that kindly, Doc, if it ain't imposing."

"It is, some, but you'll impose on everybody if you leave him out in the hot sun under that tarp much longer. I'll get my helpers to tote him inside if you want to leave your buckboard parked here for a while."

Longarm thanked the helpful county official and headed for the land office. He found Agent Chadwick lounging in the open doorway and asked if he could use the federal telegraph line again. Chadwick nodded and led him back to the wire shack as Longarm filled him in on everything but Roping Sally.

Longarm sat at the desk and got to work on the wire. Chadwick, after a time, lost interest and went back out to the front office. It took Longarm over an hour to make all his inquiries and get some answers. When he had finished he got up and went to join the land agent. He found Chadwick just saying good morning to a surly-looking man in range duds. The land agent handed Longarm a cigar and explained, "That was old Pop Wessen. He's heard about trouble on the reservation and wants to file a homestead claim out there. Got sore when I told him it was a foolish notion."

"I wanted to ask you about that, Mr. Chadwick. What would happen to all that land if the Blackfoot sort of, well, lit out for Canada or someplace?"

"You mean abandoned the land held in trust for them? Nothing, right away. I suppose the army would round 'em up and bring 'em back, in time, don't you?"

"Those the army left breathing. Would the land revert to public domain if it stayed empty long enough?"

Chadwick shifted his cigar and thought for a moment before he said, "It'd take a long time, but if Uncle Sam just couldn't get any Indians to live on that range for, oh, at least seven years . . . you know what? I don't *know* what the regulations are. I've got enough paper on the open-range questions I answer for white folks."

"Seems to me some of the Cherokee lands down Oklahoma way got taken by white settlers after the Cherokee picked the wrong side in the War. If those Blackfoot lit out and abandoned the reservation . . . hmm, seven years is a long time, ain't it?"

"I think I get your drift. You're suggesting someone's trying to run the Indians off, eh?"

"It's a natural suspicion, but planning on filing on abandoned land seven years up the road seems a right cool game for anyone with murder on their mind.

You're sure there's no way anyone could get at that range sooner, huh?"

Chadwick puffed his cigar pensively. "Not as far as I know. Find out anything about that old boy you shot last night?"

"Yeah, he had his last name in his wallet. The nickname Fats fit the wanted papers on him. He was a gunslick for hire. New Mexico has a murder warrant on him and he's suspected in other parts of picking fights for pay."

"But you said you had a fuss with him in Denver."

Longarm nodded, slowly scratching the back of his neck. "I did. What I'm trying to figure, now, is whether he trailed me up here for personal reasons or was in town on other business, saw me, and decided to pay me back. I never told him I was coming to Switchback —I disremember saying so to anyone in Billings."

"You mean someone here in town might have sent for a hired gun and the rest was just dumb luck?"

"A man could take it either way. You have any ideas on who might be fixing to start a private war, hereabouts?"

Chadwick shook his head. "Not offhand. Save for the troubles out at the reservation, we ain't had much trouble up here lately."

"You issue range permits, don't you?"

"Sure. I register homestead claims and hire out government grass on a seasonal basis. You know how most cattle outfits work. They claim a quarter-section with timber and water for the home-spread, then range their cows on the open prairie all around. Uncle Sam's supposed to be paid a range fee by the head, but they cheat a lot."

"You hear tell of anyone fighting over range?"

"Nope, I ain't. The herds are building fast, since the buffalo thinned out, but most of the locals are friendly enough about it. They let the cows mix on the open range, work the spring and fall roundups together, and cut and brand neighborly. There's maybe a little friendly rivalry, but nobody's ever taken it past fists."

Longarm chewed thoughtfully on his cigar, then said, "Let's look at it another way. Cal Durler says he's been missing cows. Any others been having trouble along those lines, hereabouts?"

The land agent looked surprised as he asked, "Are we talking about rustlers, Longarm?"

"We're talking about what I call cow thieves. If some local stockman has been building his herd the sudden way, it might account for some of what's been going on. Cow thieves get shot a mite in these parts unless they have some guns to back their play. So a dishonest cattleman might hire some guns—or on the other hand, some neighbors who aim to put him out of business might do the same."

Chadwick nodded in understanding and blew out a stream of smoke before saying, "I've heard talk about the reservation herd losing strays. Some of the locals think it's funny as hell. That kid Durler has a lot to learn. I don't think anyone's really *stealing* his cows, but you'll have to admit an unbranded calf running wild along the reservation line might be tempting fate."

"Yeah, I've been trying to show him how to herd cows properly. But if you're right about the local cattle outfits, it's odd about those hired guns."

Chadwick shrugged and said, "That one you had to shoot was likely just passing through, then. Or maybe he was trailing you personal."

Longarm put a hand on the doorknob and said, "Maybe. I thank you for the use of your wire and I'd best be on my way."

"Don't mention it. Where you headed next?"

"Thought I'd drift around town and get the feel of things before I ship some stuff East at noon and get on out to the reservation. To tell you the truth, I'm sort of stuck for some answers."

Leaving the land office, Longarm walked across the dusty street toward the saloon. In the shade of the overhang he found the army scout, Jason, talking to an older man with a tin star pinned to his white shirt. Jason thrust his bearded chin at the approaching

103

deputy and called out to him. Longarm joined them on the plank walk in front of the swinging doors and Jason said, "Longarm, this is Sheriff Murphy."

As Longarm nodded to the lawman, Murphy said, "How come you didn't report that shooting you had last night, Deputy?"

"I did. The body's over at the coroner's. We had it out on the open range and I figured it was a county matter."

The sheriff fixed him with a hard look. "I like to know when folks get killed in or about Switchback, mister. I know you federals think your shit don't stink, but I'd take it kindly if you let us poor country boys in on things once in a while."

"Sheriff, I meant no offense. I truly thought the doc would fill you in, and as you can see, he did."

"Well, yeah, he did tell me about it, but—"

"There you go. I'll tell you what. Next time some old boy takes a shot at me, I'll run right over to your office. By the way, where is it?"

The sheriff jerked a thumb over his shoulder. "Down thataway, near the station house."

"That's settled, then. I hope you boys drink before noon. I see the bar is open."

Before anyone could answer, Jason shouted, "Down!" and pushed Longarm hard, as he dropped behind the nearby watering trough.

The first shot parted the air where Longarm had been standing and crashed through the boarded-over saloon window he'd broken the last time he'd been by. The second raised a plume of spray from the watering trough and spattered Jason with water as he shouted, "Up behind that false front! The hat shop next to the land office!"

Longarm had dropped behind a barrel he hoped was filled with something. He aimed his drawn .44 at the drifting smoke cloud above the building the scout had indicated and snapped, "I've got him spotted. Watch your head!"

Another shot from above the hat shop gave away the sniper's position behind the false front lettered *Hats and Bonnets*. Longarm figured the last S was his best bet, but he crossed both Ts with bullets as he fired three times. Jason popped up and sent an army .45 round through the pine boards as, somewhere, someone screamed and they heard the clatter of a rifle sliding down shingles and a loud, wet thud.

Jason said, "He dropped between the hat shop and land office, in that narrow slot."

Longarm saw Agent Chadwick peering out of his doorway and shouted, "Get back inside, Chadwick! Jason, you and Murphy cover me!"

Then, without waiting for an answer, he was up and running. He crossed the street in a zigzag run, flattened himself against the corner of the hat shop, and quickly reloaded as he got his breath. A woman stuck her head out of the hat shop and Longarm motioned her back inside with a silent, savage wave of his .44. Then he took a deep breath and jumped out, facing the narrow slot between the buildings as he fired for effect into it. He dropped to one knee under his own gunsmoke and took a long, hard look at the body lying face-down, wedged between the plank walls on either side. Then he stood up and thumbed more cartridges into his Colt as Jason ran across to join him, saying, "Murphy lit out. I think he ran into the saloon and just kept going. We get him?"

"Yeah. I owe you, Jason."

"Don't mention it. Lucky I seen the sunlight flash on his barrel as he was fixing to do you. Anyone you know?"

"They called him Curley. He was a friend of the one I got last night. I'll be surprised as hell if he don't have a record, too."

By now Chadwick had joined them, peeking around the corner to gasp, "Jesus H. Christ! How many of these hired guns do you figure we have in Switchback, Longarm?"

"Don't know. I make it two less, right now. I'll get him out of there in a minute. Right now I owe Jason, here, a drink. He just saved my ass."

Chadwick followed them to the saloon, as did the hat shop owner and a dozen others in the neighborhood who'd heard the shooting and wanted to steady their nerves.

The scout didn't seem to think he'd done all that much, considering, but he let Longarm buy, muttering something about the way the army paid folks, these days.

As they leaned against the bar together, Longarm said, "It's lucky I found you in town. I mean, aside from what you just did for me. I've been meaning to ask some questions about the army's interest in the Blackfoot."

"Hell, they ain't all that interested, Longarm. Beats me why we're here. Likely Washington just figures soldiers've got to be some durned place if they ain't another."

"You been getting anything on expected Indian trouble?"

"From the Blackfoot? They were ornery enough, a few years back. Ain't lifted anybody's hair for a coon's age, though. They were rooting for Red Cloud back in '76, but only a few kids really rode with the Sioux. The old men kept most of the tribe back, playing close to the vest till they saw which way the cards were stacked. It's a small tribe, but they bled enough for a big one in the Shining Times."

"Were you out here then? You don't look old enough to go back to the beaver trade."

"I ain't. Came West as a hide hunter after the War. Knew some of the old Mountain Men, though. Most of 'em's getting on in years, now, but my first boss hunter was left over from the Shining Times. Used to brag on a Blackfoot arrow he still carried in his hide."

"You ever hear mention of a breed called Johnny Hunts Alone?"

106

"Hell, I *know* him. He skinned for me five or six years ago, down by the Powder River. Wasn't very good at it, though. He was sort of a lazy, moody cuss."

"Damn! You're the first man I've met who can tell me what he looks like, then!"

Jason stared soberly at his drink and said, "Maybe. But he never done me enough harm to mention, Longarm. How important are the papers you might have on him?"

"I could lie and say I just wanted to talk to your old sidekick, but you just saved my ass, so I won't. Telling it true, I aim to take him in dead or alive on a murder warrant, Jason."

The scout shifted uncomfortably. "You're giving me a hard row to hoe. Johnny once talked some roving Sioux out of taking my hair."

Longarm shrugged. "I can't make you tell me, but—"

"But you can likely make me wish to God I had, huh? All right. As long as I was fool enough to allow I knew him, and seeing he ain't around Switchback anyway, he's maybe half a head shorter than me and looks like what he is—half white, half Blackfoot."

"Can't you do better than that?"

"He's only got one head, damn it. He's just another breed. Maybe younger than me and not as pretty. Oh, he does walk with a limp. I disremember which leg—he got shot one time. To tell you the truth, we never jawed much. He was a quiet, moody cuss, like I said. Never killed anybody while I rode with him, though."

"The limp's the only thing I don't have on my papers, so I owe you another drink. Chief Real Bear told us Hunts Alone was on the reservation."

"Maybe he is. I'm buying this round."

"You said he looks half white. The Indian police say they know all the breeds out there and none of 'em is him. You figure Real Bear could have lied for some reason?"

"Beats me. I didn't know the man. I've jawed with a few Blackfoot since they sent me out here, but I'd be lying if I said I knew any of 'em well."

"You talk their lingo?" Longarm asked.

"Not enough to matter. I'm pretty good in Sioux and I can make myself understood in the sign lingo all the plains tribes use. Blackfoot's sort of like Cheyenne, ain't it?"

"Just about the same. You said Johnny Hunts Alone talks Sioux as well as Blackfoot, right?"

"Oh, that old boy could pow-wow fierce," Jason said. "He'd have made one hell of a scout if he hadn't took to robbing and such. We figured he had something gnawing at him, but like I said, he was only after buffalo when we rode together."

Longarm picked up the fresh drink the bartender had put before him and said, "I'd like you to think about this before you answer, Jason. If you were to see Hunts Alone before I did—"

"I'd warn him," said the scout, flatly. Then he added, "I'd tell him you were after him and give him a head start for old times' sake. Then I'd come and tell you true which way he'd lit out. I don't like being in the middle like this, but we're both working for Uncle Sam, so I'd do both duties as best I could. If that sticks in your craw, I'm sorry as all hell, but that's the way I am."

"A man has to stick by old friends, as long as he don't get crazy on the subject. Let me ask you one more question and have done with it. If I was to come on the two of you together, how big a slice of the pie would you be expecting?"

Jason took a swallow of his drink and said, "That's a pisser, ain't it?"

"Yeah, but I'd like an honest answer."

"Well, to be honest, I don't know. I can't see gunning you. I reckon I'd likely stand aside."

"That's good enough, Jason. Naturally, if you saw me coming before Johnny did, you'd likely mention my intentions to him?"

"Yep, I likely would. After that, the two of you would be on your own."

The officious Sheriff Murphy had circled back from wherever he'd hidden to take command once the smell of gunsmoke had faded away. Longarm was only too happy to leave him with the disposal of the bodies after wiring Denver where to send the reward for Fats. He knew Billy Vail would be discreet about bruiting Roping Sally's name and address about.

Longarm, as a federal employee, couldn't claim the reward for Curley. Jason said he didn't want blood money, so Longarm let Murphy put in a claim. If he ever got it, he'd likely brag on shooting outlaws into the next century, but what the hell—the poor idiot needed some brag to go with his badge.

Longarm hauled the mortal remains of Spotted Beaver back to the reservation for another interesting funeral. He arrived a little after one in the afternoon to discover some changes had taken place.

Prudence Lee had set up shop in the late Real Bear's house and was beating a drum and shaking a tambourine for some reason that Longarm didn't go over to find out. He joined Calvin and Nan Durler in the agency kitchen after giving the body to Spotted Beaver's kin.

He sat at the kitchen table and lit a cheroot as he told the Durlers about the interesting times he'd been having since last they'd been together. He didn't imagine they were interested in Roping Sally, but he told them everything else.

Calvin said, "That same fool calf busted out again this morning, but some Indian kids caught it and brought it back. Where in thunder do you figure that calf wants to *go*? He's got plenty of grass and water, damn it!"

Longarm thought before he answered. He had enough on his plate as it was; on the other hand, the answer to one question sometimes led to others. He took a drag on his cheroot and asked, "You feel up to hunting cow thieves, Cal?"

"Cow thieves? What are you talking about? Nobody *stole* the infernal calf. It just busted through the wire

109

and took off on its own like it had turpentine under its tail!"

"You're missing other critters, ain't you? Come on, let's get Rain Crow and some other police and see what's eating your new calf. You got a good saddle gun?"

"Got a Henry repeater, but I ain't the best shot in the world."

"Don't reckon you'll have to use it, but it pays to have one along. Keeps folks from getting sassy when they see you're armed."

Nan Durler said, "You men can't leave me here alone. I'm coming with you."

Before her husband could answer, Longarm said flatly, "No, you're not. I don't mean to get your man shot, Miss Nan. Why don't you go next door and help Miss Prudence whang that drum? What's she doing over there, anyway?"

Calvin laughed and said, "Teaching some Blackfoot the Meaning of the Word. They likely think she's crazy, but we don't have an opera house, so what the hell, at least it's entertainment."

Ignoring his wife's protests, the agent armed himself and followed Longarm outside. They saddled up, rode to Rain Crow's house, and got him and another Indian policeman called Two-Noses. Longarm didn't ask why they called him that. Two-Noses really only had the usual quota, but that one more than made up for the small size of the rest of him.

Longarm explained as they rode over to the pasture, "That new calf's not fully weaned, so he's likely looking for his mama. I figure we can turn him loose and see where he thinks she might be. Critters are good at finding one another."

Calvin said, "Roping Sally brought him to us. Do you think she held back on one of the cows we ordered?"

"Son," Longarm said, "you've got to learn to pay attention. When Sally and her hands drove that last

110

herd in, they *told* you they'd picked up a stray from here along the way, remember?"

"Oh, you mean that calf's the same one?" Durler looked confused.

"Hell, weren't you even *looking* at them when she brought 'em in? Of course it was the same calf. Has a calico left rump as I remember."

"Then what you're saying is that the calf's mother was one of the cows recently stolen, and— Jesus, you must think I'm dumb."

"You're learning. Everybody starts out dumb. There's the herd up yonder and, yep, old calico-rump's over against the far fence, looking for an opening."

Longarm led his little band around the fenced quarter-section on the outside. As they came up to the wailing calf against the fence, he dismounted and pulled down the top wire far enough for the lostling to leap over it, bawling. By the time he'd remounted, the calf was making a beeline for the southeast horizon at a dead run.

The men followed at a discreet trot. From time to time the little runaway would slow to a dogged walk, getting its wind back, then run some more. Two hours later, and nine or ten miles from the agency, Durler said, "We're off the reservation."

Longarm said, "I know. He's making for that sod house, yonder."

As the four riders approached, a man came out of the soddy with a rifle and called, "You're on the Bar K, gents. State your business and state it sudden!"

Longarm and his companions reined to a walk but kept coming as Longarm saw the calf nuzzling a cow through the wire fence on the far side of the homestead claim. He smiled and said, "We're on U.S. Government business, mister. You've got about two eyeblinks to put that weapon near your toes before I shoot you."

The man hesitated as he considered the odds. Then he leaned the gun against the doorjamb and stepped away from it, complaining, "You got no call to threaten me, durn it! I'm a peaceable settler."

111

"I can see that, now. You likely didn't know that some of those cows that maybe strayed over here belonged to the reservation, huh?"

"What are you talking about? I ain't got no reservation cows."

"You've got one I can see from here, mister. For your sake, I hope you haven't run any brands." He swung around in his saddle and said, "Rain Crow, ride over there and cut out every cow that isn't wearing a Bar K on it. If you see any marked U.S., or anything that might have been U.S. at one time, give a holler."

The young Indian grinned and loped toward the fenced pasture with Two Noses as the settler near the soddy protested, "I ain't had time to brand some of my critters, but I swear you got this all wrong."

A worried-looking woman peered out through the door and the man snapped, "Get back inside, Mother. I think these men are loco or something. They've as much as accused me of stealing!"

The woman ran out into the dooryard and got between Longarm and her husband as she wailed, "Oh, Lordy, don't you hang him, mister! I *told* him he was likely to get in trouble over them damn cows, but he ain't a bad man. Not really!"

Rain Crow rode back, still grinning. He said, "Fifteen head. Five U.S., one Double Z. The rest have no brands."

Longarm nodded. "Well, we'll take 'em all, then, after I thank these folks for their trouble."

The cow thief shouted, "Now, you just listen here!"

Longarm's amiable expression vanished without a trace as he turned toward the settler. "No, *you* listen, mister! I've got you dead to rights but I've got bigger fish to fry, so we're taking the cows and I'm letting you off with a warning. The warning is, the next time I see you within a country mile of the reservation line, you are dead."

"I aimed to bring them branded cows in when I got around to it. I was rounding up and—"

"You've got a Double Z cow in there, too. You want me to tell them about it?"

"I was aiming to return that'n, too. The ones I ain't got to branding yet—"

"Are lost, strayed or stolen, mister," Longarm interrupted. "You want to be friendly and call 'em strays, or are you just too foolish to go on breathing?"

"Damn it, half of them is really mine!"

"Not any more. You're getting off light and you know it. Go ahead, Rain Crow, cut the fence and we'll herd 'em all back. I'll say we found the Double Z critter mixed in with our stock, next time I'm in town."

As the Indian started to carry out his orders, the man shouted, "You can't do this, mister."

Longarm said, "I just did, and, like I said, this lady's a widow woman if I see you near the reservation or have to pass this way again."

"Now all I have to do is find out who's selling booze to my Indians!" said Cal Durler, feeling pleased with himself as he and Longarm sat on the back porch of the agency after riding back with the purloined cattle.

Nan was in the house, sulking together some vittles, and the mission woman was still beating her drum next door. Longarm noticed that Cal was fooling with a length of cotton clothesline as they talked. He said, "Your Indians are starting to take an interest in the herd. Old Rain Crow was tickled to hunt 'em down and sass a white man like that, but let's not get too cocky. Some cow thieves take their business more serious than that petty thief we just threw a scare into."

"Hell, let 'em come!" Durler said. "We'll dust 'em with number nine buck!" He got to his feet with the length of clothesline and started whipping it around through the air for some reason Longarm couldn't fathom.

He waited politely until the Indian agent wrapped it around his own shins and was frowning down at the results before he asked quietly, "Are you trying to hog-tie yourself, Cal?"

113

The agent grinned sheepishly and said, "It looks so easy when you fellows do it. What am I doing wrong, Longarm?"

"Don't know. What in thunder are you *aiming* to do?" Longarm chuckled.

Durler untangled the gray rope from his legs and answered, "I'm trying to learn to twirl a lassoo, of course. What's so funny?"

Longarm got to his feet, saying, "You can't twirl a throw-rope put together like that, Cal."

Durler held the length of limp clothesline out, saying, "I know I can't, damn it. Will you show me how *you'd* do it?"

Longarm shook his head as he took the improvised reata, explaining, "No mortal born of woman can twirl this thing, Cal. You've just made a slipknot for your noose. Every kid who ever played cowboy has made a creation like this. As you can see, they don't twirl for shit."

"Come on, I know there's a knack to it, but I've seen the way you oldtimers do it and—"

"Damn it, Cal, you're not paying attention. You got any bailing wire?"

"Sure. There's a coil on that nail near the screen door."

Longarm spotted the coil of thin iron wire and stepped over to it, saying, "We have to do something about the way you hold a gun on a gent, too. That settler would have gone for you, had you been alone."

Durler watched as Longarm broke off about eighteen inches of bailing wire and then, not having any idea what the lawman was doing as he started fooling with the end of the rope, Durler said, "You told me you let him off easy because he was harmless, Longarm."

"No man is harmless. He just wasn't worth my time. Takes months to get a cow thief in front of a judge, so most folks just shoot 'em and the hell with it. I didn't think he was worth a killing. Not if he heeds my neighborly advice, at least."

114

"All right," Durler said in an exasperated tone, "what did I do wrong over there with my gun?"

Longarm finished wrapping the slipknot in wire before he said, "I'll get to guns in a minute. You see what I've done here? Your noose runs through what we call the *honda* on a throw rope. It has to be heavy, like the sinker on a fish line, if you want the rope to follow where it's aimed."

Longarm shook out a modest loop of the limp line and started to twirl it. "You see? The loop part's trailing after the heavy honda, the way smoke trails behind a locomotive's smokestack. Most folks think the loop's some sort of hoop, but it ain't. You don't twirl the loop. You trail the weighted honda and the rest just follows natural."

He suddenly reversed his wrist action, swinging the honda in a figure-eight as the rope drew a pretty pattern in the air between them. Longarm said, "We call this the butterfly. You can't hardly catch anything with it, but it's good for showing off if gals are looking."

Durler laughed and said, "You know, I think I see how you're doing that!"

"There you go. Want to try her?"

He handed the rope to the agent and watched as Durler made a brave try. The loop stayed open for a few rotations and then, as Durler laughed in pleased surprise, wrapped itself around his waist.

Longarm said, "We'd best add some weight. Knew a Mexican fancy roper once, who used lead sinkers braided into his leather reata."

Durler handed back the rope and Longarm started wrapping more bailing wire around the improvised honda. As he worked, the agent said, "Let's get back to my gunmanship, Longarm. I thought I was pretty ornery-looking over at that sod house just now. Are you saying you thought I was bluffing?"

"Don't know if you were bluffing or not, Cal. The point was, you *looked* like you were trying to make up your mind what you'd do if that man pushed it to a real fight."

"Oh, hell, he was outnumbered four-to-one and you said yourself he was just a petty thief!"

"I know what I said. Know I won't be here if he should ever steal a cow from you again, too. Rain Crow looks like he's serious enough about such matters. So be sure you take him with you if it comes up a second time. He might have you down as an uncertain gunfighter, and even if he's wrong, such doubts lead to most of the trouble out here."

"Damn it, I wasn't afraid of him. If he'd made me use my gun, I reckon I would have."

"Back up and go over what you just said, Cal. You said you *reckoned* you'd throw down. Unless a man's *certain* he's out for blood with the first shot, he's better off not having a gun in his hands at all!"

Longarm finished wrapping the honda and twirled the rope experimentally, rolling the loop around him like a hoop as he turned on one heel, muttering, "This looks like I'm rolling it on the ground, but if you watch the wired knot, you'll see I'm not. Wish there was something to catch around here."

He handed the rope to Durler. "You fool with it for a while. I've got other chores to attend to. You got a survey map I can ruin?"

Durler took the rope but didn't try to spin it as he frowned and asked, "A map? I've got some maps of the reservation if that's what you mean. What do you mean about ruining one?"

"Pencil marks. I have to stop running in circles after this Wendigo critter. I'm going to mark out all the spots I've searched or know real well. Then I'm going to have a closer look-see at the blank parts. If I haven't found anything by the time I've covered the whole map with check marks, I'm in trouble."

Still holding the rope, Durler ducked inside and came out shortly with a folded survey map. He handed it to Longarm who sat on the steps and spread it out as the agent watched, idly twirling the rope. To Durler's surprise, the loop opened and began to spin easily as soon as he stopped concentrating too hard on his own wrist.

116

He laughed boyishly as Longarm drew a loop of his own on the stiff paper and muttered, "If Johnny Hunts Alone, the Wendigo, or whomsoever is inside this circle I'm blind as a bat. Rain Crow's searched most of these outlying settlements, so— What's this *X*? About five miles north of the railroad tracks?"

Durler let the loop collapse and stepped over to stare down at Longarm's questioning finger. He shrugged and said, "That's an old, abandoned sod house. A white homesteader built it back in the sixties. Before this land was set aside as a reservation."

"What happened to the nesters? Government buy 'em out?"

"No. They were wiped out by Indians. My Blackfoot say they didn't do it. Others say they did. There's not much left of the place. Just some tumble-down sod walls and a few charred timbers."

"What about the well?" Longarm asked.

Durler looked puzzled.

"The what?"

"The *well*," Longarm repeated. "You can see there's no stream bed within a mile. If they settled there, they had to have water, so there ought to be a well."

"Gee, I don't know, Longarm. I've only been out there once or twice. Don't remember seeing a well."

Longarm folded the map and put it away in a pocket, saying, "Ruined walls to cut the wind. Maybe water somewhere on the claim. Nobody living near it. Yep. I'll have a look on my way into town this evening."

"You're not staying here tonight? Miss Lee's moved into the house next door, so there's plenty of room for you, and Nan's expecting you for supper."

"Uh, I'll be staying in Switchback tonight. I'll likely be . . . investigating till right late."

"Hell, I'll be up past midnight, Longarm."

"I might be up even later. I'll hunker down in town."

"You're on to something that will keep you up past midnight?"

Longarm managed not to grin as he said, "I'll likely get some sleep, sooner or later."

Chapter 9

The abandoned ruins told their mute tale of frontier tragedy to Longarm's practiced eye as he left his mount grazing on the surrounding short-grass to poke on foot through the rubble. It was late afternoon and his shadow lay long over the weed-grown tangle of charred furniture and heat-scorched metal framed by the knee-high walls of rain-washed sod. With the toe of his boot, he gently kicked a baby's bottle, melted out of shape by fire, muttering, "Hope they had enough sense to send you away when the smoke-talk rose, little fellow."

A dozen spent brass cartridges lay in the weeds under what had once been a windowsill. They were green with corrosion now, but they still bore witness to the desperation of a long-dead stranger who'd knelt there pumping lead as hostiles circled out there on the open prairie. Longarm wondered if he'd saved the last rounds for his family and himself as the fire-arrows landed, quivering, in the woodwork.

There were no signs of recent occupancy in the ruins. Longarm circled out until he came to the deep, grass-filled depression where the well had been. The wooden well head had been hauled away. The earthen walls, unprotected, had caved in. Longarm walked over to his grazing horse, muttering, "Not so much as a dried turd. But at least we can likely write this place off."

He picked up the reins and mounted, shooting a glance at the low sun to his west as he swung the chestnut's head toward Switchback.

118

The sun was still up, but dyeing the prairie red by the time he passed a marker indicating he was leaving the reservation. The town was just over the horizon, but hidden by the scrap line where the prairie took a sudden step into the sky. Longarm spotted a distant rider a mite to his south. The rider saw him about the same time and swung his way, coming fast.

Longarm kept his mount to a steady walk, and as the oncoming rider waved a hat, he saw it was Roping Sally.

He shook his head and swung to meet her as Sally called out, "Yaaahooo!"

As she joined him, Longarm said, "I don't think you ought to be out here alone, Sally. I thought you'd be waiting for me at your spread."

"I was, God damn it! You promised you'd come at sundown!"

"You're wrong two ways, honey. I never promised and it's not sundown yet."

"Well, it's almost sundown and I was getting worried. Every time I let you out of my sight you get in a gun-fight and I—I been hurtin' for you, damn your eyes!"

"Honey, we'd best get something straight. I've got a job to do and you're not my mother."

"Does that mean I ain't your gal any more?"

Longarm muttered under his breath. Then he smiled and said, "Hell, you're the only gal worth having here-abouts. But I can't have you riding all around Robin Hood's barn after me. I want you to stay clear of this reservation, too. I've got enough on my plate without having to worry about you as well as the Indians."

"Hot damn! I didn't know you worried about me, too."

"Well, I do, out in these parts. You know there's some kind of lunatic running around out here at night, damn it!"

"I thought you'd shot all the rascals, honeybunch."

"Well, I didn't, and I'd rather be called late-for-breakfast than honeybunch. Those hired guns weren't who I came up here after. I've got one bad breed at

119

least to watch for, and if Johnny Hunts Alone isn't the Wendigo, I've got a bad breed and God knows what else to catch. So you're to stay clear of these parts, hear?"

"If you say so, sweet darling," Sally murmured.

"Oh, Lord, that's worse than honeybunch!"

"Could I call you huggy-bear, then?"

"Not hardly. Where'd you come up with all the crazy names?"

"I been thinking 'em up all day. I suspicion I must be in love with you. Every time I think of you I get all fluttery. Let's get on home. I've took me a bath and bought me some fancy French perfume and, Jesus, I am purely horny as all hell!"

He noticed she wasn't chewing tobacco, either. God! How had he gotten into this fix? More importantly, how was he to get out of it without looking like, well, the miserable cuss he probably was?

They rode side by side through the gentle evening light as Roping Sally planned their future together. Longarm didn't try to stop her; it didn't seem possible. She'd know soon enough what a shit he was unless he got lucky and somebody shot him before it was time to move on.

A distant voice called Longarm's name and he turned in the saddle to see Rain Crow riding after them at a dead run. He and Sally reined in as the Indian joined them, shouting, "Wendigo! Wendigo! He has taken another!"

"In broad daylight? Who, and where?" Longarm said, astonished.

"A boy called Gray Dog went out to hunt rabbit on foot. When he did not come home for supper his people searched. They found him as we found Spotted Beaver. His gun was taken, along with his head. The other police and I looked for sign. There is nothing. Gray Dog was killed on the open prairie in broad daylight. There is no trail to follow."

"I'd best ride back. Sally, I want you to go on home and bar your doors till I come to you."

"Damn it, I'm riding with you! I'm a fair tracker and I can whup most men fair and square!"

"You do as I say, anyway," Longarm insisted. "What these Blackfoot can't track is likely tougher tracking than most stray cows, and whatever could take an armed Indian's head off in broad daylight ain't like most men."

"Honeybunch, I want to help!"

"You'll help most by locking yourself behind a good stout door. I don't work alone because I'm a hero, I work alone because I don't read minds, and when it's time to move sudden, I don't like to guess what a side-kick's likely to be messing up."

"You promise you'll come to me soon?"

"Soon as I'm able, Sally," he assured her.

"Do you really love me?"

The back of Longarm's neck reddened as, aware that the Indian could hear, he put out a hand to chuck Roping Sally under the chin and murmur, "I ain't all that mad at you, honey."

Sally's face lit up in a sparkling smile. "You get along home pronto, sweet love. There'll be a light in the window for you and I'm taking another bath!"

She trotted east as Longarm fell in beside Rain Crow, loping west. They rode a mile in silence, then slowed their mounts to a walk to rest them in the gathering darkness. The Indian said, "The moon will rise soon. Almost a full moon, tonight."

"Yeah. About that conversation back there, Rain Crow—"

"I wasn't listening. Sometimes I have trouble under-standing what white people are saying. So I only listen when it might be my business."

"Sure you do, but if Washington ever allows you folks to drink, I'll buy you one. How'd you find me, anyway? You came over the horizon like a rider who knew where he was going."

Rain Crow shrugged. "I tracked you, of course. Agent Durler said you'd ridden to the old homestead, so I looked for you there. I saw where you'd moved things in the ruins and walked over to the old well. I saw where you'd ridden east, so I followed."

"You're good, considering I've been riding over thick sod in dimming light."

"Oh, it is easier tracking on grass when the sun is setting. The long shadows help me see where trampled grass hasn't had time to spring back up. This time of the year many stems are dry enough to break off, too."

"What about in green-up time, when the grass is springy?" Longarm asked.

"Easier. When the prairie is greenest, the soil is softer. Even antelope leave hoofmarks then."

"But you didn't find one hoofmark near that dead boy's body, huh?"

"No. The light was perfect for looking, too. The boy had left some broken stems behind him as he walked. The grass was trampled near the body, as if by a struggle. That was all. The others think Wendigo must have flown away."

"Maybe." The deputy stroked his mustache with a long forefinger. "Leaving aside notions like hot-air balloons and such, how do you feel about soft moccasins? I was wearing army heels out there by the homestead, and not trying to hide my spoor. Was this murdered kid wearing boots?"

"He wore the leather shoes the B.I.A. issues us. I see your meaning. Our people are not used to the white man's shoes, and in any case, they seldom fit right. Gray Dog may have scuffed more than a man in moccasins would have. But even so, Wendigo should have left *some* spoor!"

"Maybe he did. Meaning no offense, Rain Crow, a busted straw stem here and another one ten yards off ain't hard to miss."

"I will look some more, by moonlight. If we are lucky and there is summer frost before sunrise— Heya! Those people up ahead are gathered around the dead boy's body."

Longarm squinted against the sunset sky at the black knot of Indians on the horizon and made a mental note

122

of where to mark it on his map. Then he heeled his chestnut and snapped, "Let's go, before they trample every goddamned sign away!"

Longarm and Rain Crow loped up to the site of the latest killing and the deputy shouted, reining in, "Stand clear, damn it!" He saw Yellow Leggings in the crowd and added, "Yellow Leggings, get these folks out of here!"

The Indian policeman shouted back, "These two are the dead boy's parents."

"All right, they can stay. Everybody else, vamoose."

He saw his orders were being grudgingly obeyed as he dismounted far enough away to avoid spooking his horse, dropped the reins to the grass, and walked over through the parting crowd. He looked down at the mess spread-eagled in the grass and muttered, "Jesus, I ain't seen anyone messed up like this since the War!"

The slim, broken body was that of a boy about fourteen years old. Longarm could tell it was a boy because the body was naked except for shoes and socks. The brown flesh was crisscrossed with gaping slashes and covered by buzzing bluebottle flies as well as caked blood. The kid's clothes hadn't been carried off; they lay around in bloody tatters. It was likely that the shreds of plaid shirt had identified the victim to his relatives. There wasn't any sign of his head.

Longarm saw Rain Crow was at his side, so he pointed his chin at a spatter of blood on a soapweed clump near the body and said, "You looked for blood on the stems farther off, right?"

"Of course. Anyone walking away with a cut-off head should have left a trail of blood, but we found none."

Longarm turned slowly on one heel, scanning the horizon all around before he muttered, "Could have headed out in any direction to start with. Due south would have run him smack into the agency. There's over thirty miles of nothing to the west before you reach some cover in the foothills over that way. A man can't walk that far on foot in a day, packing a severed head or not. East would take him smack into Switchback, where folks would likely ask questions about blood and such. I'd say we should look north."

He went back to his chestnut and remounted, after telling the grim-faced father standing by a kneeling, keening squaw that it was all right to move the body now. Longarm didn't intend to take this one to the coroner. It was beginning to look like wasted effort as well as needless hardship to the victim's kin.

Rain Crow and Yellow Leggings fell in at either side of him as he walked his chestnut slowly north, noting that the crowd had made a mess of the grass for yards in every direction. The sun was down now, but the western sky was blood-red and the big moon hung like a grinning skull to the east. They were riding over untrampled grass now, and the light was bright enough to see clearly by. Longarm spotted something shaped like a cartridge near a bird's-nest depression in the sod and reined in, saying, "What's that, by the rabbit's bed?"

Rain Crow said, "I see it. Coyote turd. Coyote found the nest empty and shit because he was angry."

Longarm allowed himself a subdued laugh. "Your eyes are better than mine, then, but I'll take your word for it."

"I dismounted the first time I saw it this afternoon."

"Oh, then that pony track up ahead must be yours. I was about to say something foolish."

"There is no sign this way. I searched for sign as far north as the railroad tracks and a mile beyond."

"You look for railroad ballast that might have been scuffed by a horseshoe?" the lawman asked.

"I got on my hands and knees and even tasted a ballast rock I thought might have been turned over in the past few hours. I made sure it was only displaced by a passing train, long ago."

The deputy's eyebrows shot up. "Do tell? How'd you figure all that by taste?"

"The fresh side of the rock tasted of coal smoke. The taste settles on the roadbed when the trains run in the rain. It rained two weeks ago. That was when the rock was turned over."

124

"You can tell a rock that was turned over half a month back?" Longarm asked, astonished.

"Certainly. Can't you? The trains lay a film of soot and dust on everything they get near. Everything near the tracks smells like burnt matches or spent cartridges. That is why the buffalo herds were split up by the coming of the Iron Horse. The animals are afraid to cross the tracks. Coyote, rabbit, and antelope will, if they have to. Wolf, bear, and buffalo fear the tracks. A few years ago we had a good buffalo hunt that way. We cornered a herd in a bend of the track and ate fat cow. The old men said we should let some of the buffalo live, but the younger men killed them all, anyway. They said it was foolish to leave them for the white hide hunters. I never ate so much in my life and I got sick." Rain Crow patted his stomach and rolled his eyes upward.

By now they were approaching the right-of-way he was talking about. The railroad followed the winding grade of an old buffalo trail, since the engineers who'd surveyed it had known that buffalo follow the lay of the land better than most surveyors could. The tracks lay mostly at grade level, with filled stretches as high as ten feet over low rolls and cuts through some rises.

Longarm rode his chestnut up a four-foot bank and reined in on the gritty ballast to stare up and down the line without dismounting. A line of telegraph poles ran along the far side, and though there was no wind near the ground, the overhead wires hummed weirdly overhead. He saw the black notch of a low railroad cut to the east, and as the two Indians joined him, he said, "Let's see how high above the tracks that cut bank is." As they walked their mounts along the ties he explained, "I've studied the timetables of the railroad. No way a man could jump even a slow freight out here from ground level. But if he climbed up on the rim of a cut, and had steel nerves . . . "

They reined in between the walls of earth on either side of the track and Rain Crow said, "I don't think so. The edge up there is not as high as the tops of the freight cars and it would be a ten- or twelve-foot leap even if it was high enough. Yellow Leggings, ride up to the north side and see if there are marks of running feet. I will check the south bank."

Longarm went with Yellow Leggings, figuring Rain Crow as the better tracker. But as he and Yellow Leggings dismounted to study the grass lip of the bank above the tracks, he saw that there was nothing to see. He called across to Rain Crow, "Any sign over there?"

"No, and the ground is barren in places from runoff. To jump off here with any chance would mean a dead run, with no hope for cautious footprints."

Longarm shrugged and said, "This was a low cut, anyway. If we could find something in the way of a higher jump-off point, not too far to walk on foot . . . hell, it's too damn dark to look for sign, serious. What say we ride back to the agency and study my map some more?"

Rain Crow called, "You go and we'll join you later. We know this range. As the moon rises the light may shift and tell us something."

Longarm saw no harm in letting them have their head. So he climbed back aboard the chestnut and headed for the agency.

When he got there he found the Durlers and their guest, Prudence Lee, seated on the porch. He noticed that Calvin had his Henry across his knees as he sat on the steps, as if guarding the two women behind him in the porch rockers. Longarm tethered his mount to the rail in front and walked over to put a foot up on the steps as he filled them in on the little he knew.

The Durlers listened thoughtfully. Miss Lee said, "I've been talking to my converts. These heathens have Zoroastrian notions. According to Indian legend, the world's a battleground between Good and Evil and this Wendigo is like our Satan."

"We know that already, ma'am," Longarm said. He turrned toward the young agent. "Cal, the old ones were already jawing about a reservation jump afore this

126

happened. We'd best wire Fort MacLeod and let the Canadian Mounties know they might have visitors."

"I'm trying to hold off, Longarm," Durler responded. "Some soldiers were by a while ago, asking about our troubles out here. I got the notion they wouldn't be all that put out to chase some Indians and maybe win some citations. Alerting the Canadian authorities would likely have to be cleared by Washington, who'd alert the army, and—"

Longarm cut in, "I know a Mountie at Fort MacLeod personally. I could send him a wire as one old drinking pal to another, wording it soft."

"Do you really think you have to? Nobody's jumped the reservation yet."

"And when they do they'll be headed for the Peace River country, scared and on the prod. Wouldn't be neighborly of us to let Queen Victoria's own Assiniboine get hit by U.S. Indians they weren't expecting. Them old ways the elders are jawing about includes bad blood between Blackfoot and Assiniboine going back before Columbus. Even if your folks came in peace, there'd likely be some fur flying along the Peace River."

"But if the army heard about it in time to try and head them off on this side of the border . . ."

The lawman nodded. "That's why I aim to word my telegram to Fort MacLeod careful. I'll say something about that breed I'm after being spotted in Canada or something. The Mounties will likely send out some patrols and they'll have at least a sporting chance of heading off such trouble as might be headed their way."

"I hope so. When did you figure to send the wire?"

"Later tonight, at the railroad station in Switchback. The wire I've been using at the land office is patched in to Washington, but the railroad wire's private. I wish Western Union was in business hereabouts. Makes life complicated, with either Washington or the Great Northern reading my mail."

"You don't suppose it's possible the railroad's behind this trouble, do you?" Durler asked.

"I've studied on that. Can't see how running off your Blackfoot could benefit the stockholders all that much. They've *got* their right-of-way over federal lands. Washigton's stopped handing out big land grants for building new lines, and from the map, there's no place hereabouts to want a new line built. I've asked about the train crews, too. There's nobody riding through here regular with any reason to kill Blackfoot, unless he was crazy, and since there's at least a five-man crew on every train, odds are he'd have to be crazy with at least four sane men covering up for him." He shifted his weight and added, "I've considered someone hopping off and on from empty box cars, too. But that last kid was killed in broad daylight. I know folks doze off from time to time in the caboose, but a man would be taking a big chance counting on grabbing for the side of a boxcar on the open prairie with the sun shining. And who knows when a brakeman's going to come walking along the top of the cars between the engine and caboose? Besides, there was only one train through this afternoon, and it passed *before* the boy was last seen alive."

Longarm took a deep breath. He wasn't accustomed to soliloquizing at such great length, and it tended to make him feel lightheaded.

Prudence Lee said, "The Indians think the Wendigo walks through the sky."

"Yes, ma'am. At *night*. I'm going inside for a spell, Cal. I want to study my map some more before I run over to Switchback. And, by the by, I think Miss Lee, here, should bunk with you folks in my old room."

Durler said, "Oh, I hardly think he'd hit this close . . ." and then his voice trailed off.

Longarm nodded and said, "That's right. Real Bear was killed in the same house Miss Lee's using for . . . whatever."

Then he mounted the steps, went inside, and back to the kitchen, where he lighted a lamp and spread his survey map on the table.

He marked the latest killing and put question marks

on every railroad cut he could find on the small-scale map. There were a few contour lines, but the scale was too small to show every rise high enough for anyone to hide behind. He himself had once hidden from Apache behind a one-foot bump in the ground. A man in buckskins, lying flat behind a clump of soapweed, could be nearly invisible from as close as a quarter-mile on what seemed featureless prairie. The reservation was as big as some Eastern states, when you studied on it. He wasn't ready to buy a flying spook yet. Except for that hot-air balloon he'd seen at the Omaha State Fair, he'd never seen a man up there in the sky, either!

Prudence Lee came in and sat down across from him, saying, "That Indian policeman, Rain Crow, just rode in. Mister Durler is talking to him. I don't think he found anything."

Longarm started folding the map as the mousy little girl added, "I have a personal problem, if you have the time to listen."

"I'll listen, ma'am, but if it's about converting Indians I don't suspicion I know how."

"I face a moral dilemma. This is a privileged conversation, isn't it?"

"If you're asking if I repeat things, I don't."

"I supposed as much." She cleared her throat. "As you know, I'm duty-bound to uphold the commands of the Lord, but on the other hand, as a woman I understand her problem."

"*Her* problem, ma'am?"

"Nancy Durler's. I think she's about to run away from her husband."

"Did she tell you as much, Miss Prudence?"

"Not directly, but I know all the signs. You see I—I knew a girl, once, who ran away from a man she couldn't live with. She's tried to atone for her sin for years, but adultery is a terrible cross to bear."

"Oh? This, uh, other gal we're speaking of ran off with another man?"

"Yes. He deserted her in Baltimore six weeks later

and I'm afraid, uh, she went a little crazy. She took to strong drink and, well, other men. I'm afraid she sinned rather badly."

"It's understandable, ma'am," Longarm said compassionately.

The girl continued, "Well, suffice it to say she found the Light in time to save her soul. You understand I only know a *little* of her story, but the way Nancy's acting reminds me of when . . . this girl was about to ruin her life."

"I'll take your word for it that another woman would know such things. But there's nobody hereabouts fixing to run off with Nan Durler."

"Oh, I thought . . . well, if she doesn't run off with anyone we know, it'll be someone, sooner or later. She doesn't just look coldly at her husband. She looks right through him, as if he wasn't there. She's told me she hates it here and, Lord, I don't know what I'm to *do!*"

"You might try minding your own business, no offense intended, ma'am. I like Cal Durler. I like his wife, too. If I knew how to stop what might be happening, I'd be the first to try."

"Perhaps if you had a word with him, man-to-man."

Longarm smiled. "What am I supposed to say? 'Look here, old son, your woman is fixing to light out on you?' He'd either laugh or bust my jaw, and in the end, what could any of us do? You didn't have a woman-to-woman with Nan yet, did you?"

Prudence shook her head, forlornly. "I'm afraid it should only light the fuse. My next-door neighbor . . . I mean the next-door neighbor of this poor, sinful girl I told you about, tried to warn her what a mistake she was making, and it only made her leave a couple of nights sooner than she'd intended to."

"There you go. There's nothing either of us can do. So let's just hope it's a passing notion."

The deputy thought this might be a convenient place to change the subject, so he asked, "How are you coming with your Bible lessons?"

"I think the Indians are laughing at me behind my

back. They enjoy the music and coloring books, but they don't seem serious about learning the Word," Prudence said, with a touch of disappointment in her voice.

"Well, you've only been here a short while and at least it keeps 'em sober. If you really want to make friends hereabouts, spend a little time buttering up the older squaws. Anyone can draw a crowd of kids to a Bible meeting."

"I've invited everyone. But the adults are so cold and reserved."

"I know. They're used to us taking 'em for fools. You might start by asking questions, Miss Prudence. Most folks are proud to share what they know with strangers. Asking a body a question shows you think he or she might know something you don't."

"I see what you mean, but I don't know what sort of questions I should ask."

"Ask the squaws about medicine herbs. Ask them how to cook something."

"I tasted some Indian food. It was awful." Prudence wrinkled her pert nose.

"Takes time to develop a taste for pemmican and such. But asking a cook for a recipe beats complimenting her on her greasy stew and, hell, you don't have to *use* a Blackfoot recipe."

She laughed. Her little face was fetching in the lamplight as she said, "I'll try it. I'm not getting anywhere with that big drum I brought."

He grinned at her and excused himself to go out front and see what Rain Crow had to say. He found the Indian with the Durlers. Rain Crow hadn't found anything, as the girl had told him.

Longarm asked, "Where's Yellow Leggings? Did he go on home?"

Rain Crow shook his head and said, "No. I expected to find him here. We split up to search for sign and agreed to meet with you here for further orders. He should have ridden in by now."

Longarm looked at the moon and said, "Getting late. We'd best go see what's keeping him."

Calvin Durler opined, "Yellow Leggings has always been slow-moving. He's probably coming in at a walk. Why not give him a few minutes?"

"He's had a few minutes. We'll ride out and save him riding in all the way. Come on, Rain Crow."

The Indian waited until they were well clear of the agency before he asked, "How did you know I was worried about Yellow Leggings?"

"Didn't have to know. I worry enough myself. Any idea where your sidekick might have gone?"

"He rode east along the tracks to see if there was sign on any of the cuts you mentioned. I scouted north for a few miles until the poor light made me think I was wasting time. I thought he would be waiting for me at the agency."

Longarm didn't answer. They rode in silence until they regained the tracks and swung east. After a time they saw a pony grazing in the moonlight. Its saddle was empty.

Rain Crow said, "That is Yellow Leggings's pony." Then he called out, loudly, in Algonquin.

There was no answer, but somewhere in the night a burrowing owl hooted back at them mournfully.

Longarm followed as the Indian led, shouting for his friend. He felt as though something was crawling around in the hairs on his neck. He slid the Winchester out of its boot and held it across his thighs as they rode on. He heard a distant chuffing coming up behind them and warned, "Train's coming, Rain Crow. Let's swing wide so the locomotive won't spook our mounts!"

As the Indian ahead of him did so, Longarm saw his own shadow painted on the silvery, moonlit grass by the yellower light of a railroad headlamp. Rain Crow shouted something in his own language and moved forward at a dead run as Longarm followed. Then he, too, saw something up ahead, illuminated by the beam of the eastbound train.

The train overtook them and thundered by as Rain Crow dropped to the ground, shouting, "It's Yellow Leggings! Wendigo has him!"

132

Longarm's own mount shied as the scent of blood reached his flaring nostrils and Longarm had to steady him before dismounting. He joined Rain Crow by the dark mass on the ground and lit a match with his free hand. Then he swore and shook it out. He'd seen enough.

But Rain Crow took a little bull's-eye lantern from his saddlebags and lit it, cursing monotonously in Algonquin. He swung the beam over his dead friend's body and the trampled grass around. Then he said, in English, "It's like the others. No head. Not a drop of blood more than ten feet from the body!"

"The head could have been toted off in an oilcloth poke or something."

"Yes, but what does Wendigo want with their heads?"

"Wants to scare you, most likely. We're wasting time here. You know we ain't likely to find sign. Let's ride over to the next rise the roadbed cuts through. My map says it's twelve feet deep."

The Indian remounted and Longarm did the same. They were almost at the railroad cut when Rain Crow reined in and whispered, "Another pony. There, off to the south of the tracks."

"I see him. Looks like a big buckskin— Oh, damn you, Lord! You couldn't have let *that* happen!"

He loped over to where Buck stood, reined in, and almost sobbed, "Damn that gal! I *told* her not to come looking for me out here!"

The Indian said quietly, "Over there, near the tracks, pale in the moonlight."

Longarm raced his mount over, slid it to a stop and leaped from the saddle to kneel at the side of Roping Sally, or what was left of her. He didn't light a match. What he could see was ugly enough by moonlight. He pounded a fist hard against the sod by his knees and said, "We'll do right by you, honey. If that son of a bitch is on this earth within ten miles he's going to die Apache-style!"

Remounting, he loped to the cut, rode up to the lip,

133

and got down, calling, "Shine that bull's-eye over here, will you?"

Rain Crow did as he was asked, sweeping the rim of the dropoff with the narrow beam. After a time he said, "Nobody was up here when that train went by."

"Let's look over on the other side. A left-hander would have reached for a grab-iron from over there."

They rode down and across the tracks to repeat the same investigation on the north side of the track. The dry prairie straw betrayed no sign of blood or footprints, but when Longarm had the Indian swing his beam near his own boots, he saw that didn't mean much. The drained soil up here was bone-dry and baked brick-hard. The stubble had been grazed by jacks, judging from a rabbit turd he saw, and his own heels didn't leave tracks. Longarm took his hat off and threw it down, as he yelled, "All right, Lord! I've had just about *enough* of this shit!"

The Indian's voice was gentle as he said, "The woman back there meant something to you, didn't she?"

"God damn it, Rain Crow, shine that fool light somewhere else, will you?"

"I know what is in your heart, and there are tears in *my* eyes, too."

"Well, I won't tell on you if you don't tell on me. I got a bottle in my saddlebags. Before we go for a buck-board to transport the two of 'em, I figure we could both use a good stiff belt, don't you?"

"Indians are not allowed to drink, Longarm."

"I know. We're going to kill that bottle anyway."

Chapter 10

Longarm was still three-quarters drunk as he waited outside for the coroner to finish. He would have been drunker if he'd known how, but the numb anger in his guts had ruined his plumbing and the stuff was just going through without dulling the pain. It was bad enough to find a stranger's body mutilated and beheaded, but he knew he'd dream a spell of nightmares about that once-shapely body he'd intended to remember with pleasure.

A trio of cowhands came over to him as he sat on the wooden steps in the wan morning sunlight. One of them said, quietly, "We ride for the Double Z. Is it true Roping Sally was killed by Indians?"

Longarm shook his head and said, "No. Whoever did it killed two Blackfoot in the process. I'd be obliged if you boys would pass the word about that. The Indians have enough to worry about without other folks after 'em!"

"We heard about them other killings, Deputy. Heard there's a Paiute medicine man out there, too, stirring up a rising."

"The Indian police know about the fool Ghost Dancer. They're keeping an eye on him. Blackfoot never had much truck with Paiute in the old days. He's just flapping his mouth in the wind, I suspicion."

"Army gent was telling us Washington's worried about this here Ghost Dancing. That Paiute cuss, Wovoka, has been down in the Indian Nation selling his medicine shirts, too!"

"There you go. None of the Five Civilized Tribes has risen. We've got all sorts of folks spouting religion in these parts, but that don't mean sensible folks have to take 'em serious. Have you boys been converted to Mormons? Are you fixing to build octagonal houses or vote the Anarchist ticket? Hell, we got a white missionary gal out at the reservation trying to sell the *Bible* to the Blackfoot without much luck."

"They say Sitting Bull's interested in Wovoka's new Ghost Dance notions."

The deputy stuck a cheroot between his teeth, but made no move to light it. "I wouldn't know what Sitting Bull's interested in, but he's way the hell over in Pine Ridge and he ain't a Blackfoot. I've been bedding down out at the Indian Agency, and if we were fixing to have another war I'd likely hear about it before the boys in the saloon."

Another hand asked, "What's this Wendigo shit they keep jawing about? Did this here Wendigo kill Roping Sally?"

"The Wendigo is a spook. I'm betting on a flesh-and-blood killer. I aim to get the son of a bitch, and when I do he'll likely die slow, gut-shot and begging for another bullet, if I have my way."

"That's too good for the shit-eatin' hound! If *we* catch up with him he'll die even slower. We been discussin' whether to stake him on an anthill smeared with honey or whether we should start by stickin' his pecker in a sausage grinder first. Roping Sally was a good ol' gal, even if she was too stuck up to screw her pals."

Before Longarm had to answer that, the coroner came out, wiping his hands on his linen smock and looking cheerful, considering.

He nodded to the three cowhands and told Longarm, "We've got a break, the last victim being white. Found a contusion just below the severed vertebrae."

"You mean she was bruised on the back of her neck, Doc?"

"That's what I just told you. Looks like she was

rabbit-punched from behind, and if it's any comfort to you boys, I'd say she never knew what hit her."

Longarm frowned and said, "Doc, she was on a tall horse and likely riding at a lope! How in thunder can anyone rabbit-punch a rider from behind like that?"

"Must have ridden up behind her," the coroner speculated.

"No, Doc, not a chance. We found the hoofprints where her buckskin slowed after she left the saddle. That bronc was loping when she fell. There wasn't another hoofmark within a mile."

"You must have missed something. I'm calling it like I read it. Roping Sally was knocked off her buckskin by a hard blow from behind, then slashed, gutted, and beheaded. The how and who is *your* department. Maybe the Indians are right and this Wendigo's some sort of *flying* critter."

"You don't believe that, Doc. If any man knew how to fly he'd be too busy patenting the notion to go about killing folks. We're likely missing his method, but flying ain't it. I've been meaning to ask you something else about these killings, though. What in thunder do you reckon he wants with the *heads*?"

"Beats me. Maybe he's taking up a collection."

"You said *you* collect skulls, Doc. I don't mean I suspicion you of being the Wendigo, for I was impolite enough to ask about where you were last night. I know about those papers you write for the Smithsonian, too. But, leaving your own Indian skulls aside, can you think of any other value a human head might have?"

The coroner scratched his head. "You mean a *cash* value? Not hardly. I can get old skulls for five or ten dollars from the medical supply houses. An interesting skull like Real Bear's might be worth a little more to some museum. A white woman's skull? Maybe ten dollars, cleaned and mounted properly. A man with a shovel could ride out along the old wagon trails and dig up all the bones he wanted without having to kill anybody. Hundreds of people died and were buried in shallow graves moving West a few years back."

One of the cowhands nodded and said, "I know an old emigrant burial ground just a few miles away. Every time it rains some bones wash out of the ground where it's gullied some."

Longarm mused aloud, "No way the heads were taken to hide the identity of anyone. We know who all the victims were. Wait a minute—the killer never took Real Bear's head! He was skinned instead of beheaded. How do you figure that, Doc?"

"Longarm, the man we're dealing with is a lunatic! How should I know why he does the things he does? He'd have to be crazy as a bedbug to do *any* of it!"

The deputy shifted his unlit cheroot to the other side of his mouth, and chewed it pensively. "We both keep saying *he*, Doc. I keep calling the Wendigo a 'he' because I've never met a gal that ornery. Is there any chance I could be wrong?"

"You mean is the Wendigo a woman? You *have* been drinking some."

Longarm pressed on, "Nobody's *seen* the Wendigo. A woman, maybe smiling sweet, could get a lot closer to folks without arousing suspicion of unfriendly intentions. That young buck Gray Dog had a rabbit gun in his hand when he got jumped. Yellow Leggings was *looking* for the Wendigo, and packing a carbine. Roping Sally was riding armed and likely looking sharp about her. Not one of those folks would have just waited for a strange *man*, red or white, to announce his intentions."

"I see what you mean," the coroner said, "but a woman won't wash. Not unless she was as strong as, or stronger than most men. Roping Sally may have been strong enough to cut those deep slashes and sever a spine with one cut that way, but we know *she* didn't do it. You fellows know any other tomboys like Roping Sally hereabouts?"

The three hands shook their heads. One of them said, "Sally was as big a gal as we had out here, Doc. She could have whupped any gal and likely half the men in the county."

"That's my opinion, too," the coroner agreed. "Long-arm, your notion might work another way. What if all three victims met someone they knew? Someone they thought was a friend?"

Longarm shook his head. "The two Indians wouldn't have been all that close with anyone Sally might have. She got along with Blackfoot, but I doubt she'd have let one get the drop on her. Besides, we found no sign near any of the bodies. I'll allow a man could move across the grass on foot without leaving sign, walking creepy-careful, but wouldn't you ask questions if even someone you *knew* came tiptoeing through the tulips at you?"

The coroner impatiently waggled an antiseptic-smelling hand at the deputy. "Let's stay with *who* and leave the *how* alone for now. Can you think of anyone, anyone at all, who might have known all the victims too well for them to be suspicious?"

"Yeah, *me*," Longarm replied. "But I didn't do it. There's the agent, Cal Durler, but he has an alibi for a couple of the killings. So does Rain Crow. He was at my side when Roping Sally was killed."

"How can you be sure? You said he found you at the agency, told you he was worried about Yellow Leggings, and led you out to look for him. He could have killed his sidekick before he came for you. Could have killed the girl at the same time, as far as that goes."

One of the cowhands said, "Hot damn! Let's round that pesky redskin up and make him talk!"

Longarm laid a restraining hand on the man's arm. "Hold on! He didn't do it. He could have killed Yellow Leggings, but he was at the agency when the boy, Gray Dog, was murdered. As for Roping Sally, he didn't know she was riding out last night in the first place, and didn't have the time in the second. And even if my watch was wrong, I've ridden some miles beside Rain Crow and he leaves footprints like the rest of us mortals."

One of the hands asked, "What *was* Roping Sally doing out there last night anyway?"

"She'd said something about stray cows, last time I saw her," lied Longarm, adding quickly to change the subject, "I'm going over to the rail yards to jaw with the dispatcher. There was a train through, just before we found the bodies. Train crew might have seen something."

To his relief, the three cowhands stayed behind to jaw with the coroner about Roping Sally's funeral. Apparently the locals had taken up a collection to see her to the burial ground in style. It was just as well. Longarm wasn't of a mind to attend the funeral. He felt bad enough about the way he'd treated her as it was. He knew it hadn't really been his fault she'd ridden out there looking for him. He'd told her not to. On the other hand, if he'd kept his damned pecker in his pants . . . but what was done was done. Her soul would likely rest easier if he avenged her than it would if he just blubbered like a fool some more.

Longarm walked across the unfenced rail yards as a Baldwin switcher shunted a string of empties on to a siding. He spotted a man walking along the tracks toward the station with a sheaf of papers in one hand and dog-trotted after him, calling out, "Howdy! I'm a lawman!"

The man stopped and said, "I ain't. I work for the railroad and I got some cattle cars to move."

Longarm fell in beside him as the dispatcher walked toward a string of empty cattle cars down the line. He explained the situation and asked, "If somebody was leaping off and on your trains out yonder, would the boys in the caboose likely notice?"

The dispatcher answered, "The brakemen walk the whole train, setting the wheels for that nasty drop just west of here. How far out on the prairie are we talking about?"

"That rolling stretch just inside the reservation line. How long does it take to set the drags, headed east?"

"Well, each car has its own brake. The boys don't set every one unless they're loaded heavy, but the crews spend some time up on the catwalk on most trips."

"When would a fellow have the best chance of leaping for a passing grab-iron without being spotted?"

The dispatcher considered the question for a moment. "Headed west, he could likely climb aboard here in the yards and if he was in an empty reefer, he might leap off without busting any serious bones or being spotted. The train climbs for the Rockies without ever using brakes. Slows down some, topping rises. Yeah, getting aboard a train out there ain't that big a shucks."

"How about coming back? Could a man hop aboard without being seen, anywhere along the downhill grade?"

"He'd be one boss hobo if he could," the yardman chuckled. "Like I said, the crews start working the brakes at least twenty miles out. He'd have to pick his train ahead of time, too. A heavy freight would have a brakeman up on dang near every car. A train hauling back a string of empties would be his best bet."

"That train that passed me last night—the one I mentioned. Was it full or empty?"

"Empty. A string of gondolas coming back from delivering ballast to the new section they're building in the mountains. Only thing is, it was scheduled on an off-hour. Your man could wait out there a week for a line of empty gondolas. He'd have to be a railroader who knew the business, too. We run all sorts of mixed loads at odd hours. I keep trying to tell the front office this ain't any way to run a railroad, but will they listen?"

Longarm pulled the brim of his hat down to shield his eyes against the glare of the midmorning sun. "You said a boss hobo could do it. I noticed some cuts out there. If a man took a long run as a train was coming, then threw himself out a good ten or twelve feet—"

The dispatcher guffawed loudly. "He'd bust his fool head before a mile of freight ran over him. The only way you could do that in the dark would be to have a flat car or a gondola under you when you came down. You'd have to know where it was likely to be when you leaped, and like I said, pick a time when the brakemen wasn't walking along the tops of the cars."

"He couldn't grab the *side* of a passing cattle car or reefer?"

"In the dark, at that speed? Listen, mister, landing on your ass somewhere on a forty-foot flat car bed would be bitch enough! Reaching for a passing grab-iron in the dark, ten feet off the grade, don't take hobo skills. It takes suicidal lunacy, and impossible luck to do it once. Twice is impossible."

Longarm nodded. "I'll take your word for it. How about hoboes, anyway? You have many riding your cars of an evening?"

"Naw, not this far west. Sometimes we give a lift to cowhands or Indians who ask polite. The stops are too far apart out here for the gents of the road."

"You'd notice, then, if the same hobo kept hanging about these yards?"

"Sure, and I'd sic the bulls on him. We got a real mean yard bull over at the roundhouse. His name is Mendez and he's a Mex or something. You want to talk to him about hoboes?"

"Later, maybe. Does he ride the trains or just work the yards?"

"Mendez is only a yard bull. We got some private detectives on the passenger trains, and the train crews deal with free riders on the freights. Mendez ain't on duty this time of the day, but he bunks over by the roundhouse with the switchmen and two kids he has helping him at night."

"I'll get around to them later. You'd know if they'd been having hobo troubles. Could you tell me the next time a string of empty flats or gondolas is due down from the mountains?"

"Nope," the yard man answered. "Like I said, they run this railroad off the cuff. Sometimes I'm lucky if they wire me a few hours ahead. Some night we'll

142

have two locomotives meeting headlamp to headlamp in the middle of God-knows. Maybe then they'll listen to me."

Longarm frowned and said, "Hmm, a man using your trains to get about would have to be reading your orders over your shoulder, then, wouldn't he?"

"Just about. Who did you have in mind?"

Longarm leaned toward the man conspiratorially, and whispered "He-Who-Walks-the-Night-Winds." Then he said pleasantly, "Thanks for your time," and turned about and walked away across the yard, leaving the dispatcher to stare after him, scratching his head.

The murder of two Indians in one evening was bad enough. The murder of Roping Sally was something else. Any sign that the so-called Wendigo might have been careless enough to leave was obliterated as parties of hard-eyed cowhands and patrols of eager soldiers rode in circles all over the reservation for the next three days and nights. Calvin Durler was worried about possible misunderstandings between the races. Longarm was worried too, but the possible bright side was that a reservation jump wasn't likely until things simmered down. The Indian police made sure the Blackfoot stayed close to home and Longarm spread the word in town that he'd take it personally if anyone shot a Blackfoot without one damned good reason. The fact that the Wendigo had killed Indians as well as whites helped.

The third evening after Roping Sally's funeral found Longarm seated on the agency steps, chewing an unlit cheroot, as the army scout, Jason, rode in alone.

Jason dismounted and joined Longarm on the steps, saying, "I've been ordered to find the Wendigo. Ain't that a bitch?"

"No reason you shouldn't try. Everybody in Montana's looking for the ornery son of a bitch. What happened to your dragoons?"

"Reckon they've had enough exercise for now. The

143

lieutenant said he was reconsidering his options. That's what he calls drinking alone in his quarters. You aim to light that cigar or just gum it to death?"

"Been trying to quit smoking. What's your pleasure?"

"I thought maybe we could throw in together. I been all over this country and you know what I've found? I ain't found shit. You reckon this Wendigo's really a haunt?"

Longarm shook his head. "I reckon we're missing some simple trick. Whoever's doing it isn't completely crazy. The Wendigo's had enough sense to lay low while half the territory's out here looking for him. That leaves someone with a reason as well as some slick way of moving about."

"Well, the heat's dying down. You suspicion he'll be doing it some more?" Jason asked.

"It's not likely that he'll suddenly get religion and just quit. I figure his play is spooking the Indians, which he's done some. It'll take some more spooking to make them jump the reservation, so, yeah, he's likely planning his next move about now."

"You reckon there's a land grabber behind all this, Longarm?"

"That's an obvious suspicion, but I can't get it to wash. No way any of the local cattlemen could claim this land, even if the Indians light out and leave it empty."

"How about a buried treasure, or a mineral claim, or such?"

"Studied on that, too. The Blackfoot are spread out thin here. A man slick enough to get in and out without being spotted could dig up half an acre easier than he could kill folks watching for him. As to minerals, they've been looked for. The prairie soil's forty feet at the least to the nearest bedrock and it's been surveyed by Uncle Sam. There's some lignite coal beds to the north. Too deep to be worth mining and too poor to be worth burning, next to all that anthracite they have back East. Nope, there's nothing here but grass and water, and like I said, no way a white man could beg, borrow, or steal

144

rangeland. The Wendigo is after something, but I'll be damned if I know what."

Jason scratched his bearded jaw and said, "I hear there's a pow-wow on the reservation tonight. You reckon the War Department might be interested?"

"You're welcome to come along, Jason. I'm riding over with Rain Crow, my Blackfoot deputy. He says one of Wovoka's Dream Singers is on the reservation. Rain Crow offered to run him off, but I said to leave the rascal be, for now."

"Them Dream Singers are pretty nasty, but it's your play. I'd go along if I thought there'd be some pretty squaws, but the old men will likely just be shaking rattles and talking sulky. So I'll pass on your offer and get on back to the fort."

As Jason turned to mount his bay, Longarm asked quietly, "Before you go, would you mind if I asked you a sort of unfriendly question?"

Jason swung around and stared back thoughtfully before he shrugged and said, "Ask away. I'll let you know if I take it unfriendly."

"Where were you the night of the three murders, Jason?"

The scout laughed and answered, "At the fort. Lucky I can prove it, ain't it? I've seen how fast you can draw!"

"I had to ask. Didn't mean anything by it."

"I know you're just doing your job, Longarm. Hell, I won't even get pissed when you check my story at the fort. A man with nothing to hide has no call to get pissed, and, hell, you never even mentioned my mother."

They both laughed. Longarm relaxed the hold he'd had on the derringer in his right coat pocket.

Jason asked, "Hear any more about Johnny Hunts Alone? Or do you suspicion him and the Wendigo might be one and the same?"

"I'll eat that apple a bite at a time. If they're the same gent, I'll catch 'em both whenever I catch one. If they ain't, I'll catch 'em separately. I've been asking about for a stranger with a limp. Nobody's seen any."

"Could be Johnny knows you're here and just lit out

to other parts. As I see it, his only reason for hiding out here would be because you didn't know he could pass for an Indian. You get my drift?"

"Sure. Real Bear's the only victim who could have identified him. *You're* still breathing, too."

"What's that supposed to mean, Longarm?"

"If Johnny Hunts Alone killed Real Bear to keep from being given away, he'd have done better to go after a white man he'd hunted with than a mess of Indians and a gal who never knew him."

"I see what your meaning is and I thank you for the warning. Anyone out to skin *this* hombre and take his head had best be good at it, though. I know the breed on sight and I can get riled as hell when folks start cutting off my head!"

Longarm rose to his feet as the scout got up, remounted, and rode away with a friendly wave. Longarm was about to go into the house, but Prudence Lee fluttered out, and whispered, "Don't go in, they're fighting."

Longarm heard the sound of breaking crockery and a man's voice raised in anger through the open doorway. He nodded and said, "Maybe we'd best go for a ride or something."

"Oh, I'd like that. Calvin said something about riding out to an Indian ceremony, later. Could I go along?"

Longarm started to shake his head. Then he thought of his plan for enlivening the festivities and said, "It might prove interesting, at that, if a white gal was there watching."

Fair was fair, though. So he said, "Miss Prudence, I'm going out with Rain Crow and some other Indian police to make some folks feel foolish. I don't expect danger, but there's likely to be some cussing."

"Oh, it sounds exciting! Calvin said you were trying to expose the Ghost Dancers as frauds, and I'm very interested in Indian lore."

"Yes ma'am. Some of such lore can tend to be a bit racy. You did say you were married once, didn't you?"

"Heavens, do you expect an orgy?" Prudence asked breathlessly.

"Ain't sure. I haven't been to many Ghost Dances. If I let you come along, you've got to promise to sit there poker-faced and not say anything, no matter what."

"I think I can manage that. If you'll help me with my side-saddle . . ."

"We'll be taking the buckboard, ma'am. Indians don't laugh at wheels the way they do at white ladies riding funny. I'll be putting some bags of feed around the edges of the wagon bed. If I should say to, I'll be obliged if you sort of flatten out behind 'em while the lead flies."

Chapter 11

It was sunset as the naked Ghost Dance missionary pranced up and down in front of the assembled Blackfoot elders gathered out on the prairie. His hair was long and stringy and his penis was painted red for some reason. He was about thirty years old and chanted in English as he waved the limp leather medicine shirt he held in one hand. His own Paiute dialect would have made no more sense to the Blackfoot than it would have to a white man, so as Longarm and the girl drove up to the edge of the crowd with Two Noses and Rain Crow at either side, they could understand his meaning as he pointed the gourd rattle in his other hand at them and shouted, "Behold, the white man comes with a woman and two of his Blackfoot hunting dogs. Do not listen to their words, my brothers. The whites are ignorant of the message of Wovoka!"

Longarm reined in at a discreet distance, ignoring the sullen muttering from the crowd as he nodded to the missionary and shouted back, "You just go ahead and have your say, old son. We've come in peace to learn, not to dispute religion with a man of the cloth—if we stretch cloth to include red paint, I mean."

The missionary wiggled his hips, swinging his painted penis, but Prudence Lee didn't blanch as he and even Longarm might have expected. She sat prim and straight on the buckboard seat, looking at him like he was a bug on a pin.

He held the leather garment up and shouted, "So be it! Hear me, my brothers! Wovoka has blessed this medicine shirt! These others you see by the council fire are for your warriors. When the time comes for our dead ancestors to join us in a final battle for our lands, the bullets of the soldiers will not hurt you if you wear them!"

Longarm muttered, "Stay here, ma'am. Rain Crow, you see that nobody trifles with Miss Prudence, hear? I'm gonna mosey over and take a closer look and listen."

He climbed down and made his way to the front of the crowd, hunkering down politely on his heels and not saying anything as the Paiute shouted, "All our dead ancestors will come back from the Happy Hunting Ground to join us! All of them! The soldiers may be many, but think of our numbers if every Indian who ever lived rides at our side against the soldiers!"

Longarm called out, "Can I ask a polite question? I was wondering if you'd tell us what tribes Wovoka had in mind."

"Tribes? Wovoka makes no distinction, white man! Our Ghost Dances shall raise all the dead!"

"*White* dead, too? You mean these folks have to face George Armstrong Custer and his men *again*? If you don't mind my saying, Custer was a mean son of a bitch at Washita and some other places even before you boys killed him!"

"Don't mock me, white man. Wovoka's medicine is only intended to bring back dead Indians!"

"I suspicioned as much. Tell me, does he aim to raise the Crows, the Utes, the Pawnees?"

"Of course. Every Indian who ever was!"

The Paiute missed the worried muttering from some of the old men around Longarm. He was probably a stranger in these parts.

Longarm grinned and said, "That should be interesting. These Blackfoot get to kill their old enemies all over again, right?"

"No, when the dead rise, they shall rise as brothers. All the old fighting will be forgotten. Indian shall greet Indian, as his fellow man."

"That sounds reasonable. Wouldn't it save a lot of

fuss if such whites and live Indians as are left just shook hands and called it quits right now?"

"You mock the message I bring. My brothers, here, are not taken in by your twisting of my words!"

"Now, that ain't fair. I ain't twisted word-one. It was *you* who said they had to make friends with a mess of damn Pawnee. How about Snakes? Does Snake Killer, over yonder, get to keep his coup feather when his dead Snake brothers come to call? What if a dead Blackfoot pops out of the ground in the middle of some Crows? Does he shake hands with them, or run off with their ponies, like in the Shining Times?"

"If you won't let me speak, I will go."

"I'll be quiet, seeing as how you don't seem to know what your message is."

In the crowd behind him, someone snickered. Longarm didn't know if the laugh had been with him or at him. Neither did the Paiute. He waved the medicine shirt again and shouted, "As I was saying, your young men shall be immune to white bullets in these shirts."

Longarm asked, "How come? I mean, I don't doubt for a minute that those raggedy buckskins are bulletproof. What I don't understand is why in thunder you need live Indians to do your fighting if Wovoka has all these dead ghosts ready to fight the army?"

"The ghosts must know our people are sincere. Would you expect the spirits to fight for weaklings afraid to stand up for their rights?"

"I don't know what a spirit might do. I'd be scared as hell to charge a Gatling gun with nothing on but a magic shammy shirt, though."

"That is because you have a white man's heart. The medicine only works for those who believe."

"That sounds reasonable," Longarm said amiably. "Put the shirt on and let's see how it works for you."

"What do you mean, white twister of words?"

"Well, I thought, as long as you've got those magic shirts, and I've got a gun, we'd see how good your brag is. Put on the shirt and I'll bounce a couple of .44 slugs off it."

150

The Paiute's face clouded over threateningly, but Longarm thought he detected a quaver in the Indian's voice as he responded, "Are you threatening to kill me, white man? I have come in peace, unarmed. The Blackfoot have extended me the protection of their hospitality!"

"Well, sure they have. I'm hospitable myself. I'd never in this world gun a man I thought was likely to die from it. But you said your shirts were bulletproof. So what say we have some fun?"

Longarm heard a murmur of agreement around him from the Blackfoot as the Paiute paled and stammered, "It would not be a fair test. I am not initiated as a warrior!"

The lawman allowed a larger-than-life expression of shock to appear on his face as he said, "You mean you're standing there telling all these folks to go to war, and you're not a proper soldier? Well, I *did* fight a war one time, and *I* ain't about to tell these old Dog Soldiers or Turtle Lances whether they should go to war or get married! Hell, I'm not ashamed to admit I never had the nerve to go through the Sun Dance as a full warrior. By the way, that's likely why I see no scars on *your* chest, huh?"

"We Paiute never danced the Sun Dance."

"I know. Never did all that much fighting, either, now that I think on it. Likely that's why Wovoka's so hot and bothered about another Indian war. It's the men who never fight that start our white man's wars, too."

An old Indian near Longarm muttered something in a jeering tone and this time, when some other Indians laughed, Longarm knew they weren't laughing at him!

The Paiute licked his lips and said, "Don't listen to him, my brothers. Can't you see what he is trying to do?"

Longarm let a little scorn creep into his voice as he said, "I ain't doing anything but saying my mind. This may be a foolish time to bring it up, but I'll tell one and all I've fought Indians in my time. I mean, I've fought *real* Indians, not ghosts." He got to his feet, threw his hat down, and pounded his chest, shouting, "Hear me! I count coup! I have killed Dakota! I have killed Cheyenne! I have taken captives back from Apache and taken Comanche alive to be hanged by the government!"

Old Snake Killer asked in an interested tone, "How many Blackfoot do you count coup on?"

"None. I don't say this because of where I am and who might be listening. I say it because I wasn't here the last time you rose against the army."

"Would you have killed me, had we met in battle?"

"You're damned right I would have, unless you'd killed me first. We're both *men*, ain't we?"

Snake Killer smiled broadly. "Yes. I think it would have been a good fight. I like a man who says what is in his heart, too. But Wendigo—"

"The Wendigo has nothing to do with Wovoka's Ghost Dance, Snake Killer. I'm a white man, not a Dream Singer, so I'll not insult you by disputing about spirits. I just want to see this jasper's medicine shirt turn a bullet before any of your young men put one on to ride against the army!"

The old Blackfoot nodded and told the Paiute, "His words make sense. Why don't you put the shirt on and prove him wrong?"

The Paiute stammered, "I am not allowed to. Only a true warrior can wear the Medicine Shirt."

Old Snake Killer got to his feet, peeling off his old wool jacket to reveal the Sun Dance scars on his bony chest as he said, "I am a warrior. Give me the shirt."

Longarm swore under his breath. He hadn't planned on getting a *Blackfoot* at the wrong end of his Colt! The Paiute missionary saw the bind he was in at the same time. Slyly, he held the thin deerskin shirt out to the old man, saying, "Of course. Let us see what happens when the white man shoots you."

The old Blackfoot put the shirt on and stood there, his head cocked to one side in mild interest as he waited for Longarm to test his medicine. Longarm knew that if he killed the old man there'd be hell to pay. On the other hand, even though common sense indicated that he should back down, he knew what the Ghost Dancer would twist it into. He drew his .44, but said, "I have to think about this, boys. You see, I don't believe in this medicine!"

The Paiute jeered, "Go ahead and shoot him. Are you afraid? Behold, my brothers, the medicine is working! Snake Killer is wearing the medicine shirt and the white man can't shoot him!"

"Damn it, it ain't the same thing!"

"Yes it is! Wovoka says a man wearing the medicine shirt cannot be harmed by white man's bullets! Whether you shoot or not, the results are the same! Anyone with eyes can see this!"

Longarm had to admit that the Paiute had a point. The rascal knew he wasn't about to gun the old man and was twisting it to look like magic!

Then Prudence Lee was suddenly at his side. She held her hand out imperiously and said, "Give *me* the gun, Longarm!"

There was a murmur of surprise from the Indians. They were no more confused than Longarm. He said, "Miss Prudence, this gun is loaded with .44-40s and I told you to stay on the buckboard!"

"Give me the gun. I assure you I have no intention of shooting anyone with it."

"Then what's your play? You could miss without looking shameful, but they'd still say it was medicine, and—"

"Will you give me that damned gun and be still? You *know* I'm a missionary!"

Longarm let her take the gun by the barrel from his hand. She smiled prettily and held the grips out to the Paiute, saying, "The white man's heart is not strong enough to shoot at a friend, even a friend protected by your strong medicine. *You* will have to fire it at Snake Killer!"

The Paiute backed away, stammering, "Not I! It is wrong for me to shoot at a brother!"

Prudence Lee followed him, holding out the gun in

grim determination as they circled the council fire. She was smiling sweetly as she insisted, "But what harm can come to Snake Killer if Wovoka's magic is stronger than a white man's bullets? Surely you know how to shoot a pistol, don't you? Heavens, I should think a man who preaches war would know at least a *little* about weapons!"

Most of the Blackfoot were laughing openly, now. The Paiute stammered obtuse theology and the little female missionary cut him up and down and sideways with sophistries of her own until it became obvious that the naked Ghost Dancer had no intention of letting her hand him Longarm's revolver.

Presently, Prudence brought the pistol back to the tall deputy and handed it to him, saying, "Oh, dear, I suppose now we'll just have to take his word for it about the shirt! He doesn't seem to want to prove it one way or the other!"

Longarm grinned back at her as he holstered the .44 and said, "Yep, they'll likely have to try those bulletproof shirts without a demonstration."

Old Snake Killer asked, "If nobody wants to shoot at me, can I take this thing off? It's badly tanned and it itches."

There was a roar of laughter, and Longarm said, "Let's go, Miss Prudence. We'll quit while we're ahead."

He led her back to the buckboard and helped her up to the seat as Rain Crow leaned over in his saddle and asked, "Do you want me to run that Paiute off?"

Longarm said, "No. Don't make him look that important. This little lady just did quite a job taking the wind out of his sails and I suspicion that the more he preaches, the more they'll laugh at him."

"You may be right, for now. But what if Wendigo strikes again?"

"I see what you mean. But leave the Ghost Dancer be, anyway. If I don't stop the Wendigo pretty quickly, we'll be up to our chins in trouble, medicine shirts or no."

Longarm fingered a shiny new silver dollar as he stood in the saloon doorway scanning the bar in the dim light. Finally, he spotted the man he was looking for by the description the railroad workers had given him. The yard bull, Mendez, was a tall, lean man in a red checked shirt and peaked cloth cap. He wore an old Navy .36 in a battered army holster and looked like he could use a shave.

Longarm bellied up to the bar beside him and said, "I'm a U.S. Deputy Marshal, Mr. Mendez. They told me over at the roundhouse that I might find you here."

Mendez shrugged and said, "I'm off duty. It's none of their business if I drink or not, on my own time."

Longarm noticed he had a slight Spanish accent. "What *are* you drinking, then?"

"I'm not. Already have a skinful and I have to work all night."

"I know. What's coming through the yards tonight?"

"Your guess is as good as mine. I think they're running a passenger train through about eight-thirty. They don't discuss the timetable with us greasers."

"Oh? The two boys helping you chase hoboes are Mexican, too?"

"One's a Mex. Other's Irish. I'm a South American, if it's bothering you."

"Seems to be bothering you more than me, Mr. Mendez. I have some friends who grew up speaking Spanish."

"I know, as long as they don't want to marry your sister, huh?"

"I figure who my sister might marry would be her own business. Did some lawman give you a hard time, once, about your accent? Or do you just hate *all* us gringos?"

"*One* time might not have bothered me," the yard bull said bitterly. "It gets tedious being called a greaser after the first hundred times or so. Look, you don't have to butter me up to get me to cooperate. What do you want from me, Deputy?"

"I said it already. Trying to get a line on slow freights passing through the Blackfoot reservation at night."

"I heard someone might be shooting Indians from the passing trains. The roundhouse gang was talking about it the other evening. If any of 'em saw anything, they didn't let me in on it."

"I know you don't ride the trains. Can you think of anyone who might, aside from the regular crews?"

"Freight trains? Hoboes, if we let them. The insurance company says we're not to give rides to Indians any more. Damn fool Shoshoni fell between the blinds a few months back and his squaw sued the line. Some free passes being given out, back East, but only to ride the passenger trains. Freight crews have enough to handle without some idiot getting in the way as they run the catwalk."

"Don't suppose any hobo could get by you, maybe late on a dark night in the rail yards?" the deputy asked.

"Sure, one could, once in a while. Play hell doing it regular, though. My boys and me have orders to dust their asses with rock salt, getting on or getting off."

"All three of you carry shotguns charged with salt, on duty?"

"Twelve gauge, double barrel, sawed off. I carry a sawed-off baseball bat, too. You want to hop a freight in my yards, mister, you'd better ask the dispatcher for permission, first."

"None of the caboose hands or maybe a friendly engineer could give a pal a lift?"

"Sure they could. I only check the cars for bums. I have a helper go up one side with a lantern while I ease up the far side in the dark to dust the rascals as they slip away from him between the wheels. I dusted one boy right in the ass that way a month ago and you should have heard him holler. But I don't ask who's riding the caboose or up in the cab. It's not my job."

Longarm tapped absently on the bar with the silver dollar in his hand and the yard bull added, "This sniper or whatever would have a hard time doing mean things from the cab or caboose, though, wouldn't he?"

"Yeah. I may as well tell you, I've wired about the country for suggestions about crazy people working for your railroad. Nobody thinks it likely a full crew of lunatics are working out here."

A worried expression appeared on the railroad cop's face. "You know about that colored boy I killed in Omaha, then?"

"Yeah. Nebraska says you got off on self-defense. You said that hobo pulled a knife on you, right?"

"He did, and he had two other niggers with him. They dropped the subject when I blew his face off. I warned him twice to drop the knife before I shot him, too, God damn it!" Mendez slammed a fist down on the bar.

"Cool down, old son! You don't have to convince *me*. You already got let off by a grand jury. I know you have a rough job."

"They fired me anyway. Said I'd overstepped my authority. Ain't that a laugh? They fire you if you let the bums ride and they fire you if you get in a fuss with 'em."

"There ain't no justice," Longarm commiserated. "I see you had no trouble getting another job out here, though."

"Oh, a railroad bull with a tough rep can usually get hired somewhere. I don't get paid as much, though, and the prices out here are higher than back East. If I had it to do over, those three coons could have driven the damned locomotive and I'd have looked the other way."

Longarm shook his head and said, "I don't buy that. The roundhouse gang has you down as a good, tough bull."

"Well, I'll get tougher if they don't quit calling me a Mex. I'm from Paraguay, not Mexico, and both my mother and father were pure white!"

157

Longarm nodded and said, "I suspicioned as much. How'd you get up here from such a far piece south? Merchant marine?"

"No. Worked for a British railroad down there when I was a teenager. Paraguay hasn't got that much in the way of railroading, but I liked it better than punching cows, so I followed the trade north."

"You've been here a spell, judging from the way you speak English."

"Hell, I fought in the War for Lincoln!" Mendez said proudly. "Least I could do to get back at Texas. The first time I was called a greaser was in Galveston and I haven't learned to like it yet."

Longarm promised never to call Mendez a greaser and left him alone at the bar. He walked to the land office to use the federal wire. After he'd reported his lack of progress and asked a few questions that nobody in Denver had answers to, he sent an inquiry to the Chicago stock market. As Agent Chadwick came in to join him under the telegraph batteries, Longarm said, "Beef's up a dollar and six bits a head and one of your battery jars is leaking."

Chadwick looked at the charred black spot on the blotter next to the telegraph key and said, "Cigar burn. Them wet cell jars are glass. They leak all at once or never."

"Doesn't it make you nervous working with all that acid up there?" Longarm asked.

Chadwick shrugged. "The batteries have to be somewhere. That's a pretty stout shelf."

"I'd have 'em on the floor if this was my wire shack. It's good to have a box of baking soda handy, too. Met a telegrapher who saved his eyes with baking soda, once, when a Sioux arrow shattered a battery jar in his face and spattered him with vitriol."

"You're a cheerful cuss today. How come you asked the current price of beef?"

"Still a cowhand at heart, I guess. I thought you'd be interested yourself, Chadwick. Seems only natural

158

the land office out here would be abreast of converting grass to dollars."

Chadwick looked annoyed and said, "Stop pussy-footing around, damn it! You heard something about that trouble I had a few years back, didn't you?"

"Some," Longarm lied, adding, "I'd like to hear your side, Chadwick."

The agent smiled crookedly and said, "I might have known you were using the railroad telegraph for snooping around about us all. Did they tell you I was cleared of the charges?"

"I didn't suspicion you'd be working for Uncle Sam if he'd caught you with your pants down."

"Hell, everybody's pants were down when they gave away all that money to build the railroads West, back in the sixties. They caught Vice President Colfax making money on those watered railroad bonds, but I was only a clerk in those days. I never even got a crack at all they were giving away in the way of land grants and tax money. The only reason I was called upon to testify was that my boss was grabbing land right and left! I came out of it clean as a whistle, and believe you me, they had me on the carpet for days, going over everything I'd had for breakfast for a good seven years! They investigated my bank account and made me show 'em everything but my belly button. But what's the use of talking? You likely got my first-grade report cards from Denver when you wired 'em, right?"

Longarm laughed and said, "As a matter of fact, I never knew you were mixed up in that old financial mess till you just now told me."

"You didn't? What in hell are we raking it up for, then?"

"We're not. You are. Folks are funny that way. They get to jawing with a lawman and next thing they know, they're telling him about some gal they got in trouble once, or how much they hated their pa for whupping 'em. Had a fellow admit to incest once, and I never suspicioned him of more than murder."

Chadwick laughed and shook his head. "All right, you suckered me into revealing my dark past. Had it been a mite darker, I'd be smoking dollar cigars in my private railroad car instead of trying to live on a piss-poor wage, considering. Do you want the name of the lady I was sleeping with the night Roping Sally was murdered?"

"It ain't any of my business, but since you brought it up, Sheriff Murphy told me about it. Says you're likely to get killed if her *other* boyfriend finds out about it."

"Damn!" Chadwick exploded. "It's what I get for staying late! Who told Murphy, that old biddy next door?"

"He said he saw you himself, making his morning rounds. The old biddy next door was watching through her lace curtains when you came through the back yard just after sundown. I don't hold with small-town gossip, much, but in a way, she might have done you a favor."

"Jesus H. Christ! You don't mean you really had me under suspicion?"

"No more than anyone else in the territory. Let's get back to the price of beef. We're headed into a cattle boom after the droughts the last couple of years thinned the herds to where the price went up on such cows as are left. Everybody out here seems to want cows bad enough to steal them, lately. I've noticed the range hereabouts is getting overgrazed. Lots of spreads are overstocked, but they keep trailing long-horn north just the same."

"Jesus, are you still gnawing that same bone about someone stealing reservation rangeland from the fool Indians?"

Longarm nodded and said, "Ain't getting much marrow out of it, either. Seems odd that nobody's made an offer on damn near virgin range. The Black-foot have maybe a hundred and fifty head grazing more than fifteen hundred full sections out there."

Chadwick shook his head wearily and insisted,

"That's the B.I.A.'s problem. Who would you expect to make *me* an offer? I keep telling you I can't sell government land, damn it!"

Longarm said, "You do file claims and issue range permits, though. Yet you say no white man's approached you with any questions about all that grass going to waste."

Chadwick cut in with an annoyed snort to explain, "Hell, of *course* they've *asked* about it. But I've told everybody the same thing. Those Indian lands are not for sale, with or without Indians on 'em!"

"Could you give me a list of everyone who's interested in spreading out?" the lawman asked.

Chadwick frowned and said, "Sure, if I can remember 'em all. Let's go out to my office and I'll write down those I recall."

As he led the way, Longarm asked mildly, "Don't you keep books on such matters, Chadwick?"

"You mean, do I record the name of every man who stops me on the street to ask a fool question? No. I don't write down the dirty jokes I hear or the names of sons they seem to think I can get into West Point, either. People suck around a man in my position, Longarm. They seem to think I'm Uncle Sam in the flesh instead of his poorly paid hired hand!"

"But you don't take bribes, right?"

"I don't know. I've never had the chance. I remember how the man I used to work under retired rich, disgraced or not. It's been my misfortune to be posted to jobs that keep most men honest through no fault of their own."

He led Longarm out front, sat down, and started writing on the back of an envelope as he muttered darkly about the stupidity of people who thought he was Saint Nicholas. He handed Longarm a list of eighteen names and brands and said, "Here, this should keep you busy. Every one of these idiots has offered to buy at least a section of Indian land, should it ever be auctioned off."

Longarm scanned the list, noting that most of the

names on it were those of small local cattlemen with modest but growing herds and small home spreads. When Chadwick asked how he knew so much, he explained, "I haven't just been spitting and whittling since I came here, Chadwick. One time or the other since I got here, I've talked to just about everybody I've been able to get within a mile of."

"Any of them cowboys interesting enough to pester again?"

"Maybe. I'll keep this with my map and check them off as I get the time. Do you get any offers from bigger outfits, like the Double Z or maybe the Tumbling R?"

"Not that I remember. Why?" Chadwick asked.

"Takes a big outfit to afford hired guns, flying machines, and such."

"I see your meaning. Have you thought about the army?"

"Sure I have. They're spoiling for another go at the Blackfoot and the War Department has observation balloons, too. But some officer out to start an Indian war to advance his career wouldn't have to use spooks. He'd just dream up some incident and start blasting away."

"If some soldiers were trying to frighten the Blackfoot into a jump, and knew the when and where of it . . . " the agent suggested.

"Too damned complicated. The second lieutenant out at the fort's ornery enough to frame up some excuse to kill Indians, but why shilly-shally about with Wendigos? If he had even one man in his command willing to murder for him, he'd just have the rascal scalp some passing white, and bye-bye, Blackfoot!"

"Yeah," Chadwick agreed, "the War Department's never been too subtle. How about the B.I.A., as long as you suspect your fellow federal employees all that much?"

"Hey," Longarm said, "it was you who brought up the War Department. But I've considered whether the Bureau of Indian Affairs might have a reason to

162

scare their own charges off. They haven't got one. The minute the Blackfoot are gone, Washington cuts the funds allocated for feeding the tribe and, if there's one thing the Indian Ring doesn't cotton to, it's leaving money in the Treasury."

"Some of those funds tend to stick to fingers along the way, too," Chadwick observed. "It wouldn't make much sense for the B.I.A. to want to go out of business, would it?"

"Not hardly. Maybe now you see why I keep chewing the same bone over and over. It's boring the shit out of *me*, too!"

"So," the land agent said, "no matter where the trail seems to take you, it keeps leading back to a crazy man, or an Indian spook."

"I don't like those possibilities, much, either. I'd best be on my way and see who else I can come up with."

Longarm left the land office and headed for where he'd tethered his chestnut in front of the saloon. He saw a townie nailing up a cardboard placard and paused to read it over the man's shoulder. It was an election poster, advising one and all to vote for Wilbur Browning for county sheriff. Longarm frowned and opined, "Seems to me your man is getting anxious, considering. The coroner tells me you've never held elections hereabouts, since there ain't enough county to mention."

The man finished hammering the last nail and said, "I know. Damned Indian reservation takes up most of the county and there ain't enough of us whites to matter. But that fool Paddy Murphy's not worth the powder to blow him up with. So we're fielding Browning against the shanty son of a bitch!"

"Browning's a rider for the Double Z, ain't he?" Longarm asked.

"Yeah, he shot a Texan in Dodge one time, which is more than Murphy can say. The territorial governor's given permission for elections and we aim to vote Murphy out."

"Reorganizing the unincorporated districts, is he? That's right interesting. They say anything about, uh,

163

expanding the county, over at your party headquarters?"

"Hell," the man said, "we ain't got a headquarters. Ain't rightly got a party, either. But since Murphy's a Republican, the boys over at the livery who paid for these signs must be Democrats."

"Don't you know for sure? Seems to me a legal election has to register voters ahead."

"Shit, nobody in Switchback's all that fussy. We just aim to have us a real lawman. If Murphy won't be voted out polite, we'll just tar and feather the son of a bitch and ride him out on a rail."

Longarm cleared his throat and adjusted the brim of his hat. "Well, as I'm a federal man, it may not be my call to tell folks how to hold local elections. But you'll find elections work better if they're legal. How come folks are so anxious about politics, all of a sudden?"

"It's the killings out on the reservation. We keep telling Murphy he ought to do something about it and he keeps saying it ain't his jurisdiction. Wilbur Browning says he'll jurisdict the shit out of that Wendigo son of a bitch if we give *him* the job."

"The Blackfoot have their own police force out there. I suspicion they won't want your man's help all that much."

"It don't matter what they want. All these Indian rascals running about killing folks have everybody spooked. Seen some more damn Indians just this morning, coming up from the railroad station armed to the teeth."

A troubled look darkened the tall lawman's features. "Wait a minute," he said. "Are you saying men from other tribes are in Switchback?"

"They weren't Blackfoot. Don't know where they were headed. I ain't an expert on Indians, but one of the fellows over to the railroad said they were Sioux. They were dressed like white men, save for braided hair and likely needing a bath, but Wes Collins, who used to be in the army, allowed as how the lingo they were jabbering was Dakota."

"You couldn't say which way they rode, huh?"

"Well, they ain't washing dishes here in Switchback, or asking for a job as hired hands, so they likely went on out to the reservation."

"You say this morning, eh? They've got four or five hours' lead on me and I doubt they'll be reporting in to the agent. I'll tell the Blackfoot police about it and let them take care of it."

"How do you know you can trust your Indian police to tell you true about other redskins?"

Longarm started to say it was a foolish question. Then he reconsidered, shrugged, and said, "I don't."

Chapter 12

This time Longarm rode back to the reservation along the railroad tracks instead of taking the wagon trace from town. He didn't know what he expected to find, but he'd never ridden the entire stretch and it was possible that his survey map was missing a few details.

As he topped the rise, west of town, and started across the higher prairie rolling toward the distant foothills, a calico steer with a broken left horn stared wild-eyed at him for a moment and lit out, running. Longarm saw its badly worn hide and figured it for a queer. Sometimes something funny happened to a castrated calf and it grew up thinking it was a heifer. The range bulls thought so, too, and the poor spooked animal was all worn out from trying to get screwed. Some pissed-off bull had whupped it good for fooling him, most likely, and now it was ranging alone, too scared to let anything near it.

The range between Switchback and the reservation line was badly misused in this stretch, too. The native grasses had been overgrazed and the brush was getting out of hand along the railroad right-of-way. Prickly tumbleweed, both blowing and growing, formed dense windrows between higher clumps of sage and greasewood that had followed the tracks east out of the Great Basin beyond the mountains. Some of the brush was waist-high to a man on foot and getting too woody for even an antelope to browse. It was a hell of a way to treat a country, Longarm thought, but told himself not to worry about it. Nevertheless, he couldn't help won-

166

dering where it would all lead to. He was all for progress; the Iron Horse had opened up a continent to Europe's hungry hordes in his own lifetime, but couldn't people see there was a limit to what the land could take? The high plains had been grazed for thousands of years without being damaged by its indigenous wildlife. The longhorn probably didn't hurt the buffalo grass any more than the buffalo had, head for head. But the buffalo had kept moving, giving the grass time to grow back. The Indian had been willing to live the same way, drifting across the sea of grass from place to place. The white man's notion of staying put with his cows and crops didn't give the range time to recover. The ten inches of rain each season and the short green-up of the native short-grasses called for at least two years of fallow for every one grazed. At the rate they were overstocking, the cattle raisers would be raising more dust than cows in a few more years.

He kept an eye on the queer. It had stopped, and was staring at him from behind a clump of greasewood, now. The critter was mixed up enough between the horns to do almost anything, he knew. Cows grazing with others were usually neighborly enough, but loners, away from the herd, tended to get odd notions. When that messed-up calico didn't think he was a gal, he just might decide he was a Spanish fighting bull. That busted horn might make a nasty hole in his chestnut's hide, too.

Longarm rode on, pretending not to notice, the way one rides past a barking farmyard dog. Then, as he and the chestnut came abreast of the queer, it lowered its banged-up head, snorted, and charged.

"Son of a bitch!" muttered Longarm, swinging his mount in a tight circle to spoil the rogue's aim. Something ticked the brim of his hat as, behind him, a gunshot swore at him, too!

As the steer thundered by on one side, Longarm was rolling out of the saddle on the other, dragging his Winchester from its boot as he threw himself at the dirt. He landed on his side and rolled behind a waist-

167

high clump of sage in a cloud of mustard-colored dust, ignoring the horse running one way and the steer the other. He rolled over again and rose on his elbows with the rifle trained back the way he'd come. The second shot tore through the sage where he'd landed, and spotting the gunsmoke wafting from some greasewood near the tracks, Longarm fired back, dropped lower and snaked at an angle toward it, cradling his rifle in his arms as he walked his elbows through the dust.

Longarm heard the pounding of hooves and turned his head to see the calico queer headed his way, its good horn down and ploughing through the brush as it came!

He fired a shot into the dust ahead of the charging queer to turn it. The critter didn't even swerve, but Longarm's unseen attacker parted his rising gunsmoke with a bullet. The lawman pulled his knees up, dug his heels into the dust, and kicked himself sideways as the calico charged blindly through the space he'd just occupied, snorting like a runaway locomotive. Longarm landed on the back of his neck, somersaulted backwards, and came up pumping lead in the general direction of the greasewood clump the shots seemed to be coming from. Then he dropped and rolled out of sight without waiting to see how good the other's aim might be. There were no answering shots. If he hadn't hit the son of a bitch, then his enemy was lying doggo, or had lost interest and was crawling himself, now.

There seemed to be no way to find out which, without catching a rifle ball in the head or attracting the attention of the crazy calico. So Longarm stayed prone in a clump of tumbleweed, propped on one elbow, as he took a fistful of loose cartridges from his coat pocket and thumbed them into the rifle's magazine. He risked a look to the west and saw that his chestnut had stopped a quarter-mile away and had begun to graze, as if nothing had happened. Longarm peered through a gap in the brush and observed that the one-horned calico was broadside to him, now. The lunatic longhorn had its tail up and its head down, pawing the dirt with one hoof as it regarded something hidden to Longarm's left, closer to the railroad tracks. Longarm didn't think the calico had spotted anyone for sure, since it wasn't spooked or charging, but the calico had seen something, so Longarm started crabbing toward the tracks, keeping his head and ass down, moving as fast as he could. Before he reached the tracks, a double-header freight came over the rise between him and town, with both engines puffing, fore and aft. The one-horned queer lit out for Texas, bawling in fright. Longarm heaved a sigh of relief and kept crawling toward the tracks as the ground vibrated under him in time to the pounding drivers of the double-header. He saw a brakeman staring down at him, slack-jawed, from the top of a car. Then the train was past and he was kneeling behind some tall, dried sunflower stalks with a reloaded rifle in his hands and not much notion where to point it.

He worked his way east along the railroad bank for four or five minutes until he reached a wooden culvert that ran under the tracks through the embankment. He saw where human knees had carried someone under to the far side and, swearing, threw caution to the winds and ran up and over. He dropped to one knee on the north side of the tracks, and swept the horizon with his eyes. Then he ran toward the edge of the dropoff, rifle ready. He surmised the bushwhacker had crawled through the culvert after that last exchange, jumped up as the train covered his movements, and lit out.

At the edge, he looked down the slope toward the outskirts of Switchback. There was nobody on the gently inclined, bare, eroded slope to the first fence line. The bastard who'd shot at him had made it to the cover of those railroad sheds and the shanties past them. Longarm considered strollling on down to ask anyone he met what they might have seen, but it seemed a waste of time. If anyone had anything to say, Sheriff Murphy would hear about it, sooner or later.

The deputy recrossed the tracks, and after some coaxing and cussing, got back aboard the chestnut. He rode on his way again without further incident, chewing an unlit cheroot as he dusted himself off and tried to puzzle out what had happened. If whoever'd shot at him was the same one playing Wendigo, Wendigo's methods weren't subtle. Could those others simply have been *shot*?

That might explain why the Wendigo took the heads. If he was trying to spook the Blackfoot with spirit killings, he wouldn't want corpses left about with bullets in their skulls. On the other hand, the sound of a gunshot carried for some distance, and nobody'd heard any.

Who was that fellow back East who said he'd patented some newfangled gadget that could silence the muzzle blast of a gun? There'd been a piece about it in *Frank Leslie's Illustrated Weekly*. A silenced rifle might explain a lot, but the shots just fired at him had sounded like a plain old .44-40. Even with a silencer, the Wendigo would have to be a fancy marksman to pick folks off in the dark from any distance. Luckily, whoever'd just been blazing away at him hadn't been too good a shot.

Aloud, he muttered, "Shit, a man picks up a lot of enemies packing a badge. Could have been just about anyone."

He passed a reservation marker where, though the locals trespassed their cows a mite along the edges, the brush began to thin out, replaced by the short-grass God had put there in the first place. The Blackfoot didn't have enough stock to graze this far from the agency. The prairie hereabouts was unspoiled. The land was tough enough to take the antelope and jack's occasional attentions. With the buffalo shot off, the virgin range was fat enough to seem indecent. Lots of last summer's straw was still standing. He'd have to tell Cal Durler it was time they either burned it off on purpose or had a wildfire from the sparks thrown by a passing train.

He followed the right-of-way, noting a couple of cuts he considered high enough for someone attempting to get aboard a train without a ticket, but when he took the time to investigate each one for sign, he found none. He came to the place where they'd found Roping Sally and swung away to head for the agency. All he'd learned was that someone was out to kill him, but he'd known that much before.

He found Nan Durler alone at the agency. She said her husband had driven Prudence Lee into town and added, "You should have met them on the road."

Longarm said, "Didn't come back by way of the wagon trace. Is Miss Lee leaving?"

"No, she said she had some shopping to do. They'll likely be back for supper in a few hours. What happened to you? You look like you've been rolling in the dirt!"

"I have. The dust'll brush out of my clothes, but I could use a bath and a fresh shirt."

"We've a washtub in the back shed you could use," she offered, "if you've a mind to. I'll boil some water and fetch you a towel and soap."

Longarm left his coat and gun rig on the bed in the guest room and lugged four buckets of pump water to the tub as the Indian agent's wife put two big kettles on the kitchen range. She served him coffee at the table while they waited for the water to heat up.

He noticed that Nan wasn't having any as she sat across the table from him. When he commented on this, she brushed a strand of hair from her forehead and sighed, "It seems all I do out here is drink that goddamn coffee. Next thing you know I'll be dipping snuff. I'm beginning to feel like one of those white-trash girls I used to feel so sorry for."

"I reckon it does get tedious out here for a woman alone, but you've got Prudence Lee to talk with, now."

"Good God, she's no more company than my husband! All either of them seems interested in are these infernal Indians! Prudence prattles endlessly about their heathen souls and Calvin's up half the night fretting about his balance sheets! You'd think it was *important* that they got his model farm working on a paying basis, for heaven's sake!"

Longarm took a slow sip of his coffee. "Well, it's likely important to Cal. He's got a heap of responsibilities out here for a man so young."

"So young is right! Sometimes I feel like I'm his mother. The trouble is, I never married him to be his mother."

"Well," he tried to console her, "you'll doubtless have some real kids to mother, sooner or later."

"With Calvin?" She laughed, a bit wildly. Then she stared at the spoon she was bending out of shape between her fingers on the table and muttered, "Not hardly. A woman needs a *man* to be a mother."

Longarm rose from the table, leaving half of his cup filled, and said uncomfortably, "Uh, I'll fetch my fresh shirt and such. Water's boiling, now."

He went to his room and dug out some clean underwear before heading for the porch shed. He noticed Nan was still at the table, fidgeting with the spoon. He went out back and closed the shed door behind him before he remembered that he'd forgotten to pour the boiling kettles into his tepid well water. He hesitated, then decided he could get as clean in cold water.

He stripped, hanging his clothes on the nails Calvin had driven in the plank walls, and gingerly got into the tub, hunkering down in the well water, which was neither warm nor freezing. He lathered himself with the washrag and turned the water chocolate-brown with trail dust. It would likely dry somewhat gritty on him, but at least he wouldn't smell bad in his fresh shirt.

The door opened. Nan Durler was standing there with a kettle.

Stark naked.

Her voice was calm as she said, "You forgot the hot water for our bath."

Longarm studied the brown water between his wet knees as he answered in a desperately casual tone, "*Our* bath, ma'am? This tub's a mite small for two and, uh, your man might think me a mite forward if he came home to find us like this."

"I told you they'll be in town for hours," she reassured him. "You just stay the way you are and I'll put a foot on either side and sort of sit down facing you. I think we'll both fit right nicely, don't you?"

"Nan, you're a married woman," he protested.

"Come on, you know you want me."

"What I want or don't want ain't the point. Your husband is a friend of mine," he told her.

"Would to God he'd be more friendly to *me*! I *need* it, Longarm! I need a man inside me so bad I can taste it! Come on, we've got all afternoon. If you don't want to do it here, let's go back inside and do it right on the bed!"

She moved her blonde pubis provocatively and laughed hysterically. "You can have me on the bed. You can have me on the kitchen table. I don't care where we do it, just so we do it, right now!"

"Ma'am, I wish you'd go put some clothes on. I'm done washing and I'd like to get out and put my pants on."

"You've got a hard-on, haven't you? You don't fool me with that shy act! I'll bet you've lost count of the women you've had."

"Never occurred to me to keep a tally."

He saw she wasn't going to leave. So as she stood there, naked, watching, he got out of the tub, erection and all, and proceeded to dry himself off.

She sighed, "Oh, that's a *nice* one!"

Longarm tried to keep his voice level as he said, "I'd be lying if I said I didn't want to, for you are one handsome gal, even with your clothes on. But we'd best forget we had the notion, Nan. I know we've been acting sort of silly, but no harm's been done and let's forget it, huh?"

As he tried to dress she dropped the kettle and threw herself against him, bare breasts pressed to his naked chest as she wrapped her arms around him and insisted, "Just one time! I'm going crazy!"

"Yep, that's likely what's the matter with you, gal. Lucky I got a mite more self-control."

"Control? You must be made out of iron! What's the matter with you? Who would ever know?"

We would, Nan. Maybe that wouldn't bother you, but I ain't done here, and I'd find it sort of difficult looking your man in the eye if I was to abuse his hospitality while his back was turned."

She suddenly stepped back, jeering, "What's the matter with you? Ain't I good enough for you?"

"Honey," he said gently, "I've bedded down with gals who couldn't hold a candle to you when it comes to looking pretty. But none of 'em were married to my friends."

"Oh, my, aren't we godly and pious today? Next, you'll have me down on my knees, repenting my wicked advances!"

"Not hardly. God is one thing, fooling with a friend's wife is another. I'm going to forget we had this conversation, Nan. But, if you don't like your husband, have the decency to just up and leave him. It ain't seemly for a pretty gal like you to carry on like this."

"I just need to be pleasured, damn it! I haven't been loved properly since I don't know when and it's only natural to do what needs doing!"

"Well, sure it is. But the only thing that makes us humans better than most other brutes is, well, that we *ain't* brutes. The Lord gave us common sense to go with our desires. So let's use some, and forget this whole thing."

"I thought a real man had to have all the loving he could get."

"No, a real man doesn't. A bull in the field, a dog in an alley, or a kid with a hard-on doesn't worry much about the who and how of it, but us grown-ups study on it before we go leaping at folks. I'll tell you the truth, I'm going to have hard-ons for a month over you, now, and I'll likely kick myself for being a fool someday, when I hear you've run off with a passing whiskey drummer or been caught with some cowhand. But when you bust this marriage up, it won't be with *me*. So, while my pecker will tease me over lost oppor-

174

tunities, my conscience will be clear." He stopped to catch his breath, amazed that he'd delivered such a long-winded sermon. He felt as self-righteous as a revival meeting Bible-beater, which he took as a sure sign that his resistance was breaking down.

"Oh, shit!" Nan exploded, "you think I don't know about that half-breed girl and you?"

"Don't know what Miss Two-Women might have said while you and she were jawing, ma'am. So I'll not defend myself, save to point out that I never met anyone she was married to."

"You . . . bastard!" she shrilled, turning from him to flounce out of the shed. She looked as nice going away as she had facing him, and Longarm sighed wistfully as he buttoned up his shirt.

"Damn fool," he told himself, "she'll likely play that trick the Egyptian's old woman pulled on Joseph in the Good Book and tell Calvin I tried to screw her, anyway!"

That was something to ponder as he finished dressing. If Nan tried to revenge herself on him by playing Potiphar's wife, Cal would likely come after him with a gun. Damn. Maybe he'd been too hasty, as well as mean to his poor pecker. A man could get killed either way and she'd purely had one nice little rump!

He finished dressing and decided to let Nan cool a while before he went back inside. He went down the back steps and walked over to the corral. He didn't have anything to do there, but at least if he was out here where the Indians in the other houses could see him with his pants on . . .

Then he grinned as he spied a dot on the horizon and recognized it as Calvin and Prudence driving back from town. They were two hours earlier than Nan had expected them to be. He hadn't just been decent; he'd been goddamned lucky.

Prudence Lee had purchased a box of vittles in Switchback along with her other supplies. She insisted that everyone eat at her house that night, the house Real

175

Bear had been murdered in. Longarm didn't go into the bedroom, but he hoped it had been cleaned up since last he'd seen it. The front room was cluttered with a big bass drum and religious pictures she'd cut out and tacked to the whitewashed walls. The two women went out to the kitchen to fuss over the tinned food she'd brought from town while Longarm and the Indian agent sat on the porch steps, smoking as the sun went down.

Longarm mentioned the strange Indians he'd heard about in town and Calvin said, "I know. Rain Crow said he'd try to find out if they were staying with anyone out here."

"Isn't he with those Blackfoot that the Paiute missionary's visiting with?"

"No, not if I can believe Rain Crow. Tell me something, Longarm. You know Rain Crow as well as, or better than I do. How far would you trust that boy?"

"About as far as I'd trust most, I reckon. Why?"

"I get the feeling he's hiding something from me. He doesn't seem at all interested in catching whoever's been selling whiskey to his tribesmen; the other day, I was sure I smelled some on his breath."

"That was likely my fault," Longarm said. "I shared a bottle with him the night we found Yellow Leggings and Roping Sally."

"I'm not talking about that far back. I think he's been drinking recently."

"Maybe he has. I had a couple of drinks this afternoon. You reckon I'm fixing to scalp you?"

"It's not the same. You and I are white men."

Longarm took a drag of smoke and blew a thoughtful ring before he nodded and said, "I know. When Indians get drunk they sing funny. Most white boys sing 'O'Riley's Daughter,' or 'The Girl I Left Behind Me,' when they get falling-down drunk. Can't make head or tail out of those Indian songs."

"Come on," Durler said. "You know how many drunken Indians have gotten in trouble."

"Yep. Some Indian drunks are mean as hell. But the meanest drunk I ever met was a trail boss called Ben

176

Thompson— No, come to think of it, I met a jasper called Doc Holliday last year, who was even meaner. I do so wish they wouldn't let mean fellows drink, don't you?"

"You're funning me, but it's no laughing matter. I'm not supposed to let my Indians get at firewater."

"Hell, *you* ain't been serving it to them, have you?" the deputy asked.

"No, but if it's on the reservation—"

"There can't be all that much of it, or, if there is, your Blackfoot hold their liquor better than most folks in Abilene or Dodge. You've got enough on your plate just trying to make cowboys out of them. Try and make *sober* cowboys out of anybody and I'll show you an easier task, like walking on water or feeding the Blackfoot Nation on loaves and fishes."

The Indian agent sighed and said, "I know you think I take my job too seriously. Nan says I worry more about my Indians than I do her. But, damn it, somebody has to worry about them. They're like children. If someone doesn't help them, they're as doomed as the buffalo!"

Longarm shook his head wearily and said, "You're wrong a couple of ways, Cal. They ain't kids; they're folks. Likely not much smarter or dumber than the rest of us. As to 'the poor Indian, fading away like the snows of yesteryear,' there are more Indians now, counting breeds living as whites, than there were when Columbus found and misnamed them."

"That's crazy, Longarm!" Durler said. "Why, there's hardly an Indian east of the Mississippi and this whole territory used to be Indian land until—"

"Until we took it all away from them and packed them tighter on these reservations," Longarm interrupted. "I'm talking about population figures, not land. Before we crowded them, they were wandering hunters or small farmers, scattered in bands of maybe thirty-odd souls, hither and yon. Little Big Horn never would have happened if the far-flung bands hadn't been snow-balled into a real army-sized gathering of the clans.

177

You started here with a fair-sized reservation for Black-foot, right?"

"Of course," the agent agreed.

"Only now, you've got Bloods and Piegans on the same land, and if I know the B.I.A., they'll be shipping you stray Shoshoni and leftover Flatheads any day now, as the cattle country expands with this beef boom. I wouldn't worry about 'the noble savage' fading away on you, Cal. He's having kids like everyone else, and getting sardined on such little land as we see fit to set aside for him in odd, godforsaken corners."

"All right, what would you do, Longarm?" Durler asked.

"I'd start by treating them like *folks*. I'd give them full citizenship and leave 'em the hell alone."

"You can't be serious! Why, right this minute, the Apache are running around killing folks and—"

"I'd make Indians obey the law, like everybody else," Longarm cut in. "If a white man or a colored man kills somebody, we call it murder. When an Indian gets mean we make a policy."

Durler said, "Well, I don't make the policy, and you've got to admit these Blackfoot aren't enthusiastic to learn about herding or farming."

"Why should they be?" Longarm asked. "If you were in jail and some nice warden told you he aimed to teach you a trade, would you stop thinking about busting out?"

"I see your point. But, like I said, I don't make the policy. So there ain't much I can do about it, here."

"Sure, there is. You can ease off and ride with a gentler hand on the reins. I've smelled some sour mash on a few breaths since I came here, but what of it? Last mean drunk who came at me was as white as you are. I'd worry more about catching the Wendigo and holding the tribe this side of the border than I would about sociable drinking."

Before they could argue further, Prudence Lee came out to tell them supper was served.

The missionary was a good cook, but the meal was

uncomfortable for Longarm. He found himself facing Nan Durler across the table, and while her eyes stayed on her beans, Longarm couldn't help wondering what she'd been saying in the kitchen to Prudence. He'd learned a long time ago, the hard way, that women were even worse than men about kissing and telling. For all the fretting and fussing about so-called fallen women, he'd noticed fallen women bragged like anything about all the men they'd fallen with. Prudence Lee said something to him, so he risked a look her way. The missionary woman met his eyes innocently as she repeated her request that he pass the salt. But that didn't mean much; Nan hadn't let on she'd known about him and Gloria Two-Women, until she'd tried to seduce him in the bathtub.

He wondered what Prudence Lee would say if he asked to sleep on her couch; not that he was about to ask her such a foolish thing. There was no way he was going to get out of spending another night under Nan Durler's roof, without it looking odd as hell to her husband.

"Someone just rode up outside," said Calvin Durler, breaking in on Longarm's worries.

Longarm said, "I heard it. Sounds like an unshod pony. One of your Blackfoot, I suspicion."

The two men excused themselves from the table and went out on the porch. Rain Crow was sitting his pony in the last rays of the sun. He called out, "I have found the Paiute Ghost Dancer. He told some people he was going off alone to make medicine. He told them he was calling on the ghosts in a place where Indians had fought a good fight. When I thought about it, I knew where the place had to be."

Durler looked blank, but Longarm nodded and said, "That abandoned homestead. It's the only battleground of the Shining Days on this reservation."

Rain Crow nodded and said, "Yes. Long ago, the Indians won there. The legends say the white settler fought well before they overran him. The Paiute must have thought to meet the ghosts of those who fell in the old fight. Instead, he met Wendigo!"

Both white men looked surprised and Rain Crow nodded. "Yes, the man was dead when I found him. He was wearing his medicine shirt, too, but it did no good. Perhaps Wovoka's medicine was only meant to protect us from white people."

Longarm raised an eyebrow and said, "You sort of *grin* when you tell your tale, Rain Crow. I didn't know you found the Wendigo so infernally funny!"

"Wendigo is not what I'm laughing about. When I first found the Paiute out there, I was very frightened. But it came to me, riding in, that the Wendigo didn't want a no-good white man's Indian like me. He came for a Dream Singer who said the spirits were his *friends*."

Chapter 13

It was dark by the time Rain Crow had led Longarm and Calvin Durler out to where he'd left the body. But the Indian had his bull's-eye lantern and Durler had brought a big coal-oil lamp from the house.

The Paiute Dream Singer's beheaded cadaver sat propped against the sod walls of the old house in what was left of his pathetic buckskin medicine shirt. The garment had been slashed to ribbons, too, and the dead man's entrails lay in his lap.

Longarm left the others to fiddle with the body as he circled the entire site with Rain Crow's bull's-eye, sweeping the prairie sod with the beam carefully and walking slowly. Then he shook his head wearily and walked back to join the others, saying, "I can see where the Paiute came in. I can see where Rain Crow came and went. I found some fresh rabbit shit, too. That's all the sign there is."

Durler shook his head and said, "We're in trouble. I was just getting used to your notion about the railroad right-of-way."

The lawman nodded. "I know. I like it too, but we're a good three miles from the tracks, this time. If he wasn't riding that rabbit, he must have flown in and out on a magic carpet."

"It's black as a bitch out here, Longarm. Are you sure you couldn't have missed something?" Durler asked.

"Not a hell of a lot. We've had some wind since I was out here last."

Durler asked what that was suppposed to mean. Before Longarm could answer, the Indian snorted in annoyance and said, "There has been no rain. The dry grass is dusty. Don't you people *look* at the earth you think you own?"

Longarm explained, "There's a film of dust on the north side of nearly every stem and blade. Nobody's been over this ground for at least a full day. When was that last north wind, Rain Crow? About this time last night?"

"Later than this. You read sign well, for a white man."

"There you go, Cal. You've got two expert opinions against the simple scientific fact that what we're saying isn't possible."

He shined the bull's-eye beam near Durler's boots and added, "You see where you just walked through this dry straw, Cal? According to all the rules of evidence, before we got here, two men came in and only one rode out. If I didn't know Rain Crow had good alibis for other such killings, I'd have no choice but to arrest him. I'd have no trouble selling it to a grand jury, either. Anyone can plainly see no other human being came within a country mile of this dead Paiute before *we* got here!"

Rain Crow protested, "I did not do it! What kind of a fool would kill a man and leave his own sign? If I wanted to fool you—"

"Hold on, old son," Longarm cut him off. "I'm not accusing you. Just reading the sign as it was left for me. Hell, I know you could have dragged some brush through the dusty grass or maybe left some false sign, if that had been your notion."

"I don't like to be accused, even in fun. Everyone knows I did not like the dead man. If you keep talking like that, the people will say I killed him!"

Durler asked, "You think that was the intention, Longarm? To somehow frame Rain Crow for the killing?"

The deputy pulled at a corner of his mustache. "I

don't know. Whoever killed this poor medicine dreamer had no way of knowing who'd find the body. As far as that goes, the ants and carrion crows might well have picked this old boy clean before *anybody* ever found him. We're way the hell and gone out on the prairie and— Son of a bitch! *That* doesn't make sense, either!"

"What doesn't make sense, Longarm?" Rain Crow asked.

"The Wendigo's *reasons*. Up to now, I've been working on the notion that these spooky killings were to scare the Blackfoot. All the others were killed and messed up where they'd be found quickly. This poor bastard might never have been found at all. It looks like pure, crazy spite-work, after all! You'd best see about getting this body back to the agency for burial. I hope you boys won't take it unfriendly, but I'm riding into Switchback, straight from here."

"You think the killer's in Switchback?" said the agent.

Longarm shrugged. "Don't know where he is. Don't even know how the son of a bitch got in or out of here. Might know more if I could ask some questions. As you see, that Paiute ain't talking much."

Leaving the two of them to dispose of the remains, Longarm mounted and rode for Switchback in the dark. He didn't really have his next moves planned, but at least this got him out of spending the night at the agency, and somebody might have noticed something unusual.

The moon was rising as he rode down the slope into the dimly lit streets of Switchback. It was still early and a rinky-tink piano was playing "Garryowen" in the saloon. Some old boy had probably requested it after reminiscing about old times. The Seventh Cav had marched to Little Big Horn to the strains of that old Irish jig and every time someone said "Indian" in Montana, some fool was bound to bring up Custer.

The land office was closed, but the railroad station wasn't. He tethered his chestnut and went in to send a progress report to Denver, knowing Billy Vail was likely having a fit. Then he asked the railroad telegrapher, "When was the last train in from the west, this afternoon?"

The telegrapher said, "There was one about noon. Eastbound passenger express will be coming through in an hour or so. It don't figure to stop here, but we can flag her down for you if need be, Marshal."

Longarm shook his head. "Ain't going anywhere. Just asking about your timetable. Was that noonday train a slow freight, with flat cars and such?"

The telegrapher frowned. "Flat cars? Don't think so. It was a fast freight, bound for Chicago with live beef. I could ask Dispatch if they were deadheading any flats."

"Don't bother. What I had in mind was no cattle train highballing downgrade."

He took out two cheroots, offered one to the telegrapher, and thumbed a light, muttering, "Damn! Just as I was hoping I had it figured, the son of a bitch went and busted all my bubbles!"

"I thank you for the smoke, Marshal. But I don't know what the hell you're talking about."

"Neither do I, now. Is your yard bull, Mendez, patrolling out back?"

"He should be. Old Mendez drinks a mite. If you don't find him, you'll find one of his sidekicks. Be careful about creeping up on 'em sudden, though. That one Irish kid is quick on the trigger as well as a mite hard of hearing. Come up on him sudden and—"

"Never mind. No sense in poking around dark tracks at night, spooky yard bulls or no. You could likely tell me if there was a work train, or something slow like that, fixing to leave the yards tonight, couldn't you?"

"I could, but there ain't. Next slow freight headed west will be at ten tomorrow night. Empty cattle cars, due in from the East. They'll be dropping 'em off for loading, all up the line and through the night."

"Anything coming east? Say around midnight?"

The telegrapher picked up some dispatch flimsies from his table and consulted them before he nodded and said, "Yeah. Here's a string of flats, lowballing through as the other orders allow it. Flats empty from unloading telegraph poles, over in the Great Basin sage country. There's a midnight passenger train using the tracks, first. Then the lowballing empties will likely poke on in."

Longarm thanked his informant, and leaving his mount where it was, moseyed over to the saloon to drink while he studied on where he'd spend the night and what in hell was going on.

In the saloon, he found Jason, the army scout, talking to the piano player, who'd stopped playing "Garry-owen" long enough to wet his whistle. Jason waved Longarm over and said, "I owe you a drink, don't I?"

"Don't know who's ahead, but I'll take it."

As Jason ordered another shot for himself and a glass of Maryland rye for Longarm, the deputy asked, "Was that old cavalry tune your notion?"

"No. I just got done explaining to the professor, here, about this being a time for other songs. How soon do you figure your Blackfoot out there aim to make their move for Canada?"

"You can tell your soldier boys not to bank on any medals this summer. Somebody killed the damn fool who was trying to talk them into it."

"Do tell? Some friends of mine likely made a long trip for nothing, then. We *are* talking about a Paiute named Ishiwatl, ain't we?"

"I don't know the bird's name well enough to say it, but that sounds close. You say somebody was looking for him?"

"Yeah, out at the fort. A posse of Crow lawmen just arrived with a warrant for his arrest. I was fixing to bring 'em out to the reservation, come morning. You say somebody shot him?"

"That's close enough. He's deader than hell. These Indian police looking for the Dream Singer would sound like Sioux to folks, wouldn't they?"

"Reckon so. Crow and Sioux both talk Dakota. Why do you ask?"

Longarm chuckled and explained, "You've just

185

handed me the first good news I've had all day. I heard there were some strange Sioux hereabouts and I've had the Blackfoot going crazy trying to locate 'em on the reservation."

The barkeep brought their drinks and they downed them in silence. Longarm ordered them each another, and Jason said, "I'll tell the Crows they can rest easy when I ride back to the fort later tonight. That Ishiwatl was one bad Paiute, to hear 'em tell it. Now, if someone would just shoot that damn Wovoka himself, we'd likely have some peace and quiet. What was the killing about? More of that Ghost Dance shit?"

"Sort of. You might say Ishi-whatever got into a theological dispute with the Wendigo."

The scout whistled and said, "Another one of *them* things, huh?"

The piano player asked, "What's a wendigo?"

Longarm said, "I wish I knew, Professor. Jason, you're a professional tracker. How would you cross maybe two or three hundred yards of dusty stubble without leaving sign?"

"I'd ride around it. There's no way to *jump* three hundred yards."

"That's the way I see it. When are you heading back to the fort?"

"A couple of hours, maybe. Came into town for some tail, but the professor, here, tells me French Mary's been rented for the night by a big spender off the Double Z. I was just fixing to try my luck at Madam Kate's. You want to come along?"

"Not tonight. French Mary's the little redhead with the saucy mouth, ain't she?"

"Yeah, and she does use it nicely. But I can't wait around all night for that damn cowboy to get done and, anyway, I got delicate feelings. Don't like to kiss a gal right after she's been . . . well, you likely know why they call her French Mary."

The piano player said, "There's a new gal at Madam Kate's who ain't been used all that much. They say she ain't more than sixteen or so and still likes her new job."

Jason laughed and said, "There you go, Longarm. What say we go over there and get her while she's hot?"

"You go, if you've a mind to," Longarm said. "I've got other fish to fry."

"What's the matter, don't you like tail, or are you too proud to pay for it?" the scout gibed.

"Hell, everybody pays for it, one way or another. I've just never liked cold cash transactions," Longarm said.

"Shit, whores are the only honest women I've ever met," Jason observed. "I'd far rather give the gal the two dollars than shilly-shally about with 'nice girls' who wind up with your money anyway."

"Like I said, we all pay, one damn way or another, and I've often said to myself it makes more sense to just slap down the cash right off. I suspicion I must be a sissy."

Jason laughed, and before they could continue their discussion, the land agent, Chadwick, came in to join them. Or, rather, to join Longarm and the professor, for he didn't know Jason, except by sight. The scout, as if inhibited by the other federal man, finished his drink and left in pursuit of carnal pleasure.

The professor went back to the piano to play "Drink To Me Only With Thine Eyes," for some reason, and Chadwick said, "I have a wire for you here, someplace."

He took a folded scrap of paper from his frock coat and handed it to Longarm, who read:

WHAT'S HOLDING UP THE PARADE QUESTION STOP YOU ARE OVERDUE AND NEEDED HERE STOP REPORT TO DENVER AT ONCE STOP SIGNED VAIL

Chadwick said, "I could open up and send an answer for you." But Longarm shook his head and answered, "He's likely not in his office and you're closed for the night and God knows how long, remember?"

"Won't you get in trouble, ignoring your superior's orders?"

"Hell, I'm already in trouble," Longarm laughed.

"No notions about those killings last week yet?"

"*Had* some. They blew up in my face this evening when the Wendigo hit again."

Chadwick looked astonished and gasped, "Jesus! You must be joking!"

"Nothing funny about it. This one was *really* spooky. The others were almost impossible to figure, but this time the Wendigo outdid himself. Killed another Indian in what must have been broad daylight, then sashayed off at least three miles to the nearest cover, without leaving a single sign coming or going."

"Good God, I can't understand it!"

"That makes two of us. But I made a promise not to leave here until I caught the son of a bitch. So I'll likely write Marshal Vail a letter in a week or so."

"I don't envy you. Where are you staying tonight, the agency?"

"Nope. Figured to bed down here in town after I ask around some more."

"You're welcome to stay at my place," Chadwick offered. "I stay up late and I've got a spare room you can use."

"That's neighborly of you, but no thanks. It's early, yet, and while I'm asking questions about this job I'm on, I might get lucky and meet somebody prettier than you. No offense, of course."

Chadwick laughed and said, "Stay away from Madam Kate's. They say a couple of her gals give more than tail. The doc's been treating one of 'em for the clap, and he says there ain't no real cure."

Longarm thanked him for the warning and left. He went to get his chestnut and mounted up, then sat there, fishing out a cheroot, as he pondered his next move.

He knew he didn't have a next move. He was chasing himself around in circles to avoid another sparring match with Nan Durler. He rode slowly along the street toward the end of town where Roping Sally's spread had been. The spread was still there, just outside of town, of course, but somehow he didn't feel like it was there anymore. Had he really ever spent that wild night, just up ahead where the lights of Switchback faded into blackness? It seemed as if it had never happened, now. The poor woman was hardly cold in her grave and he remembered her as if he had known her long ago, before the War. *You've got nothing to feel guilty about,* he told himself firmly. What was done was done and the only duty he owed Sally was to find her killer. He was only feeling fretful because someone had made a fool of him. It seemed like everyone in Montana had him figured for a fool and it was getting tedious.

He rode on into the darkness toward Sally's, running the whole thing through his head again, once more stumbling over the impossibilities of this whole infernal case. He slowed his mount, knowing he really didn't want to pass the dark, empty cabin where he'd slept with what he now remembered as a beheaded horror. Maybe he'd just hunker down on the prairie some-place. . . . "Damn it!" he swore. "There's a feather bed and a warm breakfast waiting for you out there. And you've done nothing to be ashamed of!"

He reined in and swung his mount's head toward the west, his mind made up to ride back to the agency and brazen it out. As he turned, something sounding like bird wings, *big* bird wings, fluttered past his head and snatched off his Stetson!

Longarm threw himself to one side, grabbing for his saddle gun as he heard the thing coming through the darkness again! He rolled out of the saddle and landed in the roadside ditch as it flew over him, flapping.

The chestnut had been spooked by the sound, too, and ran off a few yards, snorting nervously, as Long-arm crouched in the grassy ditch with his rifle at port, ready for anything.

But nothing happened. He stayed frozen and silent as he strained his ears. He stayed that way for a very long time. For though the moon was rising now, it was

189

still nearly pitch-black around him and that thing had swooped at him like a diving eagle who'd known where it was going!

Could it have been an owl? Too big. No owl he'd ever heard had flapped as loud and mean as that. For that matter, he couldn't remember ever running into an *eagle* that size! He'd been attacked by an eagle as a kid, trying to collect some eggs for some foolish kid's reason, and the sound of its angrily flapping wings had been a pale imitation of whatever had just snatched off his hat!

He was still wondering about it when the moon pushed an edge above the horizon and he could see the pale streak of the road better. The road was empty. The overgrazed weeds lay ghostly gray around him for at least a hundred yards, and there was nothing there to see.

After a while, he rose slowly to his feet and walked over to his hat, where it lay in the road. He examined it for talon marks, and finding none, put it on. Then he clucked soothingly to the chestnut and caught the reins. The horse was still nervous, but he soothed it and remounted. He kept the saddle gun across his thighs as he resumed his way west toward the agency.

It took him a while to get there, this time. The rising moon kept telling him he was alone as he slowly rode across the prairie, straining his ears for the sound of those mysterious wingbeats. But, though there was nothing to see and not a sound to be heard out on the lonely range, he kept swinging around to look behind him.

Longarm spent the morning at the fenced quarter-section, showing a bunch of Blackfoot kids how to twirl a throw-rope. By the time he saw that their interest was flagging a bit, he had two of them getting the knack of a passable butterfly and at least five who could drop a community loop over a fence post one out of three tries. He called a halt to the lesson. If he hadn't gotten them at least curious about roping, by now, they weren't like any other kids he'd ever met.

As he ambled back toward the agency buildings one of the older boys fell in beside him to say shyly, "The white man's rope tricks are fun, but my father says the ways of the cowboy are not our ways."

Longarm said, "I don't mean any disrespect for your elders, Little Moon, but your daddy likely doesn't know that the art of roping was invented by Indians. Us American hands learned roping from the Mexicans, who learned it from the Aztec, Chihuahua, and such."

"You're making fun of me! There were never Indian cowboys before you people came here!"

"Nope. No white cowboys, neither. The cowboy was born when the Spanish horsemen got together with the Indian hunters who roped deer and antelope, down Mexico way. The vaquero, buckaroo, or cowboy owes as much to the red man as the white. Down in the Indian Nation, there are some Cherokee and Osage cowboys few men could hold a candle to. Jesse Chisholm, who blazed the Chisholm Trail, was a Cherokee."

"Oh, we know about the Five Civilized Tribes," Little Moon said scornfully. "They are not real Indians. My father says they live like white men."

"Your Daddy's right about that point, Little Moon, but I doubt if the Cherokee would agree that they weren't real Indians. In their day they were wild enough, and the Osage lifted their fair share of white folks' hair in the Shining Times. All in all, though, the Five Tribes, Osage, and such Comanche as have taken to herding longhorns are living better than you Blackfoot, these days."

The boy walked head-down, pondering, before he shrugged and said, "I don't know. I think it was better in the Shining Times, hunting the buffalo and Utes."

"Maybe," Longarm concurred, "but those days are gone forever. As I see it, you've got two choices ahead of you, Little Moon. You can learn new ways for the new times coming, or you can sit out here on a government dole, feeling sorry for yourself while the rest of the world leaves you behind."

"Wovoka says more Shining Times are coming. If all of us stood together we could go back to the old ways and—"

"Wovoka's full of shit," the deputy cut in. "I hope you won't take it unfriendly, son, but you could gather every tribe in one place, armed and mounted, and one brigade of cavalry would be pleased as punch to wipe you out. What happened on the Little Big Horn was a fluke; old Custer only had about two hundred green troops with him. The army has new Gatling and Hotchkiss guns, now, too. So at best, that gives you *three* ways to go. You can learn to make your own money, or you can take the little money the B.I.A. might dole out as it sees fit, or you can just go crazy with the Ghost Dancers and die. Meanwhile, you might work on what I just showed you about roping. You've got to loosen up and remember to swing the loop twice to open it up before you throw. Your aim ain't bad, but your throwing is too anxious."

Leaving the Indian youth to ponder his own future, Longarm walked past the agency to the back door of the cottage Prudence Lee was staying in. As he mounted the back steps to knock, she spied him through the screen door and opened it, saying, "I was just brewing some coffee. I'm afraid your suggestion about asking for Indian recipes turned out pretty dismally!"

He joined her in the kitchen as she waved him to a seat, explaining, "You forgot to tell me Indians put bacon grease instead of sugar in their coffee. Uncooked white flour dusted over canned pork and beans is rather ghastly, too!"

Longarm chuckled and said, "Lucky they didn't serve you grasshopper stew. The grasshoppers ain't all that bad, but the dog meat they mix in with it takes time to develop a taste for."

Prudence paled slightly. "Oh, dear, I did eat some chopped meat boiled with what I hoped was corn mush. You don't think—?"

192

"No, I was funning. They only eat stuff like that when they're really hungry, and old Cal's been seeing to it that the rations are fairly good. There's nothing wrong with Indian cooking. It's just that they have different tastes. I've met some who hated apple pie, and Apache would starve before they tasted fish. Some tribes look on eating fish the way we look on eating worms."

She grimaced as she put a cup of coffee in front of him and said, "I wonder if I'll ever get used to conditions out here. The Bible Society never told me what it would be like."

"They likely didn't know. Folks back East have funny notions about this part of the country. It ain't the Great American Desert Fremont said it was. It ain't the Golden West of Horace Greeley. It's just . . . different."

"I'm trying to adjust," she said with a sigh, "but I'm beginning to see how it might drive some women, well, strange."

He wondered if she was talking about Nan Durler, but he didn't ask. He said, "I came by to ask a favor, Miss Prudence. You were fixing to hold some sort of pow-wow here this evening, weren't you?"

"If you want to call it that. I've invited some of the women over for a class in infant care."

"I'd be obliged if you could leave 'em to their heathen ways with kids at least one more night, Miss Prudence. I've told Rain Crow and the other reservation police I want a tight curfew after sundown. Some of the squaws would be riding home in the dark, even if you were to cut 'em loose early. The moon won't be up before nine-thirty tonight, and I aim to have every Indian tucked in good by then."

"Oh, are you expecting trouble from those Ghost Dancers again? I thought the man behind it was just killed."

"Yes, ma'am, and what killed him might be on the prowl tonight."

193

"Oh, dear, then you do think the Wendigo may strike again tonight?"

Longarm shrugged. "Don't know. Don't aim to leave any man, woman, or child out alone on the prairie after dark, Wendigo or no. I'm going to have to ask you to spend the night next door with the Durlers, too. Rain Crow and Calvin will be sitting up all night with the doors locked and guns loaded. The Wendigo's been making me look like a fool—partly because I've been one. From now on, I ain't waiting for him to hit so I can chase him around like a bloodhound with nose trouble. I'm making sure, no matter how he's doing it or when he's figuring to do it again, that there won't be anybody out there in the night for him but *me!*"

"You can't hide an entire Indian tribe from that madman forever!"

"Don't aim to hide 'em forever. Just until I catch Mr. Wendigo."

"But even if the Indians cooperate, the reservation's so *big!* How can you hope to intercept anyone or anything out there in all those miles of darkness?"

"If I knew that, I'd know the Wendigo's methods, reasons, and likely who it was. Getting every possible victim out of the Wendigo's reach is the best first bite I've come up with. So, like I said, you'll help a heap by bunking down with the Durlers until it's safe for you to stay here all alone."

She sipped her own cup of coffee thoughtfully, and though she finally nodded, her voice was worried as she said, "I'll do it, but I won't like it. You know they've been fighting like cats and dogs next door."

"They'll be keeping company manners with you and Rain Crow listening, Miss Prudence. They weren't fussing when I came in last night."

"You should have heard them earlier! These walls are thin, and if there is one thing I can't abide, it's hypocrisy— What's so funny?"

Longarm wiped his grin away and said, "I'd be out of a job if everybody suddenly took to being truthful. We're all a mite two-faced, Miss Prudence. I know we

194

ain't supposed to be, but I reckon it's just human nature to keep our true feelings hidden."

She stared at him oddly and licked her lips before she brazened, "Well, *I* certainly try to be truthful in my dealings with everyone!"

"I know you try, ma'am. But tell me something. When's the last time you asked the lady next door why she was fussing with her man?"

"That's different. Hypocrisy's one thing, rudeness is another!"

"Maybe. But lies are what we call *other* folks' falsehoods. When it's *our* turn to bend things out of shape we generally have a more angelic reason." He sipped his coffee and added, "I suspicion the lies we tell ourselves are the biggest whoppers of them all."

Her eyes blazed defensively as she asked, "And just what sort of lies are you saying I tell myself, sir?"

He smiled gently and answered, "I never accused you, ma'am. It's funny how the less I accuse folks, the more they seem to want to tell me. I'm in a nosy line of work, so I'm probably better at reading the silences between folks' words."

"In other words, you're just fishing? Well, you can just fish somewhere else, then. For I've nothing to hide."

He nodded as if in agreement and sipped some more coffee. He didn't really give much of a damn about such secrets as a little sparrow-bird spinster-gal might have. He wasn't getting paid to find out what had driven her to reading Bibles for a living. But wasn't it a bitch how it spooked folks when you backed off just as the questions were getting close to home?

Prudence Lee said, "I suppose you think I'm as silly as poor Nan Durler, in my own way. But that really was another girl I was talking about."

"What girl was that, ma'am?" Longarm asked innocently. "The one back East who ran off on her husband? I'd almost forgotten about her."

"I'll bet you have. I'll bet you have a whole crazy story cooked up about my atoning for some dark, secret sin. But you're wrong. It was only a girl I knew, one time."

He nodded and said, "I know. Her story reminds me a lot of Madam LaMont, down Denver way."

"Who's Madam LaMont? She sounds like a—you know what!"

"Yep, that's what she was. Ran the most expensive parlor house on State Street, for a while. The poor old gal was atoning for a terrible mix-up."

Prudence looked shocked. *"Atoning?* Is that what they call being a prostitute, these days?"

"Well, some folks have odd notions on the subject of atonement. You see, Madam LaMont came West as a bride, back in the Pike's Peak Rush before the War. Her name was something else, then, of course. Her husband was a preacher. He freighted her and a mess of Bibles to the gold camps, aiming to wash the sins of the miners away. The gal was likely fond of him, for they seemed happy. Then the preacher vanished, as did a gold camp redhead at the same time, who was said to be no better than she might have been."

"Heavens, the poor girl was deserted by her husband for a dance-hall girl?" She shook her head sadly.

"That's what she suspicioned, and it sort of jarred something loose inside her head. She took to drink and then, since it beat taking in washing, she started pleasuring men for pay. She must have been good at it, for the next thing anybody knew, she had the biggest fancy house in Denver. I reckon she was trying to get as far from the preaching trade as possible. But like I said, it was all a mix-up. Her husband hadn't done her wrong at all."

Prudence's eyebrows knit in confusion. "Indeed? But you said he ran off with this redhead!"

Longarm nodded. "That's what everybody thought. But a few years later someone found the redhead working in a house in Abilene, alone. Then, a short while later, some prospectors found the skeleton of a man down an abandoned mine shaft. Nobody ever figured out if he'd been robbed and thrown down it, or if

196

he'd just fallen in, wandering about in search of souls to save."

"My Lord! You mean it was the woman's missing husband?"

"Yep. There were some shreds of clothing clinging to the bones and he was still packing the Bible Madam LaMont had given him with a sentimental inscription on the flyleaf. When they brought it to her, she went a mite crazy."

The girl gasped, and her hands flew up to press on either side of her face. "Oh, what a terrible story! To think that poor girl abandoned herself to a life of sin because of a ghastly mistake about an innocent man!"

Longarm reached out and patted Prudence's arm. "Well, it came out all right in the end. Madam LaMont ain't in that line of work anymore, but while she was, she got as rich as Croesus. So she lives in a big brownstone house on Sherman Avenue with her new husband, these days. He's rich, too, as well as understanding. They're both right happy and the Madam still helps fallen women, orphans, and such. In her own way, she's likely done more good than she ever could have as the wife of a poor wandering preacher."

Prudence Lee tried not to smile as she said, "The moral of your tale is a bit grotesque, but I think I see it. Are you suggesting I'd do more for these Blackfoot by opening a parlor house on this reservation?"

"Not hardly. They've already got a mess of gals and a saloon. Old Snake Killer's cooking sour mash over at his place, judging by the smell. Don't tell Cal Durler, though. He frets about 'em drinking."

"Oh? And you approve of drunken Indians?" Prudence asked with a frown.

"Don't approve of drunken anybody. But they're less likely to get poisoned on their own home-brewed corn than they are on trade whiskey. Saves 'em money, too. You see, some men are going to drink, federal regulations or no. I figure it's better if they stick to cheap, pure bootleg, and confine it to the reservation."

"I won't tell on them, but I must say your ideas

197

on law and order are rather cynical," the missionary observed.

"I'm a peace officer, ma'am. My job is keeping the peace, not pestering folks about what they do in the privacy of their own homes. Trouble with nitpicking over laws is that those fools in Congress write so many of 'em. When you get right down to it, everybody could be arrested if we enforced every law ever written. Lucky for us all, few lawmen have enough time or eyes at keyholes."

Prudence laughed. "I'll remember that the next time my secret lover comes to call on me with his wicked leer and French post cards." Her face reddened fetchingly at her daring little joke. She paused, gazing down into her coffee cup. When she had regained her sobriety, she looked up and continued, "Meanwhile, I've a Bible class to teach. How soon do you think it will be safe for people to move about out here again?"

"Don't know. I'm leaving in a few minutes for Rabbit Gulch. That's a water stop, up the railroad line to the west. If I start this afternoon I should make it to the foothills in plenty of time."

"You're riding off the reservation in the *other* direction? What do you expect to find in Rabbit Gulch?"

"I'm not sure. But all I've found in Switchback is a lot of dead ends."

"Heavens! Do you think it's possible the Wendigo has been working out of another town we've never thought of?"

"Anything's possible, ma'am. And as you see, I *have* thought of it."

Chapter 14

The eastbound train of empty flat cars left Rabbit Gulch late. Nobody working for the railroad seemed to care when or where it arrived, as long as it didn't get in the way of paying traffic.

The moon had worked its way clear across the sky and was shining down, now, from the west. The rolling sea of buffalo-grass all around was ash-gray, with occasional pitch-black clumps of soapweed here and there. Anything darker than the dry grass in the moonlight would be visible, if it was big enough and moving.

Longarm rode hunkered down in the shadow of the box cars behind the locomotive, facing backward with a string of six flat cars between him and the caboose. His chestnut was in one of the empty reefers. The brakemen in the caboose had been told not to come forward across the flats until it was time to crank the brake wheels, just west of the grade into Switchback. Longarm hoped his orders would be obeyed. Anybody he spotted on the rocking planks back there was in trouble.

The train passed through a railroad cut and Longarm tensed as the flats he was watching were plunged into darkness by the shadow of the banks. Then he saw that he was still alone out here in the middle of the night. He was going to feel foolish as hell if he'd ridden all that way for nothing. Worse yet, he knew he only had one chance with this plan. He'd boarded the train in Rabbit Gulch at the last possible moment, but once they reached Switchback, one of the crew was bound to blab about the lawman's sudden interest in railroading. He'd known enough about human nature not to bother telling them to keep this ride a secret. He had to assume the secret would be out, after tonight, whether it was or not.

They ran through another cut, with no results. That didn't mean much. The son of a bitch he was laying for had nearly fifty miles of leeway out here. Besides, if he'd jumped off the westbound a couple of hours earlier, he'd have found nobody outdoors to play with, and not having any real reason to cover his tracks tonight, might not even be waiting for this train. A footprint here and another sign there wouldn't mean a thing in court, unless there was a victim found nearby.

"If I was him," Longarm muttered, "I'd walk back along the tracks as soon as I discovered the Indians were all holed up for the night. I'd suspicion someone was on to me and want to haul ass out. On the other hand, I'd have quit after Roping Sally's murder had the whole territory stirred up and looking for me, too."

He spotted something loping along beside the train to the north and stiffened. Then he saw it was only a coyote pup, having fun, and after a while the animal dropped back out of sight. The train was doing about twenty on the open stretches, a bit slower up the grades. A coyote or a horse could run alongside easily enough for a quarter-mile or so. A man afoot would have to grab hold on a grade, or drop down from a cut. Yeah, he could relax for a few minutes along this stretch.

He stood and stamped his booted feet to ease his cramped thighs, then hunkered down again, bracing the Winchester across his knees as he chewed an unlit cheroot and mused, "Killing that Paiute just don't *fit*, even leaving aside the distance and the missing sign on that dusty grass. Unless the others were killed for no good reason at all, that Ghost Dance missionary was playing right into the hands of—whoever. If *I* was the Wendigo, I'd have killed almost anybody else first. Between the killings and that fool Paiute shaking his rattles, the tribe was just about ready to jump. Well, let's study on it that way and see who'd most want that Dream Singer dead."

200

Longarm suddenly brightened and said, "Hell, that's got to be it!" as the train chuffed through another deep cut. Then the flat cars were rolling along in the moonlight once more and Longarm saw he was no longer alone.

An ink-black blob crouched on the planks, two cars back. Longarm rose slowly, the box car behind his back concealing his own dark outline, as he studied the form that had dropped from the rim of that last bank. It looked like a human being, sort of. It was on its feet now, and moving his way, as if seeking the same shadows he'd been hiding in. It walked peculiarly, on great big blobby feet, but a sudden shift of the moonlight flashed on the holstered gun it wore. It moved to the break between cars and leaped across, landing as quietly as a cat in that funny footgear. Longarm waited until it sort of danced the length of another car, jumped the gap, and was coming his way, before he called out, "That's close enough! Freeze in place and grab for some sky, friend!"

The Wendigo threw himself prone on the weathered planks and a blaze of gunfire answered Longarm's voice as a bullet slammed into the bulkhead of the reefer at his back. The shot was too wild to get excited over, so Longarm said, "You've had one free shot, you silly bastard! Now drop that fool gun and behave yourself!"

The Wendigo fired again at the sound of Longarm's voice. The round ticked the tail of Longarm's coat. So he swore softly and fired back. The Wendigo's head jerked up like he'd been punched in the jaw. Then, moaning like a wounded bear, he rolled away from the pistol he'd let fall to the planks and Longarm grunted, "Oh, shit!" and ran to grab him before he could fall between the cars.

Longarm didn't make it. Up in the cab, the engineer had heard the shots and was slowing down. But the Wendigo had fallen under the wheels!

Longarm jumped off, landing on one hip and rolling over twice in the grass beside the track as, up on the

201

train, a brakeman yelled out, "You want us to hit the brakes?"

"Hell, yes!" shouted Longarm, as he got to his feet, rifle at the ready. Then the train had rolled on, its squealing brakes hardly slowing it until the caboose was winking its red lights at him from half a mile away. Gingerly, Longarm walked over to the tracks, shining silver in the moonlight. He found one leg on the ties, with its foot wrapped in rope and straw-filled burlap. It had been sliced off by a wheel above the knee.

Longarm fished a match from his coat pocket and thumbnailed it alight. The gentle night breeze from the mountains blew it out, but not before he'd spotted the trunk, a few feet to the west. He sighed and said, "Jesus, we had so much to *talk* about, too!"

The brake boss was trotting back from the halted caboose with a wildly swinging lantern, calling out, "What happened? Did you get him?"

Longarm said, "Your train helped. Wheels tore off his head, one arm, and both legs as he bounced along the ballast under it. Bring that light over here, will you? I suspicion that's his head against that rail, there."

The brake boss stopped and raised the lantern. Then, as the puddle of light swept over the battered human head lying on its bloody left cheek against a rail, he gagged and gasped, "My God! It's that Mex, Mendez! The yard bull from Switchback!"

Longarm said, "He wasn't a Mexican. He was from South America, where they rope cows different." He bent to remove something from the belt of the mangled yard bull's torso and held it up, explaining, "You call this thing a *bolo*. The gauchos use them, down there in Argentina. You hold this leather thong, whirl her around your head a few times, and let her go. These heavy balls spread out as she goes *whoom-whoom-whoom* through the air at you. He threw it at me one night, and it sounded like a big-ass bird."

"I know what a bolo is. But what in thunder was he out here throwing it at folks for? He's supposed to be tending to business in the Switchback yards!"

"Yeah, he let folks know he kept unsteady hours. Likely pretended to drink more than he really did, so his two kid helpers would cover for the times he wasn't where everyone thought he was. Nobody notices a railroad man getting on or off a slow freight. So he'd ride out here, drop off, and lie in wait like some beast of prey for anyone who came by. Then he'd hit them from behind with that bolo, rip them up and behead them, and just wait for another train going back. He didn't walk much, and he did it carefully in those big padded sacks tied over his boots."

"I can see how he got about. But why was he doing it, and what in thunder did he take those heads for?"

"Well," Longarm said, retrieving his hat from the ditch beside the roadbed, where it had landed when he jumped from the train, "I was aiming to ask him the why of it, but as you see, he doesn't have much to say now. The reason he took the heads with him was to keep us from seeing them. When the bolo thongs hit someone about the neck, the heavy balls spin in and hammer hell out of their heads and faces. Then, too, carrying off the heads was sort of spooky. You might say he was in the trade of being spooky, and I don't mind saying, he scared hell out of *me* a few times!"

The brake boss shook his head and said, "Mendez, the yard bull. Who'd have ever thought it! You reckon he was crazy, Deputy? A man would have to be crazy to do what he done, right?"

The deputy slapped his hat against his knee, raising a little puff of dust, then reshaped it with his hands and replaced it on his head, dead-center. "Maybe. I'll know more after I figure out *why* he was doing it."

The coroner couldn't tell Longarm anything he might not have guessed about the cause of the Wendigo's death, but the papers had to be filled out, so, leaving the coroner to deal with the mangled remains, Longarm got on the federal wire at the land office. This time, the results were more interesting.

As he finished and rejoined Agent Chadwick in the

front office, Longarm said, "Mendez had a record a mile long. He told me about killing a colored hobo in Omaha, but he left out some union-breaking activities and some questions the St. Joe police wanted to ask him about a lady he left in his room when he checked out sudden, owing rent."

Chadwick asked, "Really? What did she say he'd done to her?"

"She didn't. Her throat was slit from ear to ear. St. Joe thought maybe Mendez could explain this to them, but as you know, it ain't likely he'll be able to."

"But you've made the point that the man was a killer and at least a little crazy. So let me be the first to congratulate you."

"Congratulate me? What for?"

"What for? Why, damn it, you've solved your case! You caught the Wendigo and everyone can breathe easy again!"

Longarm took out a cheroot and lit it, saying, "Hell, it's just getting interesting. Did you know Mendez didn't savvy telegraph codes? I tapped out a message to him on the bar one day, and he never blinked an eyeball when I said a dreadful thing about his mother. He was a moody cuss, too."

"I don't follow you, Longarm. The man was a railyard bully boy, not a dispatcher. He wasn't supposed to know Morse code. Oh, you mean about the railroad's schedules, right?"

"Somebody had to tell him ahead of time when the slow trains were running across the reservation. He had no call to hang around the dispatch sheds, either."

"Boy! I'm glad *my* wire's not connected to the railroad's! I expect you'll be checking on that, right?"

"Already did. Our federal line's not tied in with the railroad's. I hope you understand I've got a job to do."

"I'm getting used to the idea. What did your friends in the Justice Department say about that scrape I got into a few years back?"

"Oh, you were telling me the truth. They said your

boss had been a crook but that you'd had no way of getting at the missing money even if you'd aimed to."

"Thanks, I think. If you're not arresting me, these days, who *do* you have in mind for the Wendigo's confederate?"

"I'm keeping an open mind on that. It's possible Mendez had some other way of knowing the schedules. It'd take forever, which seems a mite long, to check out every switchman and train crewman who might have gossiped about who was running what to where. While I was using your wire I got in touch with my boss. Marshal Vail says he's pleased about the Wendigo, but he's still pissed off at me for not catching that rogue half-breed, Johnny Hunts Alone."

"You know, I'd forgotten all about that?"

"Denver didn't forget. The warrant I pack on Hunts Alone was the only reason I came up here in the first damn place. You might say this crap about the Wendigo, Mendez, or whomsoever was a side issue."

Chadwick laughed and said, "Some side issue! You scattered the poor bastard from hell to breakfast!"

Longarm smiled. "Well, he wasn't too tidy while he was alive. I'm sorry I shot him, though. He died too sudden, and before he could tell me some things I wished to know."

"You still think he had a motive, then? I mean, a sensible motive a sane person might understand?"

"There's no big mystery to that part of it. Mendez was a killer by nature and a bully by profession. He was playing Wendigo to run the Blackfoot off their land."

"Damn it, Longarm, we've been over that till I'm blue in the face from explaining. There's no way anyone can claim that Indian land. I not only looked it up in the regulations, I wired Washington to see if there'd been any new rulings on the subject."

"Do tell?" Longarm raised an eyebrow. "What did Washington say?"

"The same thing I've been telling you. Even if this particular reservation was completely abandoned for a full seven years, the land's been set aside in trust for the Blackfoot Nation."

"In other words, as long as one Blackfoot's still living anywhere in the country, no white man can claim an acre of that range?"

Chadwick rolled his eyes heavenward and said, "Not even if the Blackfoot ran up to Canada and took an oath to Queen Victoria. I checked that out with headquarters while I was at it. As wards of the state the Indians are not allowed to sell, give, or even throw away a square foot of their land, once it's been allotted to them."

Longarm asked, "What about some other tribe being given an abandoned reservation?"

Chadwick looked blank. Then he went to the bookshelf and started rummaging through a buckram-bound book of regulations, muttering, "I can see it, in *time*. But that couldn't be what the Wendigo, or Mendez, had in mind."

"Why not?"

"Hell," Chadwick said disgustedly, "you know how slowly the government works. And even if the B.I.A. did assign some other tribe the lands, what good would it do any white man?"

He opened the book to the regulation he'd been looking for and nodded, saying, "Seven years with no other claims, as I thought. Besides, even if another bunch of Indians were brought in, what would it mean to a white cattleman? I agree, all that ungrazed range might tempt almost anyone who might have hired Mendez, but as I keep trying to tell you, there's no way on earth they can *get* it!"

As he put the book back, Longarm asked, "Let's try it another way. What if someone were to just *hire* the range? Doesn't the government charge a modest fee per head for running cattle on public lands?"

"Certainly. Collecting range fees is part of my job."

"All right. What would it cost me, per head and season, if I came to you for a grazing permit on those reservation lands?"

Chadwick reached for his bookshelf, hesitated as if lost, and turned to say, "I don't know. You'd have to ask Durler, the Indian agent."

"I have. He doesn't know how to *rope* a cow, either. I thought the Land Agency had the final say on all government lands not being used for anything else."

"We do and we don't. You know about interservice rivalry, Longarm. The B.I.A. would never release grazing rights to us."

"Doesn't your office hire out land in the Indian Nation, down Oklahoma way?"

Chadwick frowned and said, "I'll have to ask about that. It's my understanding the Indian Nation's a special case. As you can see, I don't have any B.I.A. regulations here. Doesn't Durler have a library of his own out at the reservation?"

Longarm sighed, "Yeah. I've been looking through those fool books, too. I never was good at Latin and they seem to have been written by some old boys who never learned enough English to matter. Durler says he doesn't know what the Wendigo wanted, either. Do you think he's telling me the truth?"

Chadwick blinked in surprise before he asked, "Jesus, do you think the Indian agent himself might have been behind the killings?"

"Somebody was. I've been going with the notion that Durler doesn't know too much about stealing money from the government, yet."

Chadwick laughed and said, "It takes a while. I'm still working on my education. By the way, how long have *you* been in the service, Longarm?"

Longarm chewed his unlit cheroot and answered soberly, "Seven or eight years. They haven't caught me stealing from them yet."

"That makes two of us. Us little fellows never get to put our hands in the cookie jar, do we? You have to know those thieves in Washington pretty well before they let you at the pork barrel."

Longarm didn't answer, so Chadwick continued, "I don't know Durler all that well, but I'll stick my neck out and say he's probably as honest as most of us field men. If he was thinking of pocketing bribes for granting range fees to any local cattleman, he'd be foolish to run his own Blackfoot off."

Longarm frowned and said, "Keep talking. How *would* a crooked Indian agent go about getting rich at his job?"

Chadwick hesitated. Then he shrugged and said expansively, "Hell, we all know how the Indian Ring worked it under Grant. They didn't chase Indians *off* reservations. They crowded 'em *in* like sardines. If Durler was a crook, he'd want all the Indians out there he could get!"

"How do you figure that, Chadwick?"

"Jesus, I thought you said you'd been reading the B.I.A. regulations!" Chadwick said impatiently "The B.I.A. gets money from Congress to take care of them. The money in mistreating Indians is in skimming off part of the government allotments for food, clothing, medical supplies, and so forth."

"Then the more Indians an agent has to work with, the more loose change there is to sort of lose in the cracks?"

Chadwick laughed a bit enviously, as he nodded and said, "There you have it. If *I* was a crooked Indian agent I'd have ten times as many Indians out on that reservation. Then I'd divert about ten cents on the dollar and retire rich!"

Longarm nodded as if in sudden enlightenment and agreed, "You'd make more that way than selling range permits for a side bet under the table, huh?"

Chadwick sighed in open envy this time as he said, "Oh, God, yes. Cows only eat grass. There's no way to fiddle with the price of beans and white bread, feeding cows. They don't wear shoes or sleep under blankets, either. I'll bet that agent Cal Durler replaced is living in a big New York brownstone, now."

Longarm frowned and said, "Back up. Are you saying the agent young Cal replaced might have been a crook?"

Chadwick grew suddenly cautious as he answered slyly, "I don't want you to quote me about a fellow federal man, but it's common knowledge he was a Grant appointee. His name was McBride and the new reform administration threw him out on his ass as soon as they went over his books."

Longarm ripped a piece of yellow paper from a pad on Chadwick's desk and wrote the name down before he asked, "Was this McBride ever charged with anything, or are we only funning?"

Chadwick said, "I told you I have no real evidence. No, they did not put him in jail. The way I heard it, they let him resign peaceably, after he had some trouble explaining why he was collecting rations for three times as many Indians as there were in all Montana Territory."

"They get a federal indictment on this McBride jasper, or is all this just suspicions?" Longarm asked, folding the piece of paper and putting it in his pocket.

"Oh, you know half of Grant's boys, including Grant, were never out-and-out *arrested* for stealing half the country. I'll allow the old general, himself, was just a fool who trusted too many old friends after he was President for a while. President Hayes has been taking things back gentle. Just firing or transferring boys caught with their fingers in the till."

"I know. I've only been allowed to arrest half the crooks I've run across in my travels. Crooked or honest, politicians like to sweep old scandals under the rug. I reckon stealing from the taxpayers is a trade secret. I'd better have a few more words with the Justice Department on your telegraph, though. Some of what you just told me is interesting as hell."

Chapter 15

When he was finished at the land office, Longarm went to get his chestnut at the livery near the railroad station. He put off his intended return to the reservation when he spotted a trio of morose-looking but well-dressed Indians, hunkered on the station platform with their backs braced against the wall.

He walked over to them, flashed his federal badge, and asked, "You boys wouldn't be the Crow policemen from the B.I.A., would you?"

The leader of the trio nodded and said, "I am Constable Dancing Pony. You must be the one who killed the crazy man who killed the man we came here to arrest."

"I'm sorry you boys came out here for nothing," Longarm apologized. "Since you're headed home, can I take it you don't suspicion any other Ghost Dance activity out at the Blackfoot reservation?"

Dancing Pony shrugged and said, "The Paiute we were after was the only one reported in the territory this summer. We are going to Pine Ridge to talk to Sitting Bull. The Sioux are more interested in Wovoka's nonsense than the other Plains tribes. The death of Ishi-watl seems to have nipped it in the bud, here. That crazy white man did a good job in killing him."

Longarm asked, "Did you boys by any chance have a look around out there?"

"Of course. The army scout, Jason, led us over to the old homestead where the Ghost Dancer was killed. Some Blackfoot said you had buried the fool. But from what we have been told, he answers the description on our warrant, so the case is closed."

"Maybe. I've got another warrant on a Blackfoot breed named Hunts Alone. He's said to be hiding out somewhere around here."

Dancing Pony nodded. "The scout, Jason, told us this. We did not meet every Blackfoot on the reservation. The Crow and Blackfoot are not friends. But those we met seem to be pure-bloods."

"Did you talk to the Blackfoot policeman, Rain Crow?"

"Yes. He seems a good man, for one of *them*. He does not have white blood."

"What made you think I thought he wasn't a good man?" Longarm asked, frowning.

"He is one of your suspects, isn't he? If I had been in your place the night the Ghost Dancer was killed, I would have said Rain Crow did it."

"He told you about the way the signs read, huh? Lucky for Rain Crow the Wendigo turned out to be another man."

"Yes," the Crow agreed. "Any other lawman would have arrested Rain Crow for the killing. They told us the crazy man wore straw-filled sacking on his feet. I think that might have hidden his tracks, most places. But I don't see how he crossed fresh dust without leaving sign. Can you tell me how he did it?"

"No, and since Mendez is dead, he can't, either."

Dancing Pony stared thoughtfully into Longarm's eyes for a long, hard moment. Then he smiled thinly, and said, "You intend to write a few loose ends off, then?"

Longarm ignored what seemed to be a leading question, saying, "*You* have the power to arrest any Indian for murder, Dancing Pony. Do you intend to take Rain Crow in for some serious questioning in the near future?"

The Indian chuckled and answered, "No. If somebody took advantage of the other murders to get rid of a dangerous troublemaker, even if I could prove it, I don't think I would want to. If one of our people would only kill that damned Wovoka, before he stirs up more trouble . . ."

"I see we're in agreement on some things, then. I'd say that the Wendigo was just one clever son of a bitch, wouldn't you?"

Dancing Pony studied Longarm for a time before he said, "You have a good heart for a white man. We shall remember your name." Then he added, "Since the case is closed, will you be leaving with us on the train?"

"Not hardly. I still haven't caught the man I was sent up here about." He might have added that he hadn't really closed the books on the Wendigo, either, but he didn't. Other lawmen tended to get in the way sometimes, since his own methods were inclined occasionally to bend the rules.

Saying goodbye to the Indians, Longarm got his mount from the livery and rode out to the reservation. As he tethered the chestnut behind the agency, Prudence Lee came out of her own place and motioned him over with a worried look.

Longarm joined her in the shade of her back porch, touched the brim of his Stetson, and said, "Ma'am? You look like you've just met up with a spook."

"Calvin Durler's out looking for you, with a gun! Thank God you didn't meet him on the wagon trace!"

"I took a shortcut across the open prairie. What do you mean, a gun?"

"It's that Nancy! She told him something about you and he's half out of his head with rage! I only heard the loud parts when they were shouting about it half an hour or so ago, but she seems to have said you, uh— you know."

Longarm swore under his breath and said, "I never. I reckon you must suspicion it too, huh?"

Prudence shook her head emphatically. "No. If I thought she was telling the truth I'd let him shoot you. I told you she was going crazy. What are you going to do about it?"

Longarm shrugged and said, "Nan will have been

watching from her back window the same as you, so she knows I'm here. Cal will ride clean into Switchback and they'll tell him I rode out. We'd best go inside your place."

"You're welcome to hide with me, of course, but if I could have a talk with Nan before he gets back—"

"No. I want you where I can keep an eye on you. I've run into crazy-jealous husbands before, and there's only one way you can handle them."

"Good heavens! You don't mean to kill the poor boy!"

"Not if I can keep him from killing me some other way."

"Oh, my God, I shouldn't have told you! I can't have a dead man on my conscience!" Prudence cried in dismay.

"Well, had you left me in smiling ignorance you might have had two. He'd have had the clean drop on me, and since I don't take kindly to getting shot, I'd have likely gone down shooting back. Let's go inside while I study my next move."

"Can't you just ride out?" Prudence asked.

"Nope. Ain't finished hereabouts. Oh, I could hide out for a day or so, but it'd make my job tedious, and in the end, he'd likely catch up with me when I wasn't set for a showdown. I think it's best we get it over with as soon as possible."

He led her inside and started piling furniture against the wall facing the agency next door, saying, "I hope he doesn't just start shooting through the wall when Nan tells him I'm in here, but you never know. When we see him coming, I want you flat on the floor behind this stuff."

"Oh, my God, I don't believe this is happening! I must be having a bad dream! You can't mean it, Longarm! You can't just ambush that poor boy like this!"

"Miss Prudence," he said, laying a firm hand on her shoulder, "I ain't all that happy about it myself. You do as I say and I'll do what I have to. He'll be coming back before the sun sinks enough to matter."

Longarm was right. It was an hour before sunset when Calvin Durler rode in at a lope, his pony lathered and his face red with rage. He swung out of the saddle with a double-barreled shotgun in his free hand and ran into his own house, shouting.

A few minutes later he was out the back door again and headed next door, yelling, "I know you're in there, you son of a bitch! Come out and fight like a man!"

There was no answer. Calvin strode, grim-faced, toward the back porch entrance, all caution thrown to the winds as he searched for the man his wife had accused. He stopped a few paces from the roof overhang and called again, "Don't hide behind a woman's skirts, you bastard! If you won't come out, I'm coming in! Defend yourself, sir!"

And then a loop of throw-rope dropped around his head and shoulders, snapping tight to pin the enraged husband's elbows to his sides as Longarm, standing on the roof above, yanked hard.

Durler was lifted off his feet, sputtering in surprised confusion, as Longarm ran the length of the eaves and spilled Durler on one side. Then he dropped to the ground, still pulling the rope. He dragged Durler, kicking and screaming, away from his fallen shotgun, then came in hand-over-hand down the rope, and as Durler struggled to rise, kicked him flat, jumped on top of him, and proceeded to hogtie him with the pigging string he'd been gripping between his teeth.

The back door flew open and Prudence Lee flew out, shouting, "Don't hurt him, Longarm! It wasn't his fault!"

Longarm finished binding his victim securely before he looked up with a grin, and still kneeling on Durler's thrashing body, he said, "I told you I'd try to take him without gunplay, ma'am."

The other back door opened and Nan Durler peered out, looking almost as confused as her husband. Longarm slapped Durler a couple of times to gain his undivided attention before he said calmly, "She wasn't expecting to have to repeat her fool story to both of us,

214

Cal. Let's see if she was trying to get *you* or *me* out of the way, huh?"

He called out amiably, "Which one did you think it would be, Nan? I know you were pissed at me, but on the other hand, you likely figured I could take your man. I know divorce is frowned on, but wouldn't it have been more Christian?"

Nan ducked inside without answering, but her husband grunted, "Get off my back, God damn you! You're killing me!"

"Not as dead as she figured I would be. What in thunder's wrong with you, old son? Even if you bought that fool tale she must have told you, did you really think you had a chance against me? Meaning no offense, the last time I rode through Dodge, Ben Thompson and John Wesley Hardin both stayed out of my way."

"You just untie me and let me at a gun, you son of a bitch, and we'll just see how good you are!"

"I know how good I am, Cal," Longarm said calmly. "Likely your wife does, too. I don't aim to let you up till you've had time to reconsider a mite. You've been fighting with her for days. Ordinarily, I don't ask what married folks are fighting over, but she's been talking about leaving you, hasn't she?"

There was a long silence before Durler said grudgingly, "That's between me and her. She said you trifled with her while my back was turned, God damn you!"

"Well, she's a handsome woman and I'm no saint, so I can see how you might have been fool enough to buy that shit. But you missed a point or two. If I'd been at her while you were out tending your chores, don't you suspicion she'd have sort of wanted to keep it a secret? Most gals do. How'd she get you so riled? Did she say I had a bigger prick?"

"You bastard! How did you know that?"

"I'm a lawman. This ain't the first time I've run across such action, though I've usually been the arresting officer. Ain't it a bitch how gals get us poor idiots to fight with that old taunt about our peckers?

I don't care if you believe this or not, but Nan ain't in a position to say all that much about my anatomy. She only saw me once in my birthday suit and it wasn't up enough to mention."

From the sidelines, Prudence Lee gasped, "Mr. Long! I'll thank you to remember I'm a lady!"

"Can't be helped, ma'am. This is man talk. You'd best go inside if it's too rich for your ears."

She didn't move. Interested in spite of himself, Calvin Durler asked, "She saw you naked? When was this?"

"When she came in on me as I was taking a bath. She likely meant to scrub my back or something."

"She told me you'd had her in our own bed. She said she'd tried to resist, but you were so strong and she was so weak, her flesh betrayed her into going all the way."

"Sure, she told you that," Longarm said. "Next to being told the other man is bigger and better, nothing steams a man like hearing it took place in his own bed. She didn't miss a trick, did she?"

"God damn it, she *must* have been telling me the truth! How could any woman admit to such a thing if it wasn't true?"

"To get her husband killed, most likely. Just *think* a mite, damn it. Even if I was fool enough to trifle with a man's wife under his own roof with miles of open country all about, why would I take even more of a chance than I had to? Hell, you've given me a guest room with a lock on the door, old son! Don't you think I'd have sense enough to use it for my wicked seductions, if such was my intention?"

Durler said, "She told me you caught her in our room, making the bed, and—"

"Damn it, she makes all the beds at the same time," Longarm interrupted. "Besides that, if I was some sort of mad rapist, Miss Prudence, here, has been all alone at my mercy without a husband to protect her. Ain't that right, Miss Prudence?"

The missionary blushed and stammered, "What are you saying? We've never been improper together!"

216

"There you go, Cal, and meaning no disrespect to your woman, this single gal, here, is no uglier. Well, never mind. The point I'm aiming at is that I'd be too foolish to be let out without a keeper if I'd been fooling with a married-up woman under her own roof with a good-looking single gal alone next door."

Prudence Lee added, "I can assure you, Calvin, Mr. Long has been a perfect gentleman the times we've been alone, and come to think of it, he's been alone with me more often than with Nan."

Longarm asked, "Can I let you up now, Cal?"

"Well, maybe I won't shoot anybody just yet, but I've got a lot of questions to ask everybody hereabouts!"

Longarm untied his wrists and ankles and helped him to his feet as Durler muttered murderously, "Somebody's been trying to pull the wool over my eyes, God damn it."

"I know. Why don't we all go over to your place and have us a pow-wow with your woman?"

But when the three of them got to the agency kitchen, they met Nan Durler with a packed carpetbag and a defiant look on her face. Durler said, "Honey, we've got to talk about this situation." But his wife snapped, "I'm through talking, you mealy-mouthed nitwit! If you were any kind of a man at all, you'd have killed him for what he did to me!"

"He says he didn't do it, Nan."

"I don't care who says what to anybody!" Nan Durler exploded. "I'm taking one of the ponies into Switchback. You can pick it up at the livery. I'm going where men know how to do *right* by a lady!"

She swept grandly out, and as Durler followed, pleading, Longarm caught Prudence by the elbow and murmured, "Stay here with me and let 'em have it out."

"I don't want her to tell him more lies about you. I've never met a woman with such an evil tongue!" Prudence said with righteous indignation.

"I have. I'd say her mind's made up and she's leaving peaceably. Her notions on collecting a government pension as the widow of a federal employee didn't pan out, but she's on her way East and he won't be turning her around."

"Oh, good heavens! I didn't even consider a pension! So that's why she wanted you both to fight!"

"Only partly. Since Cal ain't listening, I will confess she did try to get me to do what she said, only I wouldn't, and she was likely moody enough about it to not care all that much which of us got buried. Since she never figured she'd have to repeat her fool tale under cross-examination, I suspicion she's given up. He'll be fool enough to tag along all the way to town, but she's getting on that train. Her jaw was set for a long trip elsewhere."

"Well, he's well rid of her, I suppose," Prudence said. "But what's to become of her?"

"Don't know. Don't care. She'll find another man, or failing at that, take up the trade she was likely born for. I doubt she'll become a missionary."

Prudence Lee's eyes narrowed as she snapped, "Just what was *that* supposed to mean, sir?"

"Just funning."

Longarm was drinking alone in the Switchback saloon that night when Jason joined him at the bar. Jason said, "Heard you took a room at the railroad hotel."

Longarm said, "Just for the night. I'll be pulling out for Denver in the morning."

"Oh, you finished here?" Jason asked, surprised. "I thought it might have something to do with that domestic trouble out at the agency."

"Jesus, news travels in a small town, don't it? The back-fence gossips must have had a lot of fun when Durler's old woman left on the evening train."

"I heard something about her leaving him. Surprised *you're* leaving, though. When I rode in to see the Crow police off they said you had some loose ends left hereabouts."

"There's loose ends and there's loose ends, Jason. Sometimes, in my trade, it pays to leave a few be. The Wendigo killings have stopped, and I can't find Johnny

Hunts Alone. Meanwhile, there's more work waiting for me back in Denver and my boss is getting moody about it."

"I see. So we'll likely never know how Mendez pulled off some of it, or why, eh?"

Longarm said, "Oh, I got the Wendigo's moves nailed down. Like I suspicioned, he was using the railroad and those burlap boots to get on and off the reservation. Killed his victims with that South American bolo, and you know the rest."

Jason scratched at his thick-stubbled jaw. "Damned if I do! What about that Ghost Dancer, killed miles from the track, or old Real Bear, murdered right next door to the agency? No tracks near there, were there?"

"Mendez never killed those two," Longarm explained, "The Ghost Dancer was killed by . . . never mind. The point is, the Indian who got rid of a troublemaker before he could get the tribe in hot water did everyone a favor, and what the hell."

"What about the old chief?" Jason asked, puzzled.

"Oh, that was Johnny Hunts Alone. Real Bear had recognized and turned the rascal in. So he butchered the old man and skinned him. You said the breed was once a hide-skinner, remember?"

Jason snapped his fingers. "That's right, and Real Bear's head wasn't cut off, either!"

"There you go. Mendez was sent to follow up on the first spooky killing when the Dream Singers started scaring folks about the Wendigo. The idea was to scare the Blackfoot off all that open range. Mendez was a hired thug. Don't know if the grisly trimmings were his idea or not. He didn't have much imagination. Kept pulling the same fool tricks till I caught him."

Jason frowned and said, "Wait a minute. Loose ends are one thing, but this is ridiculous! You say you think Johnny Hunts Alone killed Real Bear, but you've given up on catching him?"

"I'd catch him if he was on the reservation. But he ain't. He likely lit out shortly after killing the informer. His only reason for being in these parts was to hide out.

With the Justice Department, army, Indian agency and all combing the reservation for the Wendigo—"

"I follow your drift. He's likely in Mexico by now. But what was that about someone putting Mendez up to those other killings?"

The deputy laughed softly. "Ain't it obvious? Mendez didn't kill folks as a hobby. He did it for money. He was hired to run the Blackfoot off a huge stretch of virgin range. None of the big cattle outfits would be in a position to claim or buy the land, once it was deserted, but they don't *buy* open range in the first place. They pay a fee per head to the government to graze it. Cal Durler says he's had lots of offers, but he turned them all down. Says he was offered a few bribes, too." Longarm reached for a cheroot, lit it, and mused, "Had the Blackfoot run to Canada as planned, the B.I.A. would have fired Durler as dead wood."

"Then who would they go to with an offer on the grazing rights?" Jason asked.

"Land office, of course. Bureau of Land Management has the say on all federal lands not occupied by anybody."

"You mean Chadwick could lease out grazing rights on Indian lands?"

Longarm nodded. "Sure. He says he can't, but I checked with Washington and he has the power to lease even your army post, if it ain't being used by anybody. The grazing rights are leased on a yearly basis. Land office can grant the rights to the White House lawn if President Hayes ain't there to object."

"Kee-rist! Don't you see what that means, Longarm?"

The lawman took a long drag on his cheroot and blew out a thick column of bluish smoke. For a moment, he watched it thin out and spread to merge with the pall already floating in the thick atmosphere of the saloon, then he said, "That Chadwick ain't up on his regulations? Or that he'd have been in position to line his pockets if the Blackfoot had deserted all that land?"

"Good God Almighty! Ain't you going to arrest him?" Jason asked.

"I'd like to," Longarm said. "But on what charge? Mendez is dead, so he can't be a witness. There's nothing I can prove. But what the hell, the killings are over and he'll be too scared to try again, so I'm closing the books on the case."

Jason drained his glass and held his finger up to the bartender for another as he growled, "That's raw as hell, Longarm! Can't you see Chadwick was behind it all? You know how big cattle spreads take care of government men who can grant 'em grazing rights while keeping smaller men off the free grass!"

Longarm nodded morosely, and agreed, "Sure, I know. But I can't touch the rascal. It's no crime to be a mite confused about his land office regulations. Not in court, anyway. He was never on the reservation or anywhere near the victims, so what am I to do about it?"

"By God, if it was me wearing that badge I'd *shoot* the son of a bitch!" Jason said vehemently.

"I've studied on that. The man's a federal official with powerful friends. Wouldn't be legal for me to just up and gun him down like the dog he is. But like I said, he likely won't try anything else. He was mixed up in another scandal a few years back and it took him a long time to get up the nerve to have another go at the pork barrel. So he'll retire poor but honest. It happens that way, once in a while."

Jason grabbed his fresh drink peevishly and snapped, "I thought you had more sand in your craw! Ain't you even gonna have harsh words with him over all he did to them poor folks?"

Longarm shrugged. "I could lecture him some, but he'd just laugh at me. He's had time to cover his crooked tracks better than his hired Wendigo ever did. No, I'll just leave polite and peaceable. I'm only a deputy and he's got some powerful pals in higher circles. One thing I've had to learn the hard way, Jason, is that the big shots never get caught."

"Jesus, you call that justice?"

"Nope, I call it the facts of life. I've got enough on

221

my plate with the *little* bastards they send me after."
He took out his watch and consulted it before he
added, "I've got some wires to send at the station and a
ticket to buy. If I don't meet up with you again, it's
been nice knowing you, Jason."

Leaving the scout to brood about it over his drink,
Longarm left and walked over to the station. He went
inside, then out the far door to the dark tracks. He
moved west along the railroad right-of-way until he
came abreast of an alleyway cutting behind the store-
fronts of the main street. Then he drew his .44 and
moved slowly down the alley toward the back door of
the land office.

He took his time deliberately, but he'd reached the
back fence when he heard a fusillade of gunshots,
followed by a ghastly scream!

Longarm nodded and moved in slowly and cautiously. The screams were still going on as he kicked in the
back door and moved along the dimly lit corridor in
their direction. They were coming from the telegraph
lean-to.

Longarm heard the front door slam, so he entered
the shack. Agent Chadwick was rolling on the floor
in a puddle of blood and steaming battery acid, his
hands covering his smoldering face as he wailed, "Oh,
Jesus! Mary, Mother of God, I can't stand it!"

Longarm placed one boot on a dry spot, holstered
his .44, grabbed one of Chadwick's booted ankles, and
hauled him clear of the vitriol and broken battery
glass, saying, "Don't rub it in, you stupid son of a
bitch!"

He dragged Chadwick along the corridor, leaving a
trail of smoldering carpet in their wake, and kicked out
the front door to drag the screaming land agent out into
the street. People ran from every direction as Longarm
hauled Chadwick through the dust to a watering trough,
picked him up by the belt, and plunged him full-length
into the water, soaking his own arms to the elbows as
he did so. He called out, "Somebody run for the doc

222

and stand clear of that splashed shit. Even mixed with water it's strong enough to peel you alive!"

He glanced around for Jason, but the scout wasn't part of the crowd. Longarm shrugged, and since Chadwick seemed to be drowning, reached in for a handful of his hair and pulled his head up. As he did so, the hair came off in his hand and the land agent's head banged against the soggy end planks, out of the water. He was screaming again now, so he'd probably live for a while, the poor bastard.

Longarm turned to the bartender from across the way and said, "Tell the doc somebody put a bullet in his gut, then shot out the battery jars above him. He's likely done for, but ask the doc to try and keep him alive till I get back."

Someone asked, "Where are you going, Deputy?"

Longarm said, "To arrest the man who did it, of course. A favor is a favor, but the law is the law, too."

He caught up with the scout in the livery. They were alone there, since the stable hands were up the street, attending the evening festivities around the dying land agent.

Longarm said, " 'Evening, Jason. Going someplace?"

The bearded scout smiled thinly and said, "I was wondering why my saddle was missing. You came by here and hid it before laying for me over at the saloon, huh?"

"Yep. I owe you for pushing me out of the way of a bullet, so I hope we can settle this peaceably."

"I notice you haven't drawn. Don't reckon you could see your way to just let me ride out? You know that skunk had a good killing coming to him."

"You killed him better than most Apaches might have managed. I reckon blood is thicker'n water, even if you killed old Real Bear after he recognized you. Since you had nothing to do with killing those other Blackfoot, and they were your kin, I sort of figured you'd go for Chadwick, once I told you he'd been behind the Wendigo bullshit. I want you to listen sharp before you go for that gun at your side, old son. I'd rather take you

223

in alive, but I'm taking you in, not for what you did to Chadwick, but for those other folks you robbed and killed as Johnny Hunts Alone."

"I might have known you had me spotted. Can we talk a spell before we slap leather?"

"I've got time. If you're trying to tell me you've gone straight as an army scout, forget it. I've sent some wires and there's no scout assigned to Fort Banyon. You knew it was a quiet post and just rode in with bogus orders you'd typed up under a carbon paper. That drunk C.O. out there never gave enough of a damn to check, and since you only aimed to stay a month or so, you had till next payday before anyone might have asked for confirmation. I'm surprised the Crow police didn't tumble, though. Few army posts have scouts assigned between campaigns, and when they do, it's usually a local man who talks the local tribe's lingo. I know you said you didn't talk Blackfoot, but of course you do. That part about talking Sioux was clumsy, Johnny. Got me wondering why you were scouting in Blackfoot country. Saying you didn't know your way around the reservation was foolish, too. A real scout would have known the country like the back of his hand, or there'd be no point to the War Department's hiring him in the first place!"

"You gotta admit I can pass for pure white," Jason-Johnny said proudly.

"Sure you can. That's what mixed us up, at first. They sent me looking for a Blackfoot, *on* the reservation, not a white scout right next door. Old Real Bear forgot to put that part in when he got word to us you were in the neighborhood. But as you see, I figured it out. Once I knew you weren't a real scout, the rest just sort of fell into place. Nobody'd be working as a scout just for the hell of it, and you *are* sort of dark, once folks get suspicious."

Johnny Hunts Alone nodded and said, "I still say you had dumb luck. Had that son of a bitch, Chadwick, not used my killing Real Bear to start a war of his own . . ."

"That's right. I'd have likely run in circles for a few days, found out no breed answering your description was on the reservation, and decided he'd just lit out after killing the old man. But as you see, it didn't work out that way. I had you spotted soon enough, but I didn't know if you were the Wendigo, so I left you to one side until I caught Mendez, and you know the rest. If you'd oblige me by unbuckling that gun belt, gentle, I'd be willing to take you to Denver without putting you in irons. Like you said, I owe you."

The half-breed shook his head and said, smiling broadly, "Can't hardly see my way clear to do that, Longarm. I reckon it's you or me, huh?"

"I wish you wouldn't make me kill you, old son."

Hunts Alone laughed, a trifle wildly, and staring hard at the holstered .44 at Longarm's side, went for his own.

There was a bright orange blaze of two rapid shots and Johnny Hunts Alone staggered back against the wall of a stall as the horse behind him whinnied in terror. The half-breed slid down the planks, leaving a trail of blood against them as he sank to his knees, his own gun still undrawn and his eyes riveted on the grips of Longarm's holstered sixgun. He shook his head and muttered, "What the hell—?"

Longarm took the little brass derringer from the side coat pocket he'd fired through and explained, "I was covering you with a double-barreled whore pistol all this time, Johnny. You said you wanted to talk, so I let you. But I've had men draw on me in the middle of an interesting conversation, so . . ."

"Damn it, that wasn't *fair*, Longarm! I thought we were going to settle this like gents."

"You had your chance to come peaceably. I gave you a better chance than you did when you hit old Real Bear from behind, and while we're on the subject, that last bank clerk you gunned was unarmed. But we're wasting time with this fool talk, Johnny. How bad did I hit you? The doc's right up the street."

"I'd say you killed me," answered Johnny Hunts Alone, judiciously, as he removed a blood-slicked hand from his chest and studied it calmly in the dim light.

Longarm said, "I'll be taking that gun before I go to fetch help, Johnny. You just rest easy and try not to move about."

But as he drew his .44 and knelt to take the gun from the kneeling man's hip, the breed suddenly vomited blood and fell forward on his face. Johnny Hunts Alone's body twitched a few more times, then lay very still. Longarm felt for the pulse on the side of his neck and said aloud, "You were right, old son. I purely put at least one round where it counted, didn't I?"

The man stretched out in the stable litter didn't answer.

Longarm hadn't expected him to.

Longarm knelt a while in silence, wondering why his gut felt so empty. It was all over. He'd done the job he'd been sent to do and he had done it damned well, in all modesty. So why did he feel so shitty?

It wasn't that he'd just killed another man. He'd gotten used to that part. It went with the job. He'd given this poor jasper the chance to come with him peaceably and politely, and where in the U.S. Constitution did it say a lawman had to treat a wanted killer fairly?

No, he didn't feel guilty about killing Johnny Hunts Alone. He'd owed the man for saving his ass that time, but the breed had only been acting natural when he spied that gun barrel trained on them from across the street. Nobody was all bad. The man he'd just killed had likely been decent to his friends and good to his horse, too. Had he been given more of a break than he'd asked for, he'd be riding out about now with a dead lawman lying here, and not feeling all that sorry about it.

As to tricking Hunts Alone into killing the one man the law couldn't touch, Longarm thought that had been right slick, if he said so himself. He'd file it that he'd gunned Johnny after tracking him from the murder of a government official and there'd be no scandal worth mentioning. It was all as neat as a pin. Perhaps he was feeling sad because, no matter how many of them died, poor Roping Sally would never come back with her tomboy smile and rollicking rump to brighten up a tedious world.

He got to his feet again, brushing the stable dust from his knee with his hat, and stepped outside.

More sightseers were running to the sound of the more recent shots and Longarm saw one was Sheriff Murphy. Longarm said, "Take charge of the body in there, will you, Murph? By the way, there's a reward on the cuss. I'll write you up for an assistment, if you want."

"Why, that's neighborly as hell, Longarm. But who in thunder did you shoot this time? The doc says Chadwick's done for!"

"I didn't shoot Chadwick. The man who did is inside, dead. You'll find he's that jasper who said he worked for the army, Jason. His real name was Hunts Alone and he was a Blackfoot on his mama's side. Now you know as much as I do and I've got other chores to tend to."

Leaving Murphy in charge at the livery, Longarm jogged up the street to where Chadwick lay naked on a wagon tarp near the watering trough. The coroner looked up brightly and said, "You're delivering 'em fresh these days. This poor cadaver's still breathing. No need for an autopsy, though. The cause of death was a bullet through the spleen and a shower of battery acid. I just knocked him out to ease his way out of this world. Before he went under, he said something about a double-cross."

"He likely thought one of the folks offering him bribes was spooked about it. Did he mention any names?"

"No, and he won't. Even if he'd lived—I mean for the night—he'd have been in too much pain to talk sense. Those third-degree acid burns must smart."

The deputy marshal pulled at a corner of his John L. Sullivan mustache. "Hell, I wanted him to confirm a few

227

things. No way to bring him around for a minute or two?"

"I'll try."

The coroner started to give the charred body an injection. Then he shook his head and said, "He's gone. Maybe I gave him a mite more morphine than I should have."

"I reckon it was your Christian duty, Doc. I can see the bones in his face and the eye holes are still smoking."

"Yeah, it was a hell of a way for any man to die," the coroner agreed.

Longarm shrugged and muttered, "Oh, I don't know. All things considered, I suspicion the mother-loving son of a bitch got off easier than he deserved!"

A man in the crowd marveled, "Jesus, Deputy, when you hate, you hate *serious*, don't you?"

Longarm swept the crowd with his cold, gray-blue eyes as he nodded and said, "Yep, and you might spread the word that I'll be back if anyone ever, ever raises another finger against my friends out at the Blackfoot reservation!"

He assumed, as he walked away, that they'd gotten his message. If they hadn't, what the hell, he'd meant every word.

Chapter 16

It was another midnight by the time Longarm reached the agency after one last, tedious ride out to fill Calvin Durler in on all that had just taken place.

He found the young Indian agent in a chair next to the kitchen table, sprawled face-down across it and out like a light. There were no bullet holes in Durler, but a jar of white lightning stood on the table near his snoring head, three-quarters gone.

Longarm considered shaking him awake, but decided not to. Drunken young men whose women had just lit out on them tended to be testy, even when they were able to hear you. So Longarm snuffed out the kitchen lamp to keep the poor kid from cremating himself and stepped outside.

There was a light in Prudence Lee's window, but it was late. He thought maybe he'd just light out and the hell with it. If Durler had any questions they couldn't answer for him in town, he could write to Denver when he sobered up.

But Prudence must have heard his chestnut's hooves, for she popped out on the porch to hail him, saying, "I was so afraid you'd leave without coming by to say goodbye. Is it true you're finished here?"

"Yep. I've returned the hired mule and buckboard to the livery, made arrangements to return the army's horse to Fort Banyon, and I've bought a through ticket to Denver. My train pulls out tomorrow."

"Oh? Then surely you intended to spend the night out here?"

"Not hardly. Calvin's drunk as a skunk and it gets tedious listening to folks blubber about lost love. I've got a room in town for the night—or what's left of it."

"The least you can do is come inside and sit a spell," Prudence said. "I'm so confused about all that's happened, and I'd love to have you explain it all to me."

Longarm shrugged and followed her inside, where a pot of coffee was already boiling on the stove. She'd likely put it on as soon as she'd heard him ride in.

He sat down at the table and said, "Well, I've told this tale so many times I'm sick of it, so I'll make it short and sweet."

Which he did, between draughts of Prudence's strong coffee, up to the events of the previous few hours. When he had finished, Prudence Lee said, "So the Wendigo business was all a ruse to drive the Indians away to Canada, right?"

"Yep. Almost worked, too," Longarm said, taking a sip of coffee.

"But you were waiting for the Wendigo on the train. The fact that the Ghost Dancer was murdered miles from the track never fooled you?"

"Heck, no. I could see right off who did it. When you read two men going in and one coming out, and don't believe in ghosts, there can only be one answer. Rain Crow tracked the Ghost Dancer down and killed him for being a troublemaker. Then, when he saw he might have exceeded his authority a mite, he tried to make it look like the Wendigo had done it."

"Are you going to have to arrest Rain Crow?" Prudence asked, a troubled look in her eyes.

"No. By now he's figured out what he did wrong. Had he just up and shot the jasper, as a lawman trying to make an arrest, there'd have been no crime to report. I suppose I could get picky about it, but I'm not of a mind to. I could make a fuss about Snake Killer's homemade liquor, too. But I'm a peace officer, not a man to cause trouble for peaceable folk. Besides, I see Calvin's got a jar of Snake Killer's medicine next door, likely helping him get through the first troubled nights.

So I ain't putting anything about fire-water in my official report."

As she poured him another cup of coffee, he said, "That's about the size of all that's happened, Miss Prudence. I'll just drink this and be on my way."

"Don't you think we'd be more comfortable on the davenport, out in the other room?" Prudence asked.

"If you say so, ma'am."

He followed her into the parlor, where he noticed that she didn't light the lamp as they sat down together. She waited until he'd swallowed a few sips before she said, quietly, "I'll be going into town myself, in the morning. Would you take me with you?"

"You leaving for good or just shopping, ma'am?"

"For good. Why do you ask?"

"I've returned the hired buckboard. I could ride you postern on the chestnut, if it was just a shopping expedition. Packing you and all your gear on one horse, though, is another story, I'm afraid."

"I won't be taking much. Just my personals, in one bag. I noticed when Nan left that a woman can carry all she really needs in one neat bundle."

"What about your big bass drum, Miss Prudence?"

She laughed oddly, and said, "To hell with the big bass drum! I'm so tired of beating it I could scream!"

Not meeting her gaze, Longarm asked, "Don't you want to be a missionary any more, ma'am?"

"I never wanted to be a missionary, but what was I to do? I don't know how to play one of those new typewriters, I'm not pretty enough to be an actress, and I don't know how to walk a tightrope in the circus."

"Now those are purely interesting trades for a lady, ma'am. Are you saying you just took up reading Bibles because you needed a *job*?"

"Of course. It was that or . . . work I'm not ready for. I was rather desperate when I checked into that home for wayward girls, and when they offered me a position as a missionary . . . well, damn it, what was I to do? Work in a fancy house? I may have strayed, some may have said I was fallen. But, damn it, I never fell *that* far!"

"I see." Longarm nodded sagely. "That gal you were telling me about—the one who ran off with a rascal who deserted her? She was you all the time, right?"

"Of course. Don't tell me you didn't have *that* figured out!"

Longarm winked. "The thought sort of crossed my mind, but it wasn't my business."

"So now you know. And I don't mind telling you it's a load off my mind! I was getting so sick of playing Little Miss Goody."

He chuckled and said, "A little Goody ain't all that bad, taken in moderation. If you're giving up on being a missionary, what's your next goal—learning to play a typewriter after all?"

"Anything would be an improvement over reading the Bible to a lot of people who just aren't interested. I thought I'd get back to civilization with the little I have left and . . . I don't know. That story about Madam LaMont had a moral, all right. I noticed that while she was atoning, she got *rich* at it."

Longarm drained the cup, placed it on the floor, and leaned back to observe, "You ain't as wicked as you'd have to be to take up that line of work, honey. Don't be so hard on yourself."

"What makes you so sure I couldn't be . . . one of those women?"

"You ain't cold-blooded enough. There's a poor, lonesome fool right next door, with a good income, and he's ripe for the plucking. A wicked lady would be over there right now, helping him forget his troubles while she taught him to leap through hoops. A gal who was willing to sell her favors could take that idiot for every cent he had and make him wire home for more!"

"My God! The thought never crossed my mind!" Prudence gasped.

"There you go. You just don't think like a dance-hall gal. You'll likely wind up an honest woman in spite of yourself."

232

She laughed and said, "You have a wicked imagination. Now that you've pointed it out, I can see how I could trap poor Calvin without, as you put it so bluntly, selling anything at all."

"Yep, he'd likely marry up with you if you took him under your wing. Old Cal's the marrying kind."

"Well, I'm not a mother hen and if I was I don't think he'd be my cup of tea. Nancy was an awful girl, but I could see how living with such a wishy-wash could drive most women to distraction. I don't know why I'm telling you this, but I ran away from a husband who was twice the man Calvin is!"

Longarm shifted his weight and observed, "He'll likely find some gal in Switchback. Word gets around quick about a lonesome cuss with a good job. Besides, he ain't that bad—just has some growing to do. He's already learned to ease up on the Indians and brand his livestock. He'll make some gal a good man, provided she ain't as particular as yourself."

"Could we please drop Calvin Durler? A body would think you were trying to marry her off to the nearest thing in pants! Maybe I am particular, for a woman of my age and looks, but when I *am* ready to try again, I shan't make the same mistake. I was a teenaged silly and my mother was after me to marry the boy next door and . . . no, the next time I'm going to have a much better notion what I'm getting myself into!"

"Pays to shop around a mite, eh?"

Prudence sighed, "I suppose you could put it that way. I've wasted some of my best years on a nice boy who bored me to distraction; I've made an awful fool of myself with a no-account handsome devil, and for a while, acted so crazy I hardly remember what it was like. Now that I've seen I'm just too . . . well, *healthy* to give my remaining good years to mission work— Heavens, what am I saying? Why am I baring my soul to you like this? And is that your *arm* around my shoulders, sir?"

Longarm gently drew her closer, and observed, "Lots of folks seem to tell me things they hadn't intended to.

233

Gal I knew once, said it had something to do with my not getting all excited in the middle of a quiet conversation. As to why I'm holding you friendly, I reckon I'm cold or something. I'll stop if you want me to."

She reached up to clasp the big hand cupping her shoulder as she sighed, "It does feel comforting, but you're to go no further. Just because I've let down my hair a mite is no reason to get ideas. I may be middle-aged, and not much of a looker, and I've told you far too much about how weak I've been, but—"

"Slow down! You're talking silly. You can't be thirty yet, you know you're a right pretty little mouse, and friends don't take advantage of each other's weaknesses."

"Oh, you're just saying that," Prudence scoffed. "I'll admit I'm not deformed, but 'fess up—you wouldn't have your arm about me if I hadn't confessed to being a fallen woman, would you?"

"I might have hesitated if you'd stuck to beating drums for the Bible Society, but as for being fallen, I suspicion you haven't fallen as far as you might have aimed to. Most of us have more lust than nerves. We've been brought up to think a lot of things that are only natural must be wicked. Somehow the people who wrote the rules got the funny notion that anything that felt good had to be bad for us."

Her reply, if she had one, was muffled against his lips as he gently pulled her closer and kissed her. She responded, started to struggle, then moaned in pleasure and started kissing back.

Longarm put his free hand against her firm little belly, felt that she wore no corset, praise the Lord, and started moving up. Then he decided what the hell, and slid his hand down between her thighs and began to stroke her gently through her cotton twill skirt and whatever was under it.

She gasped and twisted her lips away from his, pleading, "No! I don't want to!"

"Sure you do. Don't you think I can read the smoke signals in your pretty brown eyes?"

"Oh, I'm so bewildered! My body's saying one thing, but my head tells me this is wrong. The Bible says it's wrong!"

He noticed she wasn't pulling away all that vigorously, so he massaged her through the cloth and soothed, "Go with your body, honey. Anyway, if you really want to talk religion at a time like this, don't you reckon the Lord would never have made us like we are, or let us be together like this, if He was so dead set against it?"

Even as she stopped struggling and opened her thighs to his caress, she protested, "Damn it, you know that's pure sophistry!"

He grinned and said, "Yeah, ain't that a bitch?" as he picked her up and carried her into the bedroom, observing, "We could wrestle on that damn horsehair some more, but it ain't civilized, and all these fool clothes are in the way."

"What are you *doing*!" she exclaimed, even as she helped him with the hooks and eyes while he was undressing her. He gently stripped her to her shift and high-button shoes as she half-struggled, half-cooperated on the mattress. Then he popped a few buttons of his own, got most of his duds out of the way, and was mounting her. She sobbed, "Oh, I never should have told you about my past!" as she wrapped her thighs around him and gripped his naked buttocks with her leather-clad ankles. He moved them into a better position and started thrusting harder as she rolled her head from side to side and gasped, "Oh, this is terrible! What must you think of me?"

"I think you're more wondrous than an army in its banners. You want me to take it out?"

"You do and I'll kill you! I think I'm . . . oh, Jesus! I *know* I'm coming!"

Later, after they'd taken time to catch their breath and get rid of all the remaining clothing, Prudence held him in her arms, nibbling on one ear, as she purred, "Will you take me with you to Denver, darling?"

235

He said, "I'll take you to the moon if you want, but maybe I should have explained a few things."

She placed a finger to his lips. "Hush, don't spoil this moment, darling. I know you're not the marrying kind." She chuckled and added, "As a matter of fact, I'm not sure I am, either. Not for a while, at least. There's so much of life I seem to have missed out on. God, you must think I'm terrible!"

"No, I think you're one of the few sensible gals I've run across lately. I'll take you with me at sunup and we'll just sort of drift with the tide till—"

"No plans, dearest. I know better than to hold you to foolish promises and, well, you seem to have started something, for *I* don't mean to be held to any, either!"

She saw he wasn't going to answer and chuckled. "You're not sure if you like that or not, are you? I suppose most girls you do this with fall madly in love with you?"

"I like it best when there's less fool talk and more action," Longarm said.

She laughed as he remounted her. She responded to his first thrust, saying, "My heavens, Nan Durler really told the truth about one thing. If this be carnal depravity, I like it. I didn't mean to offend your manly pride, dearest, but I *told* you I was weak-willed."

Longarm laughed, too. He started moving faster, thinking, *Yeah, this is what every old boy says he wants —a pretty little thing that moves her tail like a saloon door on payday, with no strings or tears in the cold, gray dawn.* By jimmies, he'd take her to Denver and hold on to her for a spell! Then, as he paused, once more sated for the moment, Prudence sighed, "Roll over on your back and let me do it my way."

"I'm still up to it, honey, and I like to do things my way and I'm bigger than you!"

"My, yes, in every way," she purred. "But please let me get on top. Pretty please with sugar on it?"

So, having shown he was still the boss, sort of, Longarm rolled his back against the mattress as she took her own way with his flesh. As he suddenly laughed, she paused and asked with a frown, "What's so funny? I didn't think I was all that ridiculous with my old shimmy off!"

He laughed again and explained, "I was thinking of a gal I met, maybe a million years ago, who said I'd never meet up with another half as good."

Prudence Lee arched her petite torso back to grasp his bare ankles and brace herself on locked elbows. Then she hooked a heel in each of Longarm's armpits and began moving her tiny pelvis in a manner he found impossible as well as delicious. He gasped, "You're purely fixing to bust me off inside you, but don't you dare stop!"

"Was that other lady right in her assumption you'd never meet her match in bed, darling?"

Longarm grinned up at the gamin face smiling back at him between a pair of bouncing cupcake breasts and answered, "Honey, she was as crazy as a bedbug! Every other gal I've ever done this with was just practice for tonight. You are the very best I've ever had and that's the truth!"

That was what he liked most about women. No matter how good the last had been, each time he found himself a new one, it really did seem that she was the best he'd ever had. So no matter how often he said it, he was always telling the truth.

SPECIAL PREVIEW

Here are the opening scenes
from

LONGARM IN THE INDIAN NATION

fifth novel in the bold new
LONGARM series from Jove/HBJ

Chapter 1

Snapping awake with all senses alert wasn't anything new to Custis Long. He'd done that every morning for almost as many years as he could remember. What was new was snapping awake in a bed far softer than his own, in his rooming house. It was as different as his own bed was from the rough shakedowns on the ground that he'd gotten used to in the field. For a moment he was startled by the unaccustomed luxury of satin sheets and pillowcases brushing his bare skin, the scent of patchouli and musk heavy in his nostrils, and a soft, warm feminine form cuddled up to him.

For a moment, Longarm resisted two temptations. The first was to lever himself out of bed the way he usually did the instant he was awake. The second was to nestle down again with the woman, who was still asleep, and enjoy the pleasure of rousing her.

He didn't resist the temptation to recall the night from which he'd just awakened, and memory brought a smile of pleasure to his face. The evening had started badly. He'd swung off the train at Julesburg to find the station agent waiting for him with the yellow flimsy of a telegram. The wire had been from his chief, Marshal Billy Vail, ordering him to get back to Denver as fast as possible while Vail dispatched another deputy to take on the Julesburg case. Longarm had gotten enough messages from his boss to distinguish between the ones that meant what they said and those that gave him a choice of obeying them or ignoring them. The telegram, together with his badge, enabled Longarm to persuade

240

the stationmaster to flag the Limited, which would get him back to Denver that night.

While the westbound Limited puffed impatiently, Longarm swung aboard the baggage car, where he dropped off his saddle and gear. Then he made his way through the train, looking for a seat. There were only two chair cars, both full, and the Pullmans were just as crowded. He didn't find a seat until he'd walked all the way back to the observation car, which was also the club car, and where he'd probably have wound up in any event for a drink while he waited for the first call to dinner.

Years of riding trains to and from his case assignments had given Longarm a good eye for the recurring types of passengers he encountered. He figured the man standing next to him at the tiny corner bar while they were both waiting for service for a traveling salesman, a drummer; the back-tilted gray derby hat and the flashy stickpin in an overly ornate cravat were both earmarks of the type. It was easy to see, from the drummer's red face and unsteady hands, that he'd been spending too much time with the bottle. The man hadn't gone into the dining car when the chime-tapping steward came through making the calls to dinner. In fact, he'd ignored all three announcements. Longarm went in on the second call, and in the diner he noticed the woman. She was sitting with another woman and a man, and it would have been impossible not to notice her. She was the most attractive feature of the otherwise drab dining car.

Longarm shared a table with three other men— stockbrokers, judging from their conversation in which he took little part. Their talk of stock issues, debentures, convertibles, and options held small interest for him, and they were too engrossed in business talk to spend much time chatting idly with a stranger they'd never see again. After the meal, he returned to the observation car and took his after-dinner dram of Maryland rye out onto the platform to enjoy the crisp night air, which grew progressively crisper as the Limited huffed and swayed gently in its climb up the foothills of the Rockies. The first hint he had of trouble came when the door to the observation platform opened and the woman he'd seen at dinner came flying out.

Longarm grabbed her just as she was about to hit the brass rail that ran across the end of the platform. "Hey, now!" he said. "You ought to be more careful. You could've fallen right off the train!"

Whatever she'd been about to say in reply was lost in a bull-roar from the drunken traveling man who rushed after her onto the observation platform.

"Don't play hard to get with me!" he shouted. His face, Longarm could see in the light from the open door, was even redder than it had been before supper. "You fancy dames are all alike! Lead a man on, then run away!"

"Please! Let me alone!" the woman pleaded. "I don't know you, and I don't want to!"

"You weren't acting this way inside!" he charged.

"I came out here to get away from you!" she snapped.

"You came out here so I'd follow you, and we could be by ourselves," he retorted, with drunken lack of logic. "That's just fine, girlie. Now, we can play!"

Longarm stepped between the drummer and the woman. Obviously, the drunk hadn't noticed him before, for his eyes bugged out. Longarm said, "I heard the lady tell you she wants you to leave her alone."

"Who in hell are you to butt in?" the man demanded. "Trying to cut me out with the dame, are you?"

He swung. Longarm had no trouble grabbing the slow-moving wrist. His callused hands cut into the soft skin of the drummer's arm as he pushed the man to the side of the observation platform. Before the startled drummer knew what was happening, Longarm had grabbed his other arm and was holding him out over the edge of the platform, his legs swinging in rhythm with the swaying of the speeding train, nothing but the thin mountain air below his feet.

Looking down at the ground rushing past below

him had a very sobering effect on the drunk, especially when the wind took off his derby and sent it sailing into the dusk. He gasped, "Jesus, mister! Don't let go of me! If you drop me, I'll be killed for sure!"

"Let me hear how nicely you can apologize to that lady for troubling her," Longarm ordered.

"Now, I didn't mean anything! I was just—"

"Please!" the woman said. "Don't hurt him on my account!"

Longarm didn't answer her. He gave the drummer a shake. "Find your tongue fast, mister! If I let you go now, it'll be a long walk to Denver!"

"Lady, I'm sorry I stepped out of line," the man gasped. "If you'll overlook it—"

"Yes, yes! I'll accept your apology," she said quickly.

Longarm pulled the man back onto the platform and released his arms. The drummer wiped the sweat off his red face with trembling hands and fled into the coach.

"My goodness!" the woman said. "You certainly have a way of dealing with people who upset you. I hope I never get in your bad graces! But, I'm very grateful you stepped in to stop that man from annoying me."

Longarm took off his Stetson and made a little half-bow. "I'm glad I was on hand, ma'am, to save you trouble."

"You must be very strong," she smiled. "That man weighed at least two hundred pounds, but you handled him like a sack of peanuts."

"Well, even if he was three sheets to the wind, he ought to've been able to tell you're the kind of lady who wouldn't appreciate somebody like him trying to get fresh with you."

The woman looked abashed. "I suppose it was partly my fault. I made the mistake of coming back here to the observation car for an after-dinner glass of port, instead of having it served in my compartment."

"Your friends I saw you with at dinner didn't come back with you, then?" the lawman asked.

"Why, they weren't friends. Just people I was sharing a table with, as one does on a train."

"I guess it wouldn't have mattered to a gentleman, even if you were sitting down drinking by yourself, on a train. In a saloon, now, it might've been different."

The woman's hand flew up to her breast. "Goodness! I wouldn't go into a common saloon, even with an escort! I'm Julia Burnside, by the way."

She extended her hand, palm down. Longarm didn't know whether she expected him to kiss it or shake it, but thought it wasn't quite his style to be kissing a lady's hand, so he grasped the hand and shook it, while with his other hand, he touched the brim of his hat.

"My name's Long, Miz Burnside. Custis Long, Deputy U.S. Marshal from the Denver office." He hesitated, then asked, "Would I be presuming if I asked if you are related to the late general?"

"No." She smiled. "Though I do hope I have better luck than he did. But my father's family lives in Georgia, and I think the general came from New England. And it's Miss Burnside, by the way."

He smiled. "I wasn't aiming to be nosy, ma'am. Just wondering." Again Longarm hesitated. Then he suggested, "If you'd like to go back in the car and finish your glass of wine, I'd be honored to sit with you. It might keep somebody else from bothering you."

"Why, thank you, Mr. Long. Or should I call you Marshal Long? I'd enjoy your company."

"It doesn't matter a bit what you call me, ma'am. I don't set a lot of store in titles, but I've gotten sort of used to being called Longarm. Here, let me open that door for you."

They sat chatting in the observation car, Miss Burnside with her glass of port, Longarm with a fresh glass of Maryland rye, while the Limited steamed up the long slope to Denver. Without being obvious about it, Julia Burnside encouraged Longarm to talk of his experiences, and he enjoyed their conversation thoroughly, as would any man who finds an attractive young woman obviously interested in what he has to say.

When the conductor called the first warning for the Denver stop, they joined the flurry set off by other passengers who were getting off at the Colorado capital. Longarm decided to write off the incident as a pleasant but inconsequential evening. Even so, he hated to see it end. He'd found Julia Burnside's dark beauty and her slow, sensuous way of smiling exceedingly attractive. She was past the age of kittenish youth, but not yet overly mature. Longarm didn't expect to see her again after they parted in the excursion car, but when he'd picked up his gear from the baggagemaster and was carrying it out of the depot he saw her standing on the top step. A porter with a loaded luggage cart waited behind her. She was surveying the long line of hacks and carriages with impatient bewilderment.

"Something wrong, Miss Burnside?" Longarm asked.

She turned toward him, obviously pleased to see him, but puzzled.

"My carriage isn't here. I sent our housekeeper a wire from Omaha, telling her to have Duffey meet me." She shook her head. "The staff wasn't expecting me back so soon. I suppose they're treating themselves to a few days away from their jobs."

"Your family had to travel somewhere else, then?"

"There's only my father and me. Mother died several years ago. We'd planned to spend another week in Atlanta, but he got a telegram that called him to New York, and I decided to come home alone."

"Well, now, you ought not go to an empty house by yourself, at night. Suppose I just escort you home?"

"Really, Marshal Long—Longarm—there's no need for that. I'm not a baby. I can go home without worrying or being afraid."

"Just the same," he said, "I bet you'd feel better if somebody was with you."

"Well, if you're sure I wouldn't be imposing. The house is in quite a lonely part of town, some distance out on Sherman Avenue."

"All the more reason I should see you home. And you ain't imposing one bit," Longarm assured her. "I

245

don't have a wife or anybody waiting for me. I'll just see that you get home safe and sound."

He whistled up a hack and saw that her bags were properly stowed away, then tossed his own gear onto the rack on top of the vehicle. He was wondering if he'd been too forward in making his offer. Julia Burnside's dress and manners marked her as being prosperous, but a home on Sherman Avenue meant more than mere prosperity; it meant wealth. His conversation during the drive was somewhat inhibited, but his companion more than made up for it with a stream of light, somewhat nervous chatter as the hack passed beyond the zone of lighted streets and into the city's outlying residential section.

When he saw the Burnside house in the veiled moonlight of the autumn night, looming huge and dark in the center of an acre or so of newly planted lawn and shrubbery, Longarm whistled softly to himself. *It must look bigger than it really is,* he thought. Then the hack turned onto a semicircular driveway that led to the front door of the imposing structure, and Julia said, "I'll go on ahead and light a lamp in the hall, if you don't mind seeing that the driver gets all my bags."

Longarm jumped out of the carriage, helped her down, and then helped the cabman assemble the luggage. When they got to the house, the door was open, and a lamp was glowing in the hallway. Involuntarily, Longarm took a step inside. While the hackman was arranging the luggage on the floor just inside the doorway, Julia Burnside appeared at Longarm's elbow.

Turning back from his quick glance down the long, dim corridor, Longarm volunteered, "You've got a pretty good-sized house here, Miss Burnside. If it's been left by itself very long, it might be a good idea for me just to walk through it and make sure there's nobody lurking in any of the rooms."

"I was hoping you'd offer to do that. It'd make me feel a good deal safer."

"I'll just tell the hackman to wait." Longarm started

after the driver, who was already halfway back to the hack.

"There's no need," she said. "I've already paid him and told him to come back for you at six. And I warned him to be sure nothing happens to your saddle and other equipment."

Longarm said the first thing that popped into his mind. "I didn't expect you'd invite me to stay."

"I didn't plan to, until we were halfway out here." Julia pulled the jewelled pin from her hat and tossed the hat down the dim hall. Before his eyes, Longarm saw a prim and proper young lady suddenly transformed into a flashing-eyed temptress. She went on, "Then I asked myself, 'Why not?' And, do you know, I couldn't think of a single reason why I shouldn't, so I did!" And she threw back her head, laughing huskily.

As pleasant as he found the memory of what had followed, Longarm couldn't lie still while he exhausted his recollections of the night. Habit was too strong to overcome. He simply wasn't comfortable lying abed of a morning, with the day and his duty waiting. The soft satin sheets slithered luxuriously over his skin as he slipped out of bed. There was enough of a glow coming from the coal fire he'd lighted in the bedroom's small fireplace to enable him to locate a window. He opened the heavy velvet drapes wide enough to see the graying sky. It wasn't quite six o'clock yet, by his reckoning.

Moving as quietly as he knew how, he dressed by the grate's soft glow, adjusting his gunbelt and holster by feel, and foregoing the routine he usually followed each morning in his own room, of inspecting his weapons closely. He didn't know when Julia would wake up, but when he turned toward the bed after slipping his arms into the sleeves of his Prince Albert coat, she was sitting up, propped on the pillows, watching him dress. Her hair was tousled into dark curls around her face, her full lips were slightly swollen, and her shoulders gleamed in the fireglow which turned her creamy skin into rosy pink and accented the dark, pebbled rosettes of her upthrust nipples.

"How did it get so late so soon?" she asked, stretching languidly.

Longarm smiled. "Time's got a habit of hurrying, when you're enjoying yourself."

"I'd enjoy having you come back to bed, even for a little while."

"Now, Julia, you know I can't. It's getting on toward six, and that's when you said the hack would be back."

"Tonight, then?" she asked hopefully. "If the servants show up, I'll send them away, and we'll have the house to ourselves again."

"You know I'd like to. The only problem is, by tonight I might be headed out for God knows where. I told you my chief wired me to hurry back here, that he's got a case waiting for me."

"Yes. I remember," she pouted. "When you come back, then?"

"Sure. I don't know when that'll be, but I'll find a way to let you know."

"Let me find you, Longarm. My father resents any man with whom I make friends. He seems to want to choose all my companions himself. Of course, he always has his own 'companions' in a cozy little nest that he keeps in town, near his office. And I've decided that if he can choose his, I have a right to choose mine."

"Just have somebody ask at Marshal Vail's office in the Federal Building." Longarm stepped to the bed and bent to kiss her. "When I get back, then."

He let himself out the big bronze front door just as the hack rolled into the driveway.

A few minutes after eight, fortified by a hot breakfast and freshly shaved, Longarm walked into Vail's office in the Federal Building.

Vail looked up from his paper-strewn desk and grunted, "Time you were getting here."

"If I'd known you were in that big a hurry, I'd've

248

come right here from the depot last night," Longarm said mildly. "Only I didn't expect I'd find you here, then."

"I might've surprised you," Vail replied. He made a face, clasped his hands over a stomach that was beginning to bulge, and belched. "Damn soggy fried potatoes I had for breakfast. Nobody cooks spuds the right way anymore. Well, now that you're here, sit down and listen."

As Longarm settled into the red morocco armchair across from his chief's desk, he said, "The way that wire you sent me read, I didn't think you'd give me a chance to sit down before I had to leave on whatever job it is you pulled me back for. What's come up that's so all-fired important?"

Vail answered with a question. "Was Cady Martin in the outer office when you passed through it?"

"Cady? The sheriff from Teller County? If he was, I didn't see him. The only one out there was your pretty little sissified pen-pusher."

Pressing a button on his desk, Vail waited impatiently for the door of his office to open. When the young pink-cheeked stenographer-clerk stuck his head inside, Vail asked, "Has Sheriff Martin showed up yet?"

"He just this minute came in," the young man replied.

"Well, tell him to trot on in here." Turning to Longarm, the Chief Marshal went on, "It's really Cady's case, so I asked him to wait over in town to tell you about it."

"We're handling county cases now?" Longarm asked incredulously.

"We're handling this one, because Frank and Harry Warde have a connection with it. And if we don't take it on at Cady's request, we'll be getting one from the senator as soon as Cady gets back to Cripple Creek and the Wardes have time to telegraph Washington."

"All right. I get what you're driving at," Longarm nodded.

Cady Martin came in. A Colt swung from his hip, a leather vest with a star pinned on it hung loosely from his shoulders. Cady was a lanky, sandy-haired man with an untrimmed tobacco-stained mustache that drooped wearily down on either side of a long, protruding chin. His eyes were red-rimmed and he needed a shave.

" 'Morning, Billy," he said. "Longarm. Sorry I'm late, but I saw the elephant and heard the owl last night. Seemed to me I was entitled to cut loose after all the riding I've done the past week."

"No harm," Vail told him. "Sit down, Cady, and go over what you told me yesterday. I want Longarm to get it firsthand."

Martin pulled up a chair from the row ranged along the wall and let himself down into it, carefully. "Not a hell of a lot to tell. These three gophers, Scud Petersen and Dob something-or-other and Eddie Boyle, they got tired of scratching hardrock, so they figured they'd change their luck by robbing the Miner's Bank, there in Cripple Creek. That'd be three, close to four weeks back. Well, I don't know how much experience them yahoos had robbing banks before, but they fucked this one up real good." He pushed to squirt a stream of amber tobacco juice into the spittoon beside Vail's desk.

Longarm took the opportunity to ask, "You mean they didn't pull it off?"

"Oh, they pulled it off, all right. Got something like thirty thousand dollars, mostly in gold and silver, but a few greenbacks. Only Jimmy Clark, the teller at the bank, ran to the door and cut loose on 'em with a shotgun after they got outside. Tim Andrews heard the ruckus, and he came running down from his office, and when the smoke cleared away, they'd shot Tim and Clark both."

"Sorry to hear that," Longarm interrupted. "Tim was as good a town marshal as I ever ran into."

"Yep, he was all right, Tim was," Martin agreed. "Only good thing about it was that Tim shot Scud first, dropped him cold, and the one called Dob took so much lead from the shotgun that he died a little ways out of town.

"I was up to Gillel when it all took place. By the time I'd got word and made it back to Cripple Creek, Eddie Boyle was long gone, with all the loot. I took Sid, and we dogged after him on a cold trail. For all we knew, he might've been shot up, too, and had to hole up someplace close by."

Martin stopped to spit again and Longarm observed, "Only I get the idea it didn't happen that way."

"Sure as hell not," the sheriff agreed. "To cut it short and sweet, if Boyle was hurt at all, which I don't guess he was, he wasn't hurt enough to slow him down. He left a trail a mile wide, buying fresh horses every town he came to that had a livery stable. We didn't have no trouble following him."

Vail said, "You don't need to go through all that, Cady. Just tell Longarm what you wound up with."

"Like I told you yesterday, Billy, we wound up with what the little boy shot at," Martin snorted. "Boyle cut east to La Junta and then made tracks straight on south to the Indian Nation. Sid and me got as far as Fort Supply before we ran into a couple of Pawnee Indian policemen. They spotted our badges and told us to hightail the hell back to where we had jurisdiction."

"Well, they were right, in a way," Vail said. "It's federal territory, down in the Nation. I don't say they should've turned you and Sid back, but the Indian police never did take kindly to anybody from outside butting in on their home grounds."

Martin slammed a palm down on Vail's desk. "Damn it, Billy, it wasn't like Eddie Boyle's an Indian! He might be a breed, come to think about it, but he robbed a bank in my territory! You'd think them redskin bastards would give me and Sid a hand, instead of chasing us off!"

"It doesn't work out that way," Longarm put in. "They don't make us welcome in the Nation even if we wear federal badges the same as they do."

"Sure. I know that," Martin said disgustedly. "But that didn't leave us much legroom. Thing is, Sid had time while I was coming back to Cripple Creek to find

251

out a little bit about Boyle. Seems he used to talk a lot about a woman he was sweet on down in the Nation. Hottest piece of ass he ever had, he used to say. He was always getting ready to go back to her."

"Now that's interesting." Longarm frowned. "Whereabouts does she live?"

The sheriff shook his head irritably. "Damn it, I don't know! Sid never could find that out. But we were on a good trail, when we got pulled off it. Anyhow, we didn't come off so good when we tried to argue with them Pawnees, so we just turned around and headed home. Then, on the way back, I got to thinking. That Miner's Bank belongs to the Warde brothers, and I know neither one of 'em is going to be satisfied till they see Boyle on the business end of a hanging rope. So I figured I better come on up here and get Billy to pick up where me and Sid left off."

All three of the men sat silent for a moment. They knew what the sheriff had been thinking. The big mining and financial syndicates that had dominated Colorado's commercial life since the days when it had still been a Territory had grown even stronger with statehood. The syndicates were almost a government themselves; they'd taken the Cattlemen's Association as a model and had assembled a band of enforcers, a loosely knit small private army, that worked in parallel but not always in cooperation with the authorities. There was one big difference. The enforcers weren't bound by laws and rules of evidence, and often recovery of the loot from a mine or gold train or bank robbery was secondary to punishing the perpetrators as examples. Usually, the punishment was a lead slug.

"Well?" Vail asked Longarm. "How do you see it?"

The deputy pulled absently at a corner of his mustache for a moment, then replied, "About like you do, I guess, Billy. The Warde brothers are going to be pulling strings as soon as Cady reports back to Cripple Creek. You called the turn a while ago."

Vail said, "If their men go into the Nation looking for Boyle, they're sure to rub the Indian police raw. I want a man down there to keep trouble from exploding—to get Boyle first. You've had more cases down in the Nation than anybody else in the office. Your warrant's ready, whenever you are."

Longarm nodded slowly. "All right. Give me time to sit down a minute with Cady and find out what else I can about this Boyle fellow. Fort Reno's as likely a place as any for me to work out of, so I'll take the early train and connect up with the Rock Island spur that runs down to the Nation. Expect me back when you see me, I guess."

"And try to take things as easy as you can," Vail said. "The last time I heard, things were nice and quiet down there. Don't get me blamed for starting another Indian war, whatever else you do!"

Chapter 2

For the first two or three miles of his ride from the end
of the Rock Island spur track to Fort Reno, Longarm
couldn't make up his mind whether the seat of the
jolting army supply wagon was more or less uncomfortable than the bench in the caboose where he'd spent
the previous night and half the morning. Finally, he
decided there wasn't much to choose between the two,
and devoted his attention to the landscape.

There was as little to choose between the country
he was seeing now and that which he'd watched while
the freight train rolled south from Wichita into the Indian Nation. Both landscapes were virtually featureless,
and both bore the same kind of vegetation. The land
between the Indian agency at the Darlington railhead
and Fort Reno, ten miles further south, was perhaps a
bit more rolling, but on it grew the same blackjack
oaks, gum trees, and mesquite patches.

Although the primary reason for Darlington's exis-
tence was the Indian agency that served the Arapahoe-
Cheyenne reservation, the agency had attracted a few
other enterprises. There were a blacksmith shop, a notions store, a tintype gallery, and a pharmacy. There
was also a big authorized trading post that was also a
general store, and housed in the same building with it
were a hotel, a dining room, and a saloon. There was
no livery stable.

Not that it would make any difference, Longarm
thought as he shifted position trying to find a soft spot
on the wooden seat. *I'd pick an army-trained nag*

any day over what I might draw from a liveryman's outfit in a place like this.

"Something I've always wondered about," he remarked to the teamster on the seat beside him. "Why in hell does every fort in the Indian Nation have a railroad line running close to it, but not ever any spur tracks built right *to* the fort?"

"Beats me, Marshal," the man said around his chaw of cut plug. "But did you ever see the army do anything the easy way?" The teamster joined in Longarm's chuckle, then added, "Besides, if they built the railroads right up to the forts, us teamsters wouldn't have no jobs. And I'd a damn sight rather skin mules than get saddle sores on my ass chasing Indians all over hell and Texas."

"Still having to go out after runaways, are they?" Longarm asked.

"Maybe not as much now as we used to. The boys at Fort Sill do, though. Them Comanches and Kiowas down there jump the reservation a lot worse than the Araps and Cheyennes around Fort Reno."

"Comanches and Kiowas are a sight wilder than most, I'd say," Longarm remarked.

"Damn right," the driver averred. "And a sight meaner, too. Not that the ones up here are much better. I tell you, Marshal, I'm just as glad that agency's where it is, instead of jammed up to the fort. We don't get a lot of 'em wandering around, maybe slipping a rifle or pistol up under their blankets if they get a chance. And them Indians damn sure ain't going to be collecting their beef allotments and butchering the critters in smelling distance of our barracks."

Longarm nodded abstractedly. He was already plotting a course of action in his mind, to be refined after he'd studied the maps he'd pick up at the fort. Chiefly, he was wondering how far he was going to have to backtrack to pick up the trail of the missing Eddie Boyle. He'd forgotten a lot of the distances that he'd learned from his previous cases in the Nation, but seemed to recall that Fort Supply, where Cady Martin had been forced to leave the fugitive's trail, was a good hundred miles northwest of Fort Reno.

"How's the lay of the land between here and Fort Supply?" he asked the teamster.

"About what you'd expect. Dry and cold at this time of year, will be until the snow starts next month. Then it'll be just plain *cold*. Why? You heading up that way?"

"Soon as I can pick up a horse at your remount depot and draw some rations from the quartermaster's stores."

"Well, I wish you good luck." The teamster spat around the end of the wagon. "You're going to need it, if you're going into the open territory."